Reaching Rocky Mountain Jim

A Novel Based on the True Life Stories of James Nugent and Isabella Bird

Kari August

Mountain Track Publishing
Denver, Colorado

This is a work of fiction. Names and characters are the products of the author's imagination or are used fictitiously. Any resemblance to a living person is entirely coincidental.

Published by Mountain Track Publishing
2121 Delgany St., Suite 1427
Denver, Colorado 80202

Printed in the United States of America

Copyright © 2013 by Kari August
All rights reserved.

Cover design: Caroline S. Christner

ISBN: 978-0-9915466-0-2

Inquiries should be sent to:
mountaintrackpublishing@gmail.com

If you purchased this book without a cover you should be aware that this book is stolen property. It was reported as "unsold and destroyed" to the publisher and neither the author nor the publisher has received any payment for this "stripped book."

*For my husband, kids and dogs
who inspire me daily
with material*

Acknowledgments

A special thanks to my husband for all the encouragement and humor he provided throughout the writing process.
I will be eternally grateful for the guidance and support of my editor whose expert opinion was invaluable.
I could not have done it without you.

Reaching

Rocky Mountain

Jim

Chapter One
Colorado Territory
1871

Jim could never say the attack was unexpected, not the way he lived his life. Yet it was one of those experiences he imagined would never happen to him. Or if it did, the ending would turn out better. He'd be able to outwit and overcome the challenge.

If only he was superstitious, the omens sent his way last night might have warned him. A Great Horned Owl had swooped down just inches from his nose, trying to grab the rabbit Jim had snared for his supper. An hour later the smells of the roasting hare drew a pack of wolves boldly circling his campfire. Jim had merely shrugged their behavior off as starving aggressiveness after such a brutal winter.

The next day he was in Middle Park, a high meadow surrounded by snow-capped mountains. Jim glanced around at the brilliant colors the early morning light helped produce. The few spring flowers took on an intensity that dulled as the day went on, but returned to stunning proportions again toward evening. Yet it was the Colorado air that invigorated Jim the most. It was fresh and arid and seemed to suck him in as if it were a hollow trying to fill its own void. The moist Canadian air where he grew up had always seemed to push and shove at him. Jim smiled to himself. His former mountain men friends would have called him touched in the head by such musings. Time to get to work! His meat supply was low and living alone in his Estes Park cabin, he had only himself to replenish it.

Jim spotted a large buck and silently crouched down, rifle in hand. He watched as the curious deer started inching its way over to investigate a toppled pine sticking out of the ground. Once it got closer, he planned on taking careful aim. He wasn't going to lose this quarry.

Jim's dog Ring was intuitive enough to know not to disturb Jim when he was at work and wandered off after interests of his own. A few minutes later, Jim heard Ring bark furiously once, then twice. The deer raised its head, ears alert, and fled. Jim stood up and swore loudly, but nearly dropped his gun from shock when he saw Ring barreling toward him, being chased by a huge grizzly with a couple stumbling cubs in tow.

Run! For a fraction of a second the thought raced through his mind as his legs quivered. To hell with saving his beloved dog. But Jim steadied himself, took aim, and squeezed the trigger. The bullet hit the grizzly's chest, dazing her for a second, and Ring darted off at an angle away from the bear. The young cubs stopped abruptly and stared.

Things happened so fast there was no more time to think, just to act on instinct.

Recovering quickly from the shot, the grizzly charged at Jim. He dropped his rifle and grabbed his knife. She advanced with a ferocious roar, jaws snapping, and Jim tried to make a slashing stab, but the bear slapped the weapon away. Searing, stinging pain exploded on the right side of Jim's scalp as she smacked his head. Ring ran back and attempted to bite the bear's ankle, but was sent flying and rolling near the cubs. After righting himself, the dog snarled until the cubs started wandering away.

Realizing with terror, the mother grizzly was not going to follow her cubs, Jim took a couple deep breaths, letting them out quickly, before the bear attacked again. With another powerful swat, he fell to the ground, and the huge grizzly pounced and clawed, shredding through Jim's layered clothing. The bear finally took a moment to glance at her cubs, and Jim scooted backward, staggering quickly to his feet. He angrily reached for his rifle and with the stock of the gun took a slug at the bear's head, infuriating the grizzly more. She advanced again, swinging widely with both paws, and Jim's left shoulder dislocated from its socket. Jim gasped, the throbbing was so intense, and he recognized with a sinking sense of horror that he was losing the fight. He was going to die if the bear attacked again, and there was increasingly little he could do about it.

Weaving with pain, he dropped to the ground. The grizzly growled, but saw Jim lying still, appearing lifeless, and the bear ran to her cubs. With grumbling snarls, the bear staggered away, her cubs following behind. Jim tried to focus on the retreating forms but found his eyes wouldn't cooperate, and the world around him gradually receded.

Jim awoke slowly, heard a hawk screech in the distance and, without thought, tried to turn toward the sound. Pain instantly assailed him in every part of his body. Jim lay still and kept his eyes closed as he waited for the agony to abate. The bear attack. How long had he been out?

A rough, wet tongue swiped at his cheek, and Jim winced from the new pain. Ring. At least his dog had made it. Figured Ring, never missing a chance to paint his face with slobbery kisses, was now trying to clean his wounds.

Pushing the dog away, Jim struggled to his feet, his left

arm hanging uselessly by his side. Blood oozed from his scalp, dripping down his cheeks. Jim wiped it with his torn right sleeve and felt a huge gash stinging across his back. He looked around with his left eye, his right eyelid too swollen to open. Jim saw that his white mule Sassy was still in Middle Park but grazing a distance away. With his right hand on Ring's head for support, he staggered over to Sassy, dropping from exhaustion a few feet away. Sassy gazed at him warily, but continued to chomp on a clump of grass. Jim again hauled himself awkwardly up, grabbed Sassy's reins and guided the mule over to a group of rocks. After climbing a smaller one, he flopped over Sassy's back, causing fiery pain to radiate from his shoulder.

He fainted again, sliding to the ground off Sassy.

Jim came to later with Ring curled at his side. He awkwardly reached over with his good arm to pet his faithful dog and realized for the first time there was a swelling on Ring's head. Why hadn't he checked Ring earlier, and just how badly hurt was he? Jim stroked the dog's back and legs and let out a sigh of relief when he realized Ring had nothing more serious than a few small cuts and bruises.

Woozy and aching, Jim got up and slowly pulled himself over Sassy's back, managing to swing his leg astride. He kneed Sassy to get the mule going, but even that small movement caused pain. He looked around and noticed the lengthening shadows on the ground. At least another hour had passed. He needed to get moving. He clicked his tongue and, when Sassy started walking, Ring followed.

The ride was too shaky, the ground too tempting, and Jim slid off Sassy again, falling into an exhausted sleep. When he awoke, dusk was approaching, and he knew he couldn't spend the night helpless on the ground. He had no choice but to get back on Sassy, a task made even more difficult by the swelling that had set into his injured joints.

Jim tried to attach himself to his saddle. Fumbling with a rope, he placed one end in his mouth and attempted to swing the remaining long end around his waist with his good arm. The rope hit his already sore back and fell slack at his side. On the third try, Jim managed to swing the rope all the way around his body. Grabbing the end he held in his mouth, he clumsily made a one-handed loose knot at his waist. Placing the short end back in his mouth, he pulled with his jaw and tightened the knot. After twisting the long end of the rope around parts of the saddle and awkwardly tying more knots, Jim succeeded in securing himself to his saddle, but knew the effort had cost him. He was even more exhausted.

Every mile became a torture, but when at last he raised his slumped head off of Sassy's neck and squinted through his eye, he saw that he was within shouting distance of the small town of Grand Lake.

"For God's sake, somebody help!" Jim tried yelling, but his voice was too weak. Nobody noticed him.

He nudged Sassy a few steps closer, took a deep breath and tried again. "I need help!"

Two fishermen on the town's lake looked over and started rowing toward Jim. Ring started barking and ran toward the shore.

Hours later Jim felt large hands prodding and poking at his injured left shoulder. He forced his left eye to open briefly and caught a glimpse of a man and woman standing over his bed. He was so tired. Couldn't they leave him be?

He heard the woman whisper, "It must be him. Who else rides a white mule in these parts?"

"Well, let's ask him. He seems to be rousing."

This time a soft hand cupped his cheek. "Can you tell us your name?"

The sweet voice was worth the effort. Jim blinked his

eye open again and cleared his throat before answering hoarsely, "James Nugent."

Her eyes widened. "Oh, my Lord, you *are* Rocky Mountain Jim."

Chapter Two
Grand Lake
Colorado Territory

Jim sat up in bed and swallowed hard. Today was either going to be the worst day of his life or his best. He was anxious to get the day started so he could find out which one it would turn out to be.

After the fishermen had found Jim at Grand Lake, he had been taken to the local doctor's office. Doctor Charles Schodde's place of work had turned out to be his home. While he and his wife Henrietta used the upstairs for their personal sleeping quarters, the first floor was divided between a front parlor and kitchen on the west side and Charles's examining room and two recuperating rooms on the east side. Jim had been placed in the middle room directly across from the kitchen. He had a window that allowed him to view the morning light each day.

Jim looked around his cheerful surroundings. It had Henrietta's touch everywhere. There were clean sheets on the bed and a patchwork quilt neatly folded over the top of an adjacent chair. Lacy curtains hung from the window, and there was even a vase full of flowers next to his bed. Jim chuckled and shook his head. It was a ridiculous and yet wonderful room in which to mend—a far cry from recovery rooms at any army fort.

He had been at the Schoddes' house for the last fifteen days. He only knew that because yesterday he had stopped taking anything for the pain, his mind had cleared, and he remembered what Henrietta had told him. Otherwise, the last couple weeks were mainly a blur of falling asleep, waking in discomfort, eating a little, taking something more for the pain and falling asleep again.

He also remembered very well what Charles had told him yesterday. Jim opened his right hand and then clenched his fist, trying to steady his shaking nerves. Today Charles would remove the bandage from his head. Soon Jim would find out if he still had eyesight in his damaged right eye the bear had gouged. He reached up to rub his face and felt the thick bandage covering his right eye. My God. If he lost sight in one of his eyes, what would he do? Would he even be able to shoot straight?

There was a soft knocking at the door that jolted Jim away from his fears. Jim sat up straighter. This was it. He took a deep breath.

"Jim? May I come in now?"

Henrietta. Not Charles. He wasn't sure if he felt disappointment or relief. "Come on in, Henrietta."

They had agreed yesterday to start calling each other by their first names, which made sense, considering how much they saw each other. Jim watched as Henrietta pushed through the door, balancing a tray in her hands.

"I hope you have more of an appetite today than you did yesterday."

Jim started to answer truthfully that he did not, but caught himself, sensing that his answer would disappoint her. As sick as he still was, he oddly wanted to please her. Henrietta placed the tray on the bedside table, lightly stroked his hair back off his forehead, flicked open a folded towel, and, as if he were a child, tucked it under his chin. Enjoying Henrietta's touch, Jim allowed it.

"There you are. Eat up. I had time to bake this morning now that you're the only one left recuperating in the house." Henrietta looked at him expectantly.

Jim glanced down and saw a couple of fluffy biscuits on the plate, a dab of butter melting enticingly on the top of each. He took a bite of one. Lord, this woman could cook. He briefly wondered what it would be like to be married to her. He stopped chewing for a second. Where had that thought come from? He hadn't seriously thought about settling down with a woman in years. "It's delicious."

Henrietta smiled and straightened the covers. "Gracious, you were a sight when you first arrived. The town still hasn't stopped talking about it. With all your yelling and bloody scalp, some people thought you had been attacked by Indians."

"Wish it had been Indians. I might have stood a better chance than against that grizzly."

Jim focused on her for the first time. He'd been too sick up until now to notice anything beyond her caring ways. Her face was appealing, with a ready grin always lurking beneath the surface. She was probably in her twenties but looked younger, engulfed by a dress that threatened to overwhelm her petite frame. There wasn't a smudge or stain on her clothes. How did she do that, taking care of sick people all day?

Jim was good with languages, and he realized she had a faint German accent. Perhaps her goal was to look and act the part of the perfect hausfrau, and she succeeded except for one small issue: She wore her hair in a loose bun that Jim realized was always lopsided. He had never seen the bun perfectly centered. It made her seem more approachable to him.

Henrietta walked to the flower vase and started

removing the wilted heads. "I need to ask you a question, Jim. The editor at our local paper wants to know if he could interview you. He already wrote a short article about your bear attack, but he wants to write one with more detail. Do you think you feel up to him coming for a visit?"

"Maybe in a couple days."

Henrietta smiled widely. "Oh, that would be great!" She suddenly blushed. "I mean . . . well, I mean you're already so recognized in these parts being such a skilled hunter and tracker that Charles is becoming more famous, also, just by taking care of you. He's such a good doctor and well . . . it would help build his practice . . ." she trailed off turning redder. Henrietta reached to straighten her bun. She succeeded only in pulling the bun looser, still lopsided.

Jim smiled. "It's fine, Henrietta. Glad my bear attack can be of some help."

She gasped. "Oh, Lord, I didn't mean it like that!"

Jim chuckled, but then suddenly couldn't stand the wait anymore. He needed to know about his eye. "Just where is Charles?" *Charles* was a pleasant and amiable doctor. So friendly in fact, that he also had told Jim to call him by his first name.

Before she could answer, her towering husband walked into the room, ducking slightly to avoid banging his head at the doorway. "Here I am." Charles briefly studied Jim and grinned broadly. "I see you've gotten some of your color back."

Jim glanced up at the doctor and frowned slightly. My God, Jim realized for the first time just how young Charles really looked. He was at least a decade younger than Jim's close to forty years of age. How could someone so young be an actual doctor? Maybe he shouldn't trust his opinion about his eye.

Jim caught himself and inwardly shook his head. He had to stop it. Charles had taken good care of him so far; he knew that. The man had saved his life.

Charles walked over to the bed. "Let's see if you've gotten some strength back in your arm. Try pushing against my hand."

Jim bit back a curse. That exercise first? Couldn't he see Jim was a bundle of worries waiting to find out about his eye? Charles placed his hand on Jim's left upper arm. He was able to weakly raise his arm against the pressure.

Charles nodded. "Better every day. Ready to remove the bandage?"

Jim couldn't answer and only nodded, he was so uneasy.

Charles cut away the linen wrapping and studied his right eye. He didn't speak for a moment but just stared at Jim. Finally he said, "There's an adhesion between the lid and cornea. The scar tissue is preventing you from being able to open your eye fully."

Jim rubbed his eye a few seconds and tried to open it himself. It wouldn't open. He rubbed it again. It just wouldn't open. This was bad—as bad as it could get. He implored, "Can't you do anything about it?"

Charles shook his head. "Not I. Perhaps a specialist back East could help; it'll be tricky business cutting through the scar tissue though."

Jim was speechless, inwardly shuddering at the thought.

Charles sighed. "Well, you have time to think about it. I realize this is troubling news, and I'm sorry for it. I wish there was more I could do to help."

Jim quickly looked up and with a twist of his lips said, "Show me to your liquor cabinet. That'll help. I need a drink. No, I need a whole bottle. What you got?"

Charles shook his head. "Drinking's not the answer."

Jim put on a false smile. "Wanna bet? Tying one on would do wonders right about now."

"No, for now just concentrate on building up your strength. Get out of bed more if you can. I'll be back later to check in on you." He started to pick up the dirty bandage and scissors on the side table.

Henrietta stepped forward. "Charles, let me get that."

Charles nodded silently and walked out the door, again leaving Jim alone with Henrietta.

She looked at him anxiously. "It's really not so bad. Here, let me get a mirror so I can show you." She hurried out of the room.

Jim sighed. There was so much lacking in his life already. He lived alone in Estes Park, no wife, no kids, his few truly close friends far away. Now he could only see out of one eye? What if he lost sight in his other eye? He'd be completely blind and helpless. It wasn't inconceivable anymore, not after being attacked by a grizzly. He never thought that would happen to him either. What if he met up with a mountain lion next or, or . . . a crazed bull moose or . . . a badger with drooling sickness? Anything could happen.

Henrietta returned with a small hand mirror and gave it to Jim. He studied his eye. She was right; it wasn't so bad—it was horrific.

He sighed again and brushed his hair back with his hand. Besides the eye that wouldn't open, now the right side of his face was scarred with a huge gash across his forehead. Perhaps it would be less noticeable with time, but for now? It looked gruesome.

He had always taken particular pleasure in being noticed by the ladies. His solid, muscular frame and shoulder-length tawny curls had gotten him his fair share of attention. He doubted the women would be running to greet him as he entered a town now. He knew he was being stupidly vain, but he was only human.

He glanced up and frowned, noticing Henrietta looking at him worriedly. Yes, he was plenty upset, but he didn't really want her sympathy. He cleared his throat. "You realize, Henrietta, that this scar over my eye completely ruins a wink."

Henrietta let out a breath of air and visibly relaxed.

"I've worked hard to get a wink just right." He went on. "Not too flirty, not too sly, just the right amount of playful. You tell me, just how am I going to wink now?"

Henrietta smiled softly, walked over and gave Jim a hug. He was shocked at first by the close contact, but then he realized Henrietta had known *exactly* what he needed. He reached around with his good right arm and awkwardly squeezed her back. She softly patted him. If ever there was a woman who loved her husband, Henrietta was she, and he knew the embrace meant nothing other than to give him comfort. But oh, it felt so soothing right now.

A tear came to his left eye. He pulled away and wiped it with his right hand.

Henrietta grabbed his hand in hers, looked earnestly into his face, and said, "You know what, Jim? I think what we should do now is get you out of bed, try walking across the hall, and make a cup of tea in the kitchen. Would you like that?"

A cup of *tea*? Of course not. He needed a stiff drink. Hadn't she heard? But Jim found himself answering untruthfully again. "Sounds fine."

After a winded shuffle, with Jim leaning more than he thought he would need to on Henrietta, he landed with a grunt in a corner chair in her kitchen. "Thanks for your help. You're a stronger woman than you appear."

Henrietta smiled. "People always underestimate my strength." Henrietta poured water from a pitcher into a kettle and placed it on the stove to heat. "Shouldn't take too long."

She sat down on a chair across from Jim. He briefly studied her, before saying, "Sometimes I hear a slight accent from you."

Henrietta sighed. "I guess I'll never fully lose it. My parents were German immigrants. I only learned English, when I started going to school, back in Pennsylvania."

"How did you end up in Colorado?"

"My parents died young, leaving just us kids. My brother decided to try gold mining, and my sister and I followed." She waved her hands in the air. "Pikes Peak or bust!"

Jim smiled and she continued. "My brother Herman actually made a little nest egg for himself, and my sister Clarisa and I didn't do too badly either, cooking and baking for the men. I once had a silly notion I wanted to own a bakery."

"Not foolish at all. Why didn't you? Didn't your brother think it was a good idea?"

"Oh, it wasn't that. I met Charles, we fell in love, got married and settled in Grand Lake. Now my brother's working cattle way north of here, and my sister's married to a butcher in Fort Collins."

Jim nodded. Even though Henrietta had lost her parents, she still had some family living relatively close by and also a husband to care for her. As an only child, Jim had no family left in this country or Canada. No parents, no aunts and uncles, no cousins. Nothing. His parents had died years ago while he had been away, working as a trapper. The last time he had even seen them was when he had left to join the Hudson Bay Company at age seventeen.

Jim sighed. He never missed his parents more than he did right now. He never felt the absence of a wife more than presently. What was it about Henrietta and the Schodde household that brought on these yearnings? It wasn't that having a family would bring back his eyesight, but it was the thought of sharing this news with someone that truly cared for him that he missed.

The next day in his room, Jim was reading the brief article about his bear attack in the local paper when he heard a faint barking noise outside. As the sound grew louder he smiled, recognizing it. He heard a commotion in the backyard, a door opening and slamming shut, and Henrietta pleading, "Wait. Wait!"

Ring appeared in the doorway, huffing and straining at a leash around his neck, practically dragging Henrietta at the other end of the rope. She couldn't hold him back. Ring, with the head of a mastiff and the body of a collie, was a powerful dog, and he forced his way into the room.

"Ring, old boy! How ya doing?" The dog bounced around Jim.

"He's so excited I'm afraid he'll hurt you."

"Down." Ring instantly sat, but panted adoringly up at Jim.

"They were taking good care of him at the stables, but I thought you might want to see him for yourself."

"Can't think of a better surprise." Jim ruffled the fur at Ring's neck.

"Oh, but guess what? I asked Charles and since you're the only one here right now, if Ring behaves he can stay in your room with you. Isn't that great?" Henrietta stopped abruptly and looked at Jim with excitement in her eyes. "I love dogs. I had one growing up and wish we could have one now, but not everyone we care for would like a dog around."

"He won't cause any trouble."

"What should we feed him? Maybe I could get some old blankets to make a bed for him."

Jim smiled. "If you spoil him too much, he's never going to want to leave." And if Jim stayed here much longer, he was certain he would feel that way himself.

"Maybe he'd like some of my biscuits. I'll go get some." Henrietta scurried out of the room. Jim started to pet Ring's head while he listened to Henrietta fumbling with the biscuit tin in the kitchen.

She appeared in the doorway again. "This is so fun, isn't it?"

Jim chuckled. He'd fed his dog many times before and would hardly call it thrilling, but he loved watching Henrietta enjoying herself. Henrietta held out a biscuit to Ring. He gobbled it down in one bite.

Henrietta started giggling. "He loves it. Let's try a second one."

Ring wolfed down another. Henrietta smiled. "I'm going to make a whole new batch of biscuits. Do you think he'd like cookies, too?"

"Undoubtedly. But you don't have to go to all that trouble. A portion of regular food is fine."

"Oh, that won't do. Ring's our guest of honor."

Jim shook his head and smiled. How easy it would be for any man to fall in love with a woman like Henrietta. He could honestly see himself happily settled with a woman such as her.

Jim sat up straighter. Good God. What was happening to him? But the simple fact was, that Henrietta made him crave a kind of life he hadn't contemplated in years. He thought he had accepted living his isolated existence, but perhaps not. Perhaps he had always known that it had never been enough.

Charles walked into the room. "What's going on?"

Henrietta started giggling again. "Ring loves my biscuits!"

Jim watched as Charles smiled warmly and gave a fond light tug on her bun. "Sweetheart, you're a nut."

Eyes sparkling, Henrietta smiled back.

Ah, the mystery of the lopsided bun solved.

Jim closed his eye, not wanting to view this brief moment of intimacy.

Later that evening Jim had trouble falling asleep. After tossing and turning for a few hours, he made a decision. As soon as he could at least walk, without leaning on someone, he would head for home. He didn't need this constant reminder of what he didn't have in his life.

But before he left the Town of Grand Lake completely, he would stop by the newspaper office and ask the editor to publish a note thanking Charles and Henrietta for all their care. They deserved the special thank-you.

A week later, despite Charles's and Henrietta's protests, Jim left Grand Lake and headed for home. The first thing he did, when he entered his cabin, was walk straight to the whiskey he kept on top of his bedside table. He grabbed the liquor and collapsed on his bed.

After opening the bottle, he took a long hard swig. Hell and damnation, the ride home had been endless. Charles had been right. He had left too early and was still weak. If he wasn't feeling woozy and dizzy with any quick motion to his head, he was feeling off-balance. He couldn't get his seat just right on his mule Sassy. He knew he leaned slightly towards his injured left arm, but his view seemed off also. Half his world was cut away by his scarred right eye, and why that made riding so difficult, he wasn't exactly sure, but he knew it did.

After savoring another long drink from the bottle, Jim got up and grabbed his rifle as he headed out the door. His left arm being too weak, Jim crouched down and rested his rifle on a rock. He took careful aim of a nearby tree trunk. He slowly squeezed the trigger. The bullet didn't even come close to the target. Just as it hadn't every time he had tried it on the way home.

Jim threw the rifle a few feet away, got up, walked back into his cabin, slammed the door shut as hard as he could and collapsed on the bed again. He reached for the bottle, took another fortifying drink and then rubbed his forehead. He had a choice here to make. He could either give up with his current way of living or try to make it work despite his limitations.

He looked around his cabin at all his possessions,

probably trivial to other people, but precious to him. At least nobody had broken into the place while he was gone. He took another drink and sighed. He loved his home.

The cabin he had built a few years before was in Estes Park, more precisely the beautiful valley in Estes Park known as Muggins Gulch. He'd never met Muggins, who had previously run cattle for one of the local ranchers, but if he ever did, he would tell him that he couldn't have picked a better home site.

His cabin was surrounded by an incredibly pretty grass and flower covered meadow, with a shimmering creek for water, meandering nearby. But the best feature was the fact that the surrounding hills were steep enough to provide just the right amount of protection. On the east end, there was only one way into his valley from the surrounding towns, and on the west end, only one way out of his valley; and this west end led to the main part of Estes Park where the other settlers lived. Jim saw exactly who traveled to and from Estes Park because the other way into Estes Park, by way of the Big Thompson River, was too rough passing. It was like being the gatekeeper to one of the most fantastic wilderness areas in the world.

Jim took another drink. No, he wasn't leaving this place. It was just too cherished. Besides, even if he couldn't hunt right now, he could still probably trap and . . . fish. He could still probably fish. And when he learned to ride better, *and he would*, he would return to guiding visitors to the area. He still had his knowledge of all the surrounding mountains to escort them on hikes, and he knew better than anybody else where the best hunting was. He'd figure out a way to make it. He just had to, the alternative was too depressing even to contemplate.

The next morning, despite a throbbing headache, Jim began the process of adjusting to his limitations. He practiced for hours with his guns and finally started hitting some targets. He exercised his left arm lifting logs. He rode

Sassy up and down the meadow. By evening he was exhausted, but at peace. He would repeat what he did today, tomorrow, and try as best he could to conquer this new challenge. His very essence depended on it.

Chapter Three

Jim always liked visiting Fort Collins, but as he rode into the dusty frontier town, he was especially excited. After months of honing his riding and hunting skills—adjusting to his limited vision to the point that he was now confident of his shooting ability—he was going to guide his first client in a long time on a hunting trip. Not only that, he was going to see his best friend Hugo Jaska.

Though the original Camp Collins, built by the Kansas Volunteer Cavalry about ten years ago to protect settlers, had been abandoned, the former fort site now called the town of Fort Collins had a small hotel, one general store with a post office, and a mill.

Jim headed straight to the general store. He found Hugo at the end of the second aisle, trying on a hat. Hugo had his back to him, but he recognized his friend's short, muscular frame.

Jim walked quietly down the aisle, then smacked Hugo on the back. "I just knew I'd find you here."

Hugo turned around and smiled. "Meaning?"

Jim laughed. "Meaning, it didn't matter if we were just trappers, or buffalo hunters, or guides at the time. If we came into some money, you always had a taste for the finer things in life whether it was a set of custom-fitted clothes or boots of the best leather. I hardly understood why since we weren't traveling in high society, to say the least."

Jim reached for the tag on the hat Hugo was wearing. "Just how much is this ugly thing?"

Hugo slapped his hand away. "Never you mind. I think it makes me look distinguished."

"Distinguished? Since when has that become important?"

"Since I bought my sporting goods shop in Cleveland. You can't be a business owner and look like a beggar you know."

"Guess not. Hell, if it helps entice more clients like Reginald Whene to use my guiding services, then I guess you should buy it. First, you draw the client in with your fancy store, selling your expensive hunting equipment, and then you tell them about the bountiful hunting out my way. I'm just glad you decided to come along yourself. Where is our client anyways?"

Hugo bit his inside cheek. "Reggie's sleeping."

Jim chuckled. "Can't wait to meet him."

"Be nice, Jim. He's actually a good guy. Come on—let's get out of here and go get something to eat. Now's our chance for just the two of us to catch up."

Jim studied Hugo's face across the table at the hotel restaurant. "You look the same. How long has it been since we've seen each other? I've been trying to remember."

"Fifteen years. Lindsey and I have been married fifteen years."

Eyebrows askance, Jim said, "I still can't forgive that woman for taking you away from me."

Hugo shook his head. "It was time. The beaver creeks were getting trapped out, neither one of us liked obtaining bloody hide after bloody hide of buffalo, and there wasn't enough guiding business to keep us going despite all those wagon train settlers."

"Remember that wagon train we guided when you first

met Lindsey? Her husband wasn't the only one to shoot himself by accident."

Hugo nodded. "But he was the only one to die from his drunken mistake."

"You're just lucky he left Lindsey with some inheritance."

Hugo shook his head. "Yeah. If it wasn't for her fool of a first husband, I wouldn't have my store."

"But why'd you have to open Oxford Sporting Goods all the way over in Cleveland? I could have used your company here." Jim pushed his hand through his hair. If Hugo only knew how much he had missed him those first few years after they had separated. Hugo had been his steadying rock. Sure, Jim's reputation had continued to rise on his own as a skilled hunter and guide, but without Hugo's calming influence he had celebrated more . . . enthusiastically. He also became known as an unpredictable drunk, turning rowdy and violent at the drop of a dime if he became upset. But Hugo didn't know much about that time period in his life, and he wasn't going to tell him now.

Hugo gave Jim a long look as if he knew he was missing some of the story. Jim briefly looked away and then turned back to Hugo. Let him look. Let him see how he had aged, the worry lines, his new scars. He had survived—at least he had survived.

Hugo cleared his throat, then said, "I fell in love with Lindsey and wanted to make her happy. She wanted to return back East where her parents lived. Moving out West had been her husband's dream, not hers."

"And now? Do you have any regrets?"

Hugo shook his head. "No, we've made a good life for each other. She's a great mother."

Hugo smiled. "And besides, if it wasn't for her, you probably wouldn't get half the letters that you get from me. Luckily, she doesn't mind writing them for me. With my limited education, writing a lengthy letter is a struggle."

Jim smiled back. "You might be kind of short and only have limited *formal* education, but you always seemed wiser and taller than the rest to me, starting from the first day you bossed me around at the Hudson Bay Company."

Hugo grunted. "Don't have any regrets about leaving that company. Even if I was your boss, we both were like slave labor, turning all our furs over to them for profit."

Jim nodded. "Thankfully, you loaned me the money to buy the equipment so we could go out on our own."

"You paid me back every cent."

Jim smiled. "That I did. So tell me, what did Lindsey think about you coming out for this visit?"

"Oh, she was fine with it. She thinks I work too hard. She's been encouraging me to take a hunting vacation for years and when I told Reggie about you being a guide out here, and he decided to come, it a was like a spur in my saddle that I couldn't stop thinking about. I knew I had to come myself." Hugo pointed at Jim. "But let's talk about you. I'm sure you have some interesting Indian fighting stories, working as a scout for the army, that you didn't write me about. Or how about afterwards during the Civil War? What about some of those stories?"

Jim inwardly groaned. More bad times in his life. More excessive drinking. Despite his reputation as an erratic drunk, the army had needed his fighting and scouting skills and had offered him a job. Then later during the Civil War? He had been involved in the Kansas border fighting, and there was nothing he could be proud of there. Some of those events might have occurred over a decade ago, but the memories were still torturing Jim now. He gave a half smile to Hugo. "We'll get to those in time. We have a whole week together. Let's order and eat and then go rouse up this Reggie. I want to meet him."

Jim had taken one look at Reginald Whene and sized him up immediately. If there was one thing Jim had learned guiding previous clients that usually proved true, it was the better the state of a man's hunting attire, the worse his skill.

Reggie, as he liked to be called, had stood there on that boardwalk this afternoon in brand-spanking-new hunting clothes.

Sitting next to each other in front of their evening campfire, Jim looked over at Hugo and made a face. Across the blaze Reggie was in the middle of a lengthy explanation about his family's shipping business.

Jim whispered, "Does he ever shut up?"

Hugo lowered his voice, "You mean you didn't like hearing about all the places he's traveled in the world and his previous big-game hunts?"

"I can barely keep my eye open, and that's saying a lot since I only have one eye to keep open."

"Well, I like him. I appreciate his eagerness. He makes things kind of fun."

Jim listened to Reggie a bit longer and conceded Hugo had a point. Reggie's enthusiasm was kind of refreshing. Reggie paused to take a deep breath, and Jim jumped in, "Hey Reggie, what do you think about trying some elk hunting tomorrow with Hugo and me?"

Reggie's face lit up, and he answered in his customary nasal voice, "That'd be great, fellows. Can't wait to try it, fellows!"

The next day Jim leaned across his mule Sassy and whispered to Hugo, who sedately sat on his own mount, "My God, he's clumsy. He may have gone on big-game hunts around the world, but in what capacity—as the cook? There was no way he could hit a single elk running, or walking, for that matter. No, we needed to find an entire herd."

Hugo answered back quietly, "That was smart thinking on your part. Now that we've chased the whole herd that weak one over there has dropped to the ground. He can hit that elk, I'm sure of it."

Jim watched Reggie dismount and stealthily stalk closer to the downed elk. Jim smirked. "Maybe if he gets close enough. Tomorrow we better find a huge herd of buffalo."

Hugo smiled. "God, you were glorious to watch years ago, hunting buffalo on horseback. Remember how you'd identify the leader of the herd and get him circling, and the rest would follow behind? Then you'd shoot the buffalo that spun off from the circling mass."

Jim smiled. "It's more of a sport if a chase is involved. I'd shoot while guiding my horse just with my knees. There isn't even a question whether Reggie can handle my preferred method. Hell, I don't even know if I could do it anymore." Jim glanced down a moment before gazing back at Hugo.

Hugo frowned. "Does it bother you much?"

It was a painful question to answer. Jim pretended he didn't understand. "Does what bother me?"

"Not being able to do everything you took for granted before."

Jim sighed. "I suppose—but only if I think on it too long. I try not to think about it."

Hugo slowly nodded. "Good answer. Hey, what's up with Reggie now?"

Jim frowned as he watched Reggie having trouble shooting his rifle. He shook his head before shouting, "Hey, Reg, don't forget to load your rifle first."

Hugo tried not to laugh.

Jim rode Sassy up alongside Hugo's horse. "Today's as crazy as yesterday. I just can't watch this anymore. I'm putting myself out of my misery." He pointed his finger at the back of his head and mockingly pulled the trigger.

Hugo leaned his elbow on the front of his saddle, before answering, "Well now, if you're going to try killing yourself, you need to shoot yourself in the mouth. Shooting yourself in the back of your head won't guarantee that you'll die."

"My God, you can pick the strangest moments to make a teaching point sometimes."

Hugo shook his head. "Jim, Jim, Jim. You need to have more patience with Reggie. Just think, if Reggie has a good time, then he'll go back East and tell his friends, who'll tell their friends that you're a good guide."

Jim looked appalled. "What if his friends are like him?"

Jim watched Reggie try shooting several more times the weak appearing buffalo on the top of the hill. The bullets ricocheted off the surrounding rocks. The buffalo stood still as if he knew Reggie was no threat. Jim dismounted and walked over to where Reggie was crouched behind a sage bush. Jim blurted out the first made-up excuse that came to his mind, "Hey, Reg. I think the wind has changed directions, and you need to be positioned just so. Follow me."

Reggie nodded sagely and followed Jim to three feet in front of the buffalo. Reggie smiled. "Thanks, Jim. I'll do my best."

Jim hurried back to Hugo and watched from a safer distance. Reggie shot and shot until finally the buffalo dropped. Reggie turned around and shouted, "That was great, fellows! When can we do that again, fellows?" Reggie jumped up and down a couple times with his arms raised over his head, but abruptly stopped and widened his eyes at something on the ground.

Jim rushed back over and heard the familiar hissing sound before he spotted the rattlesnake near Reggie. Keeping his eye pinned on the snake, Jim motioned for Hugo to ride over.

Hugo trotted over and shook his head. "I sure don't miss those vipers. You want to get it or should I?"

Jim glanced at Hugo. "I got it. Hand me your rope,

Hugo. Hold perfectly still, Reg."

Reggie nodded vigorously up and down. "You bet, Jim. I won't move a muscle."

Jim quickly took the rope from Hugo and with a swift snapping motion, stunned the rattlesnake by hitting its head with the end of the rope. Once the snake lay subdued, Jim ground its head with his boot heel. He pulled his knife from his belt and cut off the crushed head. He then severed the rattlers off the tail and handed them over to Reggie. "A present from me."

Reggie glowed. "Thanks, Jim! Can't wait to try that next!"

Jim couldn't hold it in anymore. He collapsed on the ground and rolled over laughing. Hugo bit back a smile.

"When am I going to see you again?" Jim grinned at Hugo, but he knew he wasn't fooling his best friend. Jim was hurting inside, having to say good-bye. The stage heading to Cheyenne was leaving Fort Collins in just a few minutes, and Hugo would be on it. Reggie had already left on the stage heading to Denver.

Hugo grabbed Jim by the shoulder and looked at him earnestly. "Whenever you decide to travel to Cleveland, you'll always have a place to stay at my home."

Jim exhaled hard. Yeah, Hugo would say that. Hugo still didn't know much about what kind of man Jim had turned into as a scout for the army and during the Civil War. There had always been some other topic to talk about the last week. His drinking had been moderate as well—he hadn't gotten drunk the whole week. He hadn't any desire to either. Except for Jim's obvious scars, Hugo still saw him as he once had been, that better version of a man than Jim considered himself now. Could he be that man again? Or, was it possible . . . had he always been that better man, but a man who had just gotten caught up in the events occurring around him? Jim sighed. He didn't know.

Jim cleared his throat before asking, "No more hunting trips out West?"

Hugo looked around wistfully. "Maybe in a few years—I'd like to show my sons this area before it gets too settled. They would like to meet you, too, I'm sure."

Hugo's sons. What was it like to have a son of your own? Jim pulled at his lower lip and studied the ground. He'd probably never know. The thought hit him in a sadder way than it ever had before. If he had settled down the way Hugo had, how much more filling would his life be now?

Jim shook his head. What's done was done. He couldn't erase his past. But what he needed to do now was cut off all these embarrassing emotions coming at him. He looked up and pasted a smile, while playfully punching Hugo on the arm. "Be sure to bring Reggie with you also."

Hugo grinned. "Hey, at least he gave you a big tip when he left."

Jim beamed. "A huge tip—I should give you some of it for helping to keep me sane."

Hugo shook his head. "Keep it; you deserve it all. I can't believe it's been just a year since that griz attack and you're doing so well."

"Maybe not so well, but I'm getting by."

He grabbed Jim in a bear hug. "More than getting by"—Hugo slapped Jim on the back—"You take care of yourself. I'll write when I get back."

Jim swallowed hard and nodded.

Back at his cabin, Jim looked at Ring stretched out on the floor in front of the fireplace. "Did you miss me, Ring? Did she treat you well?"

Ring quizzically raised his head, then yawned and slumped back down to sleep. Jim usually left Ring at Maggie McTeekey's house when he couldn't take Ring with him on one of his trips. The widow could be trusted to take good care of Ring. Jim had offered some of his bonus money when he had picked Ring up from her house on the way home from Fort Collins, but she had declined, telling Jim to bring her some fresh fish instead, when he headed her way again. She was tired of eating venison. He had left her a huge haunch of deer when he had left Ring with her to guide Reggie.

Jim rubbed his chin. Hmmm. She wanted fish, did she? Well, that's what she was going to get.

Jim hailed her cabin while mounted on Sassy, "Grandma, come on out. Look what I got for you. Don't let all my hard work the last couple days go to waste."

A stout appearing, gray-haired woman emerged from the open door, smiling broadly. "Lord, what you up to now so early in the morning? You got that Irish devilment in you today, I see."

Jim's parents had emigrated from Ireland to Canada before he was born. He had never met his grandparents, but if he could pick a woman he would want for his grandmother, it would be sweet Maggie. Her thick Irish accent always reminded Jim of his parents, and he had gotten into the teasing habit of calling her Grandma. She didn't seem to mind.

Jim smiled. "Look behind me. I brought you a few fish."

Maggie walked over and peeked in the sack full of trout tied behind his saddle. "Mercy me. How many are in there?"

Jim chuckled. "Maybe a couple hundred—I didn't count. You said you wanted fish so I brought you some."

She shook her head. "Now what am I going to do with all those trout?"

He dismounted. "Eat some, smoke some, and the rest I'll give away to others."

She grinned. "But first, I'll fry some up for you and me to enjoy."

Ring appeared from the trail behind Jim, panting heavily. "Guess he gave up on chasing that rabbit."

Ring nuzzled Maggie's hand, and she stroked his fur. "Ring, you know you'll get some, too."

Jim smiled. "I'm sure that's exactly what he was counting on."

Jim looked up at the sky, gauging the time, as he drew rein in front of the Christner's cabin. This would be his last stop for the day before heading home. They were a young couple who were new to the area. Jim didn't know them well, but the wife always gave a pleasant wave when Jim passed by their home. Usually he was on his way to Denver and anxious to get there, so he never chatted for any length of time. He had only a few trout left, since he had stopped at several homes after leaving Maggie's place, but he figured, why not? No better time to get to know them.

"Ring, you stay here." Ring gave a small grunt and rested his head on his paws as he lay down on the bare dirt in front of the cabin.

Jim dismounted, climbed the porch stairs, and softly knocked on the cabin door. No one answered, but he could hear their baby softly crying within. He knocked again more loudly and after hearing some shuffling inside, the door opened a crack. The tear-streaked face of Sady Christner appeared around the edge of the door. "Oh, Mountain Jim. I'm so glad it's you. I didn't need any more trouble."

She opened the door wider. "Come in. Come in. I'm just so worried, I don't know what to do." She wrung her hands together as she walked over to her sobbing baby, lying in the wooden crib in the center of the cabin floor.

Jim entered and watched as Sady lifted the child against her shoulder, cooed to it softly, but the baby continued to hiccup and whimper.

Jim walked over and touched his hand to the baby's

head. "What's wrong with her? Has she got a fever?"

"Alma's burning up. She has been all day. My husband left for Denver yesterday for supplies and is supposed to be back tomorrow, but I'm not sure if Alma can wait that long. She needs a doctor now. Ned has no idea that Alma even is sick. Whatever she has—came on suddenly."

"Sady, don't worry, I'll fetch the doctor for you. Did Ned leave you a horse? My mule is tired."

Sady looked at Jim with relief. "Our mare is grazing in the back meadow."

Jim headed quickly towards the door, but turned around abruptly. "Ring shouldn't cause any trouble and I'll tie Sassy up in your barn. I've brought some trout if you're hungry."

Sady shook her head. "Just hurry, please."

He nodded and ran out the door.

It took Jim longer than he would have wished to gather the skittish mare, get her saddled and be on his way. All the while as the wind whipped around and changed directions, he caught snatches of Alma's sobbing.

Jim kneed the mare to hurry her along the trail. Lord, he hated to hear babies crying. It was a sound he just couldn't abide anymore. More times than not, it triggered memories of other babies crying—pitiful babies in Indian villages watching their parents, grandparents, aunts, uncles, sisters, and brothers getting slaughtered. Wars were supposed to involve just men, but they never did. Innocent women and children always suffered as well.

Jim urged the mare into a faster trot. Of course, babies were wailing also throughout the Civil War, but it was always images of those Indian babies during his scouting days that crying seemed to trigger now. The Indian babies just seemed a bit more pathetic being left alone in a white's man world.

Jim slowed the mare down. He needed this horse, and he couldn't run her into the ground or risk breaking her leg in a hole he didn't see at this pace. God, for once in his life he was going to help one of these crying babies.

He gazed at a point on the horizon and shuddered at the flood of memories. No, it was bonfires that triggered images of the Civil War in Jim's mind—recollections of homes or whole towns in Kansas burning to the ground, being swallowed by enormous, spreading flames, innocent women and children standing outside in bewilderment, their menfolk lying dead on the ground—and for what? Sometimes all it had taken was a mere rumor, not even a substantiated fact that a man held a different opinion, and the killing and blazes had started. Jim shook his head. How could he have been involved in such brutal craziness? What kind of man did such atrocious things? But as he noticed buildings appear in the distance, he forced his mind away from his disturbing memories and concentrated on the problem at hand.

Jim walked through the batwing doors and found Doc Ernest standing at the bar in the High Horse Saloon. The crusty doctor had opened a small office a few years ago on the outskirts of Denver, but was rumored lately to rarely actually be in his office.

Jim strode up to the man. "I got a sick child I need you to see."

Shaggy grey eyebrows arched his way. "Now there's sick and there's really sick. This child better be really sick or I'm not helping. I need some strengthening here myself after the long day I've had."

"It's Alma Christner. The baby's been burning up all day long, and her mother can't get her to stop crying."

The doctor turned his head toward the painting of the nude lady above the bar. "Never heard of the Christners." He turned back toward Jim. "They live around here?"

"They're new folks about an hour from here."

The doctor shook his head. "Too far away." He waved

his hand disinterestedly. "The baby's probably teething. Just give her a shot of whiskey."

Jim grabbed the collar of the doctor so quickly and tightly, the man almost fell on top of him before catching his balance. "Now listen, you low-life son of a gun. If I had time to find another doctor, I wouldn't let you anywhere near this child, but you're all I got. So sober up, get on your horse and get over to the Christner's." He let go of the man's collar.

The doctor straightened his shirt and vest. "I'll have you know, I had training in one of the best schools back East. What's it to you anyways? You the father?"

Jim drew back his arm, but halted mid-swing. "Ned Christner is the father of Alma Christner and don't you forget it. I'd be tracking Ned down right now if I could trust you to get out there, but I see I can't. So grab your bag and let's go."

As they got closer to the Christner's cabin, the doctor cleared his throat before speaking up, "I apologize for my behavior at the saloon. I haven't been myself since my wife died. I will do my best for this child, Mr. uh—what did you say your name was?"

"I didn't. We never got a chance to introduce ourselves properly. My name's James Nugent or you might have heard me called Mountain Jim."

"Ah, so you're Rocky Mountain Jim. I have heard a story or two about you. How did you get your nickname?"

"From Indians—there were a lot of trappers in the West named Jim. I worked mainly in the Rocky Mountains so they started calling me that to distinguish me from the other Jims. The name has stuck all these years."

"Well, Mountain Jim, I apologize again for my behavior."

Jim nodded. "No apologies necessary as long as you take good care of that child."

"I promise I'll do my best."

Jim studied the doctor a moment. "That must have been tough losing your wife."

The doctor's face revealed his sorrow. "Wasting sickness." He shook his head. "The one person in the world who I would have wanted to save, I could not heal."

Jim remained quiet. What was there to say after a statement such as that?

They walked into Sady's cabin after softly knocking on the door. Sady jumped up from her rocking chair, clutching Alma in her arms. "Thank the Lord, you made it. Alma just fell asleep."

At the sudden motion and sound of her mother's voice, Alma began crying again. Jim backed out of the door. "I'll let the doctor do his work. I'll just be outside if you need me."

Ring followed Jim, and the two headed to the barn to check on Sassy.

Much later, Jim sat in the dark on a wooden bench on Sady's front porch, wondering what was going on inside the cabin. The crying had stopped about fifteen minutes ago. It was turning into an endless wait. Could Alma have died already or was she just sleeping? Jim rubbed his forehead. He couldn't believe how worried he was for a baby he barely knew—had to be a million times worse for an actual parent.

Jim had thought about having children; who hadn't? Other than crying babies, he loved being around kids. He enjoyed their antics. But when he was younger he had thought he had years ahead of him before he would need to, or even want to, settle down. Then during the war years he was just trying to survive, let alone start a family.

But what had stopped him after the war from finding a wife and beginning a family? He'd always gotten attention from the ladies and shockingly, despite his scarred face, he still did attract interest; but then Jim had always felt a man's personality was ultimately more important than looks in finding a partner. But perhaps the reason he didn't have children of his own was that, deep down, he didn't think he could ever be a good enough father to raise a child.

But was that actually true? A father should be like Hugo and he would need to be that better version of a man that Hugo saw in him . . .

The cabin front door squeaked open, pulling Jim from his thoughts. He watched as Sady, carrying a lantern, walked over and sat down next to him on the bench. She stared straight ahead and sat quietly for a moment before speaking, "I don't think I've ever been so scared in my life, and I don't know how I'll ever repay you."

"Is Alma going to be all right?"

She looked at Jim. "The doc thinks so. He says the problem's in her right ear. He gave her some syrup that he says usually helps. He's spending the night and plans to leave in the morning if she's doing better."

Jim smiled. "Well, hearing that good news is the only payment I need."

Sady nodded. "You're a wonderful man, Mr. Nugent. I hope we can be better friends in the future. Ned and I will always be grateful."

Jim shifted in his seat. *Wonderful?* He knew he wasn't that. He'd only done what was right.

The clip-clop of an approaching horse drew his attention. Ned soon appeared in front of the cabin. Jim watched as he jumped off his horse and shouted, "Sady girl! I decided to surprise you by coming home early."

Sady was off the porch in an instant, running towards him. "Ned, oh Ned, you don't know what's been happening. Alma was in a real bad way."

Ned started running to the cabin, but Sady caught his arm. "Wait! She's doing better now. I don't want you to wake her."

Ned turned and gave a puzzled look at Jim. He stood up from the bench. "Sady will tell you all about it. Sady, I'll get going now that you're in good hands."

Sady turned to Jim. "You're not leaving, are you? I haven't given you anything to eat, and you can sleep in the barn if you wish tonight."

"Nah, I'd better start heading back home. I can bed down some place comfortable under the stars tonight."

She nodded. "If ever you need anything, anything at all, let us know."

Jim silently nodded and waved before heading towards the barn.

Jim gazed up at the full moon and sighed. What he had done today had felt right. He *was* a decent man and perhaps had always been an honorable man. Maybe that was why his misdeeds in the past bothered him so.

He took a drink of whiskey and then held the flask up in front of the moon to study it. Would he have done anything remotely as horrible as the acts he had performed if he hadn't been rip-roaring drunk at the time? No, probably not. He couldn't think rationally when he drank too much, and liquor could turn a simmering temper into an unreasoning rage for him.

Jim tossed the flask a few feet away from him. He would cut back on the liquor. He had told himself that before, but this time he really meant it. He turned onto his side and tried to go to sleep.

After tossing and turning several minutes, Jim sat up and rubbed his forehead. And yet, how did one forget massacred Indian villages and whole towns going up in flames . . . he didn't want to remember, he just didn't. Why was he tortured by these memories, and other men, who had done things just as bad, didn't appear bothered in the least?

As Jim slowly lay back down, he wondered whether there would ever be a time when he would be able to forgive himself. He shook his head—probably not.

Chapter Four
Scotland

Isabella absently tapped her fingers on the windowsill and gazed out at the quiet harbor, the small fishing vessels bobbing lazily up and down with the current. The view had once enchanted her. Now she didn't know how she felt about it. Bored? Trapped? She shook her head. Why couldn't she abate this feeling of restlessness?

She looked across the cozy sitting room at her sister Hennie, reading a novel of ancient myths in Latin, nodding and smiling to herself, clearly enjoying a particular passage in the book. Isabella knew some Latin herself, but it never engrossed her the way Latin could captivate her younger sister's attention. Isabella took a deep breath. Well, no time like the present.

She straightened her shoulders, walked over and stood in front of her sister. "Hennie, I need to travel again. The new doctor I consulted in London, the specialist I told you about, has agreed that it would be a good idea."

Hennie looked up and narrowed her eyes. "Oh, no, you don't. You went last time. It's my turn."

Isabella inwardly groaned. She had been afraid that might be Hennie's reaction. She sat down on the settee facing her sister. "It's not that it's anybody's turn, Hennie. It's for my health, you know that."

"But I thought our latest move from England to Scotland was supposed to have done you good."

"It helped for a while, but my headaches are back, and I feel the same lethargy in the mornings. Some days I can barely get out of bed."

Hennie shook her head. "When is all this going to *stop?*"

Isabella frowned. "I don't know. But if Father and Mother, God rest their souls, were still around, they would agree another excursion is in order. Don't forget years ago it was my doctor who originally suggested traveling may improve my health, and it did wonders back then."

Of course, with Isabella single and in her twenties at the time, looking to be a confirmed spinster, Father had suggested where she travel and picked areas where there were decidedly more men than women–such as North America—but that was never the reason discussed for her trips, and traveling did fortify her health. She only felt sick when she had been back home for a while.

Isabella straightened her skirt. "Besides, after I returned I published not one, but two books, that both sold well, making the trip even more worthwhile."

"Ah, yes. What were they again? *The Englishwoman in America* and *Aspects of Religion in the United States of America.* How could I forget?" Hennie raised one corner of her mouth. "Well, perhaps if you had let me accompany you on your travels, I could have published some books myself, and maybe my health also would have improved."

Isabella sighed with exasperation. "You know it was more complicated than that. After all, who would have helped Father lead the flock? Mother couldn't be the only one to assist him. Anyway, you've never suffered health issues as severely as I have. If you were ailing now, too, then it would be proper for you to travel also."

"Perhaps I just suffer in silence more than you."

Isabella crossed her arms but said nothing. She lifted one brow and waited for Hennie to come to her senses.

Hennie frowned. "Maybe I'm also . . ."

Isabella cocked her head back and gave her sister a good stare.

Hennie sighed. "Oh, all right. I admit it. I'm feeling fine right now. I guess I don't need to make the trip." She arched both brows and smiled. "But wouldn't it be nice if we could just travel because we felt like it and not because we needed to?"

Isabella sat straighter. "Never, Hennie! It would appear too selfish. Our parents raised us to devote our lives to improving the common good, to helping the poor, to relieving suffering—why it would ruin our reputation!"

Hennie raised her chin and pitched her voice slightly higher, "And we *must* respect our reputation at all times."

Isabella softly smiled. "You sounded just like Mother then. I really do miss her."

"As do I." Hennie closed her book. "Anyway, let's get back to your proposed trip. Where do you plan on travelling this time?"

"I've heard that the dry air and climate in western America are excellent for one's health. Consumptives are being cured in the Colorado Territory."

Hennie looked perplexed. "Consumptives? You're not consumptive, not even close to it."

"Hennie, that's not the point."

"What is the point then, pet?"

Isabella sighed. Hennie was certainly in one of her contrary moods. Isabella took a deep breath and reminded herself that she loved her sister and continued patiently. "We don't know what illness I have, correct? But maybe the pure air will do me good."

"Well, perhaps. But tell me, how do you plan to get to America?"

"Hmmm." Isabella tapped her upper lip with her finger. "This time I ought to see whether traveling by way of the Pacific Ocean helps my health."

Hennie suppressed a chuckle. "I knew that was coming. Of course you wouldn't want to travel where you've already been if you could tour another part of the world."

Isabella frowned and started to counter another of her sister's incautious remarks but instead decided to ignore it. She forced a smile before asking, "Will you help me plan my trip, Hennie? Research the Pacific Islands with me?"

Hennie rested her elbow on the reading table and slumped her head in her chin. "I suppose so, I do enjoy scholarly activities"—She smirked—"Of course, that could help explain why I'm in my thirties and still unmarried, as are you."

Isabella was aghast and put her palm on her forehead. "Hennie, what has gotten into you today with all these cavalier comments? We just haven't found the right men yet. We both need someone who can challenge us, intellectually and otherwise. When we find them, we'll be married."

"If you say so."

Isabella shook her head. "Now back to my trip. Of course, my primary concern will be to improve my health, but listen to this"—Isabella clasped her hands together—"I also plan to write a book about my adventures, a travelogue of sorts that would aid any future visitors to the area."

"Isabella, you do realize that there is already an abundance of travelogues for sale."

Isabella smiled smugly. "But mine will be especially well written because you're going to help me. I'll write letters back to you, and you can help me edit them into book format."

"I'm going to help you with your writing again?" Hennie sighed. "Well, considering our forebears were always more titled than wealthy, I suppose if you manage to sell any books at all, it will help defray some of the costs of the trip. We don't want to dip into our inheritance money more than necessary."

"Indeed, Hennie. Father was only a preacher after all, and he certainly didn't inherit a substantial amount of money from his father. Now tell me what you know already about the Hawaiian Islands."

"First off, Captain Cook was killed there by the natives—"

Isabella cut her off. "A long time ago, I'm not worried about that."

"Well, you should still be careful about not offending the indigenous peoples. Watch what you eat, beware of what you drink, and by all means don't fall from the ship on the way over and get eaten by sharks."

Isabella frowned. Was Hennie just trying to tease her now or was she being serious? "Hennie, stop trying to scare me from this trip. It won't work."

Hennie shrugged. "If you go, I just want you to be careful, that's all."

Isabella scoffed, "I'm always careful."

Hennie coughed. "This is your sister to whom you are speaking. I know you. Once you get something into your head that you want to do, you completely disregard the dangers. Why I'd even call you reckless at times."

"Reckless? That's absurd." Isabella blew out a deep breath. Christian women shouldn't fight and especially not with their sisters.

Hennie studied her nails. "You've always been that way."

Isabella shook her head. "I'm sure I don't know to what you refer."

"How about when you climbed that tree far too high and needed to be rescued."

Isabella stood. "I was saving the cat!"

"Tommy down the street could have retrieved it much more easily than you. I remember telling you that at the time."

"We were just children." Isabella waved her hand dismissively. "As if I would have listened to a sister three years younger than me."

"Then how do you explain your behavior when you were nineteen and Father bought you your first horse?"

Isabella put her hands on her hips. "Mohawk? I was proud of my equestrian abilities. I enjoyed having a reputation as a fearless rider."

"You started riding any horse, even those no woman had attempted mounting before."

Isabella rubbed her forehead. "Are you through?"

"All that I'm saying is, don't try to be another David Livingstone no matter how impressed you have been by his heroism."

Isabella gasped. "Who wouldn't be enthralled by his missionary work in Africa while trying to find the source of the Nile?"

"He needed to be rescued by Henry Stanley this year."

Isabella raised her voice, "That arrogant Yankee reporter didn't rescue—Hennie, you can be so—" Isabella shook her head. "I wasn't going to say it, but Hennie you can be so irritating at times."

Hennie ignored her. "We haven't even talked about what dangers you will face in the Colorado Territory."

Isabella ground out, "What now?"

Hennie started counting on her fingers. "Mountain lions, wolves, savage Indians, wild mountain men, drunk miners, blizzards"—Hennie stopped and frowned at Isabella—"I hope you don't get it into your head to go exploring on your own. Make sure someone accompanies you there at all times and—"

"Enough, Hennie. I know what I'm doing." But as Isabella started pacing the floor, she had to admit to herself that maybe Hennie had made a few valid points.

No matter—she needed to travel as much as she needed to breath, and nothing was going to stop her from this new excursion.

Chapter Five

Jim looked up from stretching a pelt across its wooden frame and noted the few aspen that were already changing color. The golden yellow of their leaves against the blue sky and emerald pine forests was striking. He hoped this fall would be as successful as this summer had been.

His eye caught a movement in the distance, and Jim focused on a couple of gentlemen, riding horses in the meadow, heading towards his cabin. As they got closer he saw they rode fine horseflesh, not as fine as the Arabian mare Jim had bought recently with his new earnings, but close. One of the gentlemen spurred off toward the west end of the valley which led to the settlement in Estes Park where Griff Evans ran a guesthouse. The other gentleman rode straight towards Jim. He stood up, and asked, "How may I help you, sir?"

The gentleman dismounted and stood very erect, one foot forward. "*Lord*, not Sir. Lord Dunraven to be exact."

Lord Dunraven? He remembered reading some article about Dunraven a few months back when the man first came to the States and the Colorado Territory. He couldn't remember much of it right now, but he knew the guy was rich, filthy rich. Jim briefly looked Dunraven up and down. If not for his finely made clothes and boots, he could have passed for any average man with his unexceptional looks, medium height and weight.

But what really distinguished Dunraven was the condescending attitude he exuded as naturally as a tree shedding its leaves—head cocked back, hands on hips, he started asking questions, "And who might you be?"

Jim stepped forward and shook his hand. "Nugent, James Nugent."

"You own this property?"

"I have a squatter's claim."

"How much land do you contend is yours?"

"From where you entered this valley to where you leave this valley, heading to the main settlement in Estes Park. It's called Muggins Gulch."

"Are those your cattle we passed when we entered, uh . . . Muggins Gulch?"

"Yes, I bought a few head recently." Jim frowned. Why was he answering this guy? Lord or not, a man never asked a stranger blatant questions. Too many people in the West had secrets either now or in their past that they wanted to hide. A man volunteered information on his own or you didn't ask. Everyone knew that.

"How long have you lived here?"

Jim shook his head—another impertinent question. Damn lucky he hadn't just asked that of a drunken and more volatile James Nugent. Jim hadn't touched a drop today or Dunraven would be flat on the ground now.

While he waited for Jim to answer, Dunraven's mouth fell back into the oddest expression. Jim couldn't help staring. He finally decided it was a "smurse," a combination of a smirk and a pursing of his lips, and how he managed to do it so easily was just plain mystifying.

"I asked how long you've lived here."

Jim focused on Dunraven's eyes. They were cold, unfeeling eyes. "I heard you the first time. It's none of your business."

Dunraven cocked his head back even further. "I'm

thinking about purchasing land around here. I like to become acquainted with an area first before making any decision."

Jim folded his arms over his chest. "Well, that's all fine and dandy, but I'm not going to be of any help to you. I'm not selling my property, and if you want any more information, ask somebody else."

Who did this guy think he was talking to? Some backwoodsman who didn't know what was going on in the world? No, sir, Jim wasn't dumb. Americans were broke. The Civil War had dragged on for too many years and not only drained the government's funds, but nearly everyone else's savings as well. The British were the ones who had the money to buy the West and had already started doing so.

He knew a pretentious ass such as Dunraven would never be satisfied with a small stretch of land. These British had vast, private game preserves back home. That's what Dunraven had to be after—either a game preserve or turning the area into a huge cattle ranch. Jim shook his head. The rich son of a gun probably wanted both a game preserve *and* a cattle ranch and probably also thought he could manage both better than the average American.

Jim looked Dunraven in the eye. "Get off my property. We're done talking."

Dunraven smiled a smirky smile. "Mr. Nugent, I didn't mean to offend you. Could you be so kind as to just tell me how far it is to Mr. Griffith Evans's establishment?"

Jim frowned. He could do that; but that was the very last question or he was punching the guy out whether he had drunk anything today or not. The son of a bitch was just too obnoxious.

"About five miles west." Jim turned his back on Dunraven and walked into his cabin.

Jim knocked on Griff Evans's door and entered without

waiting for a response. He considered Griff a friendly neighbor, to a degree. They didn't always see eye to eye on every matter, but Jim was always welcomed into Griff's home.

Griff had lived in Estes Park with his family for about five years, having settled a year before Jim by the Fish Creek and Thompson River. Griff had purchased his spread from a wild individual by the name of "Buckskin," but before that it had been the original homestead property of Joel Estes, the town's namesake.

Griff ran a guesthouse and made money hunting. He also owned a few hundred head of cattle, as opposed to the fifteen that Jim owned, but Griff also took care of several hundred more. Colorado ranchers hired Griff to run their cattle, having learned that the area had sheltering valleys and a climate mild enough year-round for the livestock to survive.

Griff should have been a man well-off, but money seemed to just flow through his hands. His drinking didn't help either. Jim had heard that Griff was getting hard up for cash again. That made Jim nervous about just what might have transpired between Griff and Lord Dunraven in the last week. Jim had seen Dunraven leave Estes Park a day ago, but had kept his distance from the man. Now his curiosity was getting the best of him.

Ellie paused in her sweeping. "Everyone's out hunting, Jim. Let me reheat some coffee for you."

"Thanks, it'll take the chill off."

Normally the fact that Griff's wife Ellie was the only one at home would have disappointed Jim. In a world of colorful characters Ellie was a dull gray. She was like a plaid shirt so faded you couldn't tell what the original shades had been or whether there had even been any colors. Jim could never seem to muster up much enthusiasm to converse with her.

But today Jim was glad Ellie was the only one present

at the guesthouse. Jim wanted to reread that newspaper article Griff had about Dunraven without drawing undue attention to his inquisitiveness, and furthermore, if he was lucky, Ellie might spill the beans without realizing it about any transactions that had occurred between Griff and Dunraven.

Jim helped Ellie stoke the fire. He picked up a log by the hearth, and the bark fell away from the crumbling pieces of wood underneath. Just like Dunraven: appearing solid on the outside, but rotting inside. He tossed the pieces in the fire and started sorting through the stack of old newspapers Griff always kept for his visitors. He found what he wanted near the bottom.

He began reading. Born in 1841, the lord's official title was the Right Honorable Wyndham Thomas Windham-Quin, the Earl of Dunraven and the Earl of Mount. Jim shook his head. Wasn't that a mouthful of dung. Jim paused and tapped his finger. Let's see, born in 1841 . . . that made the ass thirty-two years old. Too young as far as Jim was concerned to be putting on such airs even if he was a lord.

Jim continued reading. Dunraven had a large landholding, about forty thousand acres including Dunraven Castle in Glamorgan and a manor in County Limerick. He was an adventurer. Fresh out of Oxford, he had been a reporter on the front lines during the Franco-Prussian War.

"What are you reading about?"

Jim looked up. "Oh, just an article about Lord Dunraven."

Ellie smiled. "He's so nice."

Jim rubbed his forehead. She had just done it again—said something that made it so hard for Jim to converse with her. Couldn't even bland Ellie come up with something more interesting to say than just that he was *nice?* But it wasn't only that—Ellie could be so completely oblivious to people's faults, the way pet owners were to their home's smell and lodging Dunraven here must have been like owning a skunk. Jim took a deep breath. He knew he should make the effort with Ellie. After all, she had a generous heart, caring for her family and guests the way she did.

"Oh, I'm sure he acted polite," he managed, "but there can be a difference between being polite or nice."

Ellie smiled at him, quizzically. He went back to reading his article. Dunraven was a capable yachtsman, had traveled the world and accompanied Henry Stanley on his famous trip to Africa. He knew General Phil Sheridan and had hunted buffalo with William Cody.

Jim stopped reading and shook his head. It figured. His friend Buffalo Bill never could turn down an easy way to make a dime. Next time he ran into Billy in Denver, he'd have to ask him about it. Now if Billy had any business dealings with Dunraven, Jim wouldn't have any problem finding out what it was and any other specifics he wanted to know. But Griff, oh no. Griff usually kept his business dealings close to his sleeve; and of course Jim couldn't ask Griff outright what was going on when he did run into him next. Asking personal questions such as that just wasn't done.

"Coffee's ready," Ellie said. "Come sit down and let's chat a while."

Perfect. Now he would see what he could get out of Ellie. "So you liked Dunraven. Did Griff find him pleasant also?"

Ellie smiled. "Griff makes friends with everybody, doesn't he? They spent a lot of time hunting together. His companion, Mr. Laurence, also seemed to enjoy hunting. I think Lord Dunraven said they knew each other since their college days."

"Did Griff and Dunraven do anything else together?"

Ellie looked up at the ceiling a moment then back at Jim. "Well, I suppose Griff might have shown him his cattle. Oh, and they went fishing one day. I remember that."

Jim inwardly sighed. He wasn't going to get anything out of her—might as well switch to their normal conversation together.

But as Jim talked to Ellie about the weather, he couldn't help wondering if he had seen the last of Dunraven or not; and if not, what did it mean for the future of his beloved Estes Park? He certainly didn't need any future neighbor the likes of which was the Right Honorable Pompous Earl of Damnraven.

Chapter Six
Longmont
Colorado Territory
1873

Isabella sat in a chair on the front porch of the Big Elk Lodging House and swatted a bothersome fly away. She watched as a miniature storm cloud of them buzzed around the manure-encrusted boots of the dusty stable hand walking down the street. She shook her head; nobody had warned her how pesky all these flies could be. Of course, nobody had told her a lot of things about the Colorado Territory that she had learned the hard way the last few weeks—such as the lack of adequate tourist hotels in many areas and the filthy conditions in the homes she was forced to stay in out of necessity.

    She stared at the distant mountains. Perhaps the most distressing fact she had not known beforehand was just how difficult it would be to actually get to the mountains. Isabella sighed; it hardly mattered now. She was leaving for home tomorrow.

    Her trip had started out so promising. From Scotland

she had traveled to Australia, then New Zealand, and finally glorious Hawaii, and her health had really improved. No more morning headaches and feeling as if she couldn't get out of bed from overwhelming lethargy. The lush foliage and dramatic scenery had been stupendous, not to mention the exhilarating horseback rides and splendid hikes up mountains. She had even been entertained by a Hawaiian chieftain.

She supposed the rough, dirty town of Cheyenne, Wyoming, should have been her first warning that this last leg of her trip through western America was not going to progress as pleasantly as she had hoped. She wished she could have just skipped Cheyenne altogether, but it was a necessary resting stop in her journey from the Pacific coastline to her ultimate destination of the Colorado Territory.

Fellow travelers talked about the surrounding plains as being captivating, but it was hard for her to view them as anything but monotonous, and she had quickly determined that she would try to reach the impressive snow-capped mountains as soon as possible. She had read that the mountains surrounding Estes Park were especially beautiful, and there was some sort of actual guest lodging in the settlement. Even though the first time she had ever hiked a soaring mountain was the volcanic one in Hawaii, she thought she might try her hand at even steeper and higher ones. She just hadn't realized how difficult reaching the mountains and Estes Park would prove to be.

Despite the Colorado Gold Rush, in 1859, which flooded settlers into many areas of Colorado, including the city of Denver, this particular northeastern section of Colorado where she was traveling was sparsely settled. In her first attempt to make it closer to the mountains, she had endured staying with that nasty, rude family about five miles west of the town of Fort Collins. They had been the only ones whom she could find to take her in as a lodger when she had been in a pinch. Narrow-minded, zealot in their Christian religious beliefs, they had looked down upon everyone else, despite the fact that they barely eked out a living themselves. She had stayed in a snake-infested hovel with a hole in the roof. Granted, the husband once tried to guide her to Estes Park, but he had proved to be a bumbling idiot, and she had met nobody who could give her specific enough directions so she could go herself.

At least she had made friends with one of their neighbors, the Murells, a nice couple who hailed from the same area in England as her own family, before her sister Hennie and she had moved to Scotland. But they had made her feel a little homesick, and the last straw was getting bucked off their horse. Her back still ached. Now she was in the small town of Longmont on the first leg of her trip home.

Supper at the lodging house would be served soon. She just hoped it wasn't some greasy fare covered with more flies. Tonight she would write Hennie explaining that she was cutting her trip short, returning to Scotland sooner than expected.

A few hours later Isabella lay in bed, staring up at the ceiling, wondering just how things could have gone so wrong. She had been filled with such anticipation about this trip as if something big was going to happen. She hadn't been sure what, but something exciting and special as if she was going to meet someone or see something that would be life changing. Her family used to tease her that she had inherited her grandmother's special senses for predicting events, her "fairy blood," as the family liked to call it; not that anybody in her family had really believed in silliness such as spirits or ghosts or fortune telling. But Isabella would get funny feelings sometimes, and she had learned not to ignore them. She would start thinking about a friend she had not heard from for a while, and a letter would arrive or they would show up for a visit. Her grandmother used to say her ears were burning when she had experienced similar feelings. She remembered one trip with her family, in particular, when Isabella had warned everybody to pack up early and leave the inn where they were staying. They had done so begrudgingly, but were glad when they heard it had caught on fire after they left. But her fairy feelings concerning this trip must have been wrong—way off target.

She heard a knock at her door and rose to answer it. She opened the door a smidge and found the plump innkeeper, affectionately called "the Captain" because of his prior military experience, grinning broadly. "Miss Bird, I overheard you saying at supper that you wanted to travel to Estes Park. I think I've found a solution to your problem."

She opened the door more widely. "Indeed. How so, sir?"

"Two new lodgers just arrived who told me they were traveling to Estes Park tomorrow. I hope you don't mind, but I took the liberty of asking them if you could accompany them and they agreed."

"That's brilliant! But who are they?"

"Two young gentlemen who have stayed here before. College students, I think."

"But can I trust them?"

"Now, I don't know them well, but they seem most obliging."

Isabella was skeptical and imagined there had been some heavy persuasion, maybe even coercion, on the gregarious innkeeper's part. But that wasn't going to stop her from taking up his offer.

"The only problem is I don't have a horse or mule to travel on. Do you think one may be found on such short notice?"

The innkeeper smiled. "I'll inquire for you now."

Within an hour all necessary arrangements were

settled, and Isabella retired for the evening, deciding to meet the gentlemen in the morning when she couldn't find them readily that evening to introduce herself.

Isabella had trouble falling asleep that night. She was too excited about the next day's trip. She just loved that her excursion was not ending so soon, but she also fretted about being able to keep up with the two young men. She would not only be riding an unfamiliar mount, but her back still ached from getting bucked off the Murell's horse. After several hours of tossing and turning, she finally managed to drift off to sleep.

At first light, Isabella washed her face, pulled her hair back in a tight bun and put on her special riding outfit, the one she had bought and used in Hawaii: a jacket and loose skirt covering trousers. She would never be caught dead wearing it in a major city but this frontier town was another matter. She knew it looked a bit odd, but it allowed her to ride freely like a man, astride instead of sidesaddle.

She heard voices outside as some people passed under her window. She suspected they were probably the men who she would be traveling with that day. She hurried over to the window to eavesdrop on them.

"I can't believe we agreed to this."

"Definitely a stupid move on our part."

"We could get there so much faster without some woman in tow."

"Well, maybe it won't be so bad. Perhaps she's young, beautiful, and vivacious."

Hardly. Isabella had no illusions as to her appearance. She knew she wasn't ugly, but she definitely was not the female for whom they were hoping. She was short, a bit overweight, had unexciting, thin brownish hair, a sharp nose, and slightly protruding teeth. She could at least take pride that she looked younger than her close to forty years.

Isabella finished packing up and headed outside. The innkeeper introduced her to her new companions, Mr. Platt

Rogers and Mr. Sylvester Downer; both tall, but whereas Mr. Rogers had blond hair and a roundish face, Mr. Downer was dark haired, with sharp, angular features.

She caught Mr. Downer giving a pointed look over at Mr. Rogers. Mr. Rogers smothered a cough with his hand and smirked back.

The innkeeper spoke up, "Miss Bird, the only horse I could obtain for you is a little high-spirited. But when the Murells dropped you off in Longmont, they told me about your famous riding skills despite getting thrown off their horse. I am sure you will make do just fine with this steed."

Isabella had been amazed when she first realized she was talked about so much. It was as if this whole Colorado frontier was one big gossip circle, and she was the current topic of interest. But on reflection, she knew women didn't usually travel on their own without chaperones, and she was English and not American; and she supposed the articles in local papers mentioning her arrival and her extensive traveling experiences were a source of chatter—so maybe it wasn't so strange after all that she was such a novelty for these Coloradans.

She mounted up with the innkeeper's assistance. The horse threatened to buck, but Isabella dug in her heels, and the horse took off at a gallop. Sharp back pain prevented her from gaining her seat, and it took an embarrassingly long time for her to get the horse to halt.

She turned her horse back around and headed toward the men who had also mounted up by now.

Mr. Downer commented first, "Miss Bird, this is quite an adventure for a little lady like you." He looked over at Mr. Rogers and both snickered.

Something along that line had been uttered to Isabella many times, but she never remembered taking such offense to the remark. She knew she needed to make the best of the situation, however, and politely asked, "Have you been to Estes Park before?"

Mr. Rogers spoke up, "On break from college we did some hunting and hiking in the area."

Mr. Downer added, "Don't worry. We remember the way."

Isabella shook her head. "Not worried at all. What are you studying?"

Mr. Rogers looked bored with the question, but answered, "Not sure yet."

Mr. Downer replied, "Law. Shall we get going?"

A half hour later, Isabella couldn't help taking pleasure in the fact that they were backtracking after making a couple of wrong turns. Several hours later, however, she just wanted the trip to end. Every jarring step the horse took hurt her back. She was forced to slow her pace, which clearly didn't please the men. It irked her that they made little effort to disguise their feelings with their petulant facial expressions.

Eventually the two just rode on ahead of her, making little effort to share their conversation. She knew things were going really badly when they lowered their voices and their exchange ended with Mr. Downer stating, "You owe me, Platt."

Mr. Rogers trotted off, and Isabella asked Mr. Downer, "Where's he going?"

"Platt can't take the slow pace. He's meeting us at Jim's."

"Jim who?"

"Jim Nugent. He's famous around here. A mountain-man type. Supposedly a bit rough around the edges."

Isabella inwardly groaned. This was the last straw. She was going to speak up now and show her discontent whether Mr. Downer liked it or not. "Personally, all I want is a warm room with a soft bed. I most definitely am not in the mood to meet anyone else—and especially not some frontier ruffian."

Mr. Downer snorted. "Sorry, Miss Bird. I happened to

miss meeting Jim the last time I was here because he wasn't home; but if Jim's at his cabin right now, you probably have no choice."

Chapter Seven

Jim listened with half an ear to the young pup bragging about his previous hunting experiences. He was more absorbed with his current job of cleaning his rifle. He gave an occasional "uh-huh" to not appear too rude. The guy, whose name he had already forgotten—something Rogers—had hailed the cabin a short while ago and joined him inside for a cup of coffee. He acted as if they were well acquainted, but Jim couldn't even remember whether they had met before. This guy would make a good politician.

"So anyways, as soon as we drop off the lady we plan on hunting and hiking some more."

That got Jim's attention. He obviously had missed something interesting.

"What did you say? I thought you were traveling with just a mate."

"Oh, I had been, but today we were forced into escorting the prehistoric Miss Bird with us. Well, maybe not forced, but close enough. The stiff English bitty should be here shortly if she doesn't slow down even more."

Jim glanced down at his clothes. He had an extensive wardrobe as far as he was concerned. In fact, he could divide it into three categories. The first he considered his best. They were his old but worth-cleaning-once-in-a-while clothes. His next-best were his torn clothes. They merited a washing depending on the size of the rip. Category three were his worst: stained working clothes so ripe they could stand upright on their own. Odd how visitors always seemed to arrive when he was wearing his category-three clothes. Jim shook his head. Too bad it was a lady this time.

Before Jim could ask more about the woman, Ring ran out the open door, barking loudly. Jim could differentiate Ring's various barks, and something had really roused him. Rogers walked out of the cabin, coffee cup in hand, and headed towards his young, smiling friend as if nothing unusual was happening—such as Ring barking in a complete frenzy around some strange-looking woman on a horse.

Jim stood in the doorway of his cabin a moment, scratching his neck, and stared at the scene in front of him. No wonder Ring was so spooked. Jim couldn't see much of her face as she watched Ring run around her, but she didn't look as old as Rogers had made her out. She looked about his age or a little younger.

But what the hell was that outfit she was wearing? The jacket was normal enough looking except maybe a bit long, ending mid-thigh instead of at her waist. But what was underneath that jacket? Her skirt looked as if it had a rip up the center. Was that intentional so the skirt would stretch wider when she mounted her horse *astride like a man*? Jim scanned her outfit further down and covered his hand over his mouth as he gaped. Her bloomers were showing. Of course they were showing because the skirt was clearly too short. Were those bloomers supposed to look like men's trousers? But they were pinched with ruffles on the bottom. What on earth . . . ?

He shook his head and walked toward the woman. He snapped his fingers, and Ring obediently sat at Jim's feet, uttering soft growls.

With a slight bow, Jim said, "Welcome, how do you do? I'm James Nugent. It's a pleasure making your acquaintance."

The woman briefly gazed at him, wide-eyed. Undoubtedly he seemed like a savage to her, wearing his dirtiest buckskins, but then, she didn't appear too normal either. Jim held back a smile. He took secret pleasure in watching people's reactions when he looked his worst, but acted his most polite. She probably hadn't expected him to have any proper manners but little did she know.

Oh! With sudden awareness, he realized he had forgotten to hide his scarred face. Normally on first acquaintance with a person, especially a woman, he would remember to turn slightly when speaking so only the good side of his face showed. The scar on his forehead had faded, but his right eye had a slightly crinkled indentation on the upper lid and still would not open. He just had been so surprised by her crazy appearance he had forgotten to conceal his disfigurement. Well, too late now. He had to give her credit though. At least she wasn't cringing at his appearance.

She straightened on her mount. "How do you do? I'm Isabella Lucy Bird."

"May I help you dismount?"

"No need."

Jim turned and introduced himself to Rogers's companion, Mr. Sylvester Downer. He was as clean and fresh-faced looking as Rogers. They both had clearly lived an easy life, very different from the one Jim had lived at their age.

As they talked about their college vacation, Jim kept glancing back at Miss Bird. He had to refrain from helping her as she grimaced and awkwardly lowered herself to the ground. But when she looked as if she was going to topple sideways as her foot hit the dirt, Jim lunged forward to steady her at the elbow. He shook his head as Rogers and Downer obliviously kept up a conversation between themselves.

"Miss Bird, I have hot coffee if you desire."

"Some water instead, please." She bent down to let Ring sniff her hand. Ring kept snarling.

"I'm afraid I've trained him to be my faithful watchdog. Your appearance is a bit—" Jim caught himself before he said the word *strange*. "Uh . . . unexpected. Be right back."

Jim sorted through his cabin until he found his least dented tin cup and filled it from a pitcher on the table. He headed back outside only to stop in the doorway again. Miss Bird was crouched down, stroking Ring's belly, cooing, "You're a tough dog, aren't you? Protecting your master from the mean lady." Ring panted and tried to lick her hand.

"Oh, for the love of . . ." Jim walked out and Miss Bird straightened.

"I apologize for the cup, but I can assure you the water's the best. It's from the fresh creek in back of my cabin."

She took a sip. "It tastes just like melted snow! I always loved eating snow as a child."

Jim chuckled and watched as Miss Bird's face first smiled, then blushed, then stiffened all within a few seconds. He guessed her remark was a bit too open and unguarded for a proper Englishwoman. What was she doing here?

As if sensing his question Miss Bird volunteered, "I've traveled to Colorado for my health. I hope to spend a few weeks in Estes Park. I've heard it's a lovely place to recuperate with splendid scenery and hiking. There's also lodging up ahead if I'm correct."

"Yes, at Griff Evans's house. You'll be made comfortable there."

Miss Bird glanced around the dirt-covered yard that surrounded his cabin, lingering at his stack of hides. "You hunt and trap, Mr. Nugent?"

"Yes, and I do some guiding for people visiting the area."

Miss Bird turned and surveyed the pine-covered hills surrounding his wildflower meadow. "It's certainly beautiful here. I imagine, also, the hunting is bountiful."

"Enough to make a living." Jim noticed that Downer and Rogers had walked over to the part of his pasture where his cattle were currently grazing. Jim frowned; he hoped they didn't do something stupid that might scatter them. He turned back to Miss Bird. "But I'm trying to raise a herd if the hunting and trapping fail."

"I see." She looked over at his cabin and studied it a moment, before asking, "Are those paws hanging from the roof?"

On impulse, Jim walked over to the side of the cabin, grabbed a pair of beaver paws and looped them around her saddle. "With my compliments."

She looked at him startled, then laughed and said, "Why, thank you."

Jim smiled; Miss Bird smiled back and kept her smile this time instead of tightening. Jim noticed that Downer and Rogers were strolling back towards them. He was surprised to feel a touch of disappointment that his conversation with Miss Bird would be interrupted.

Shortly thereafter, the three departed and Jim returned to cleaning his rifle. He'd probably see Miss Bird occasionally over at Griff's. Not that she was the type to truly interest him, but he would try to remember to wear his category-one clothes the next time he saw her.

Chapter Eight

After riding five miles west of Mr. Nugent's place, Isabella, Mr. Downer and Mr. Rogers arrived at the main settlement in Estes Park. From atop a small rise, Isabella viewed the valley below.

By a glistening pond was a trim, one-story clapboard house surrounded by three smaller log cabins. There were several outbuildings; one she surmised to be the milking shed as she watched a young woman carry a bucket back to the main house. Two young boys chased each other around the yard before climbing a split-rail fence to pursue each other in the surrounding grass-covered meadow where a small creek and a larger river converged nearby.

The scene was charming and picturesque, but it was not the most striking part of the view. The snow-capped mountains that Isabella had seen for weeks at a distance were now much closer and vivid. They were powerful looking and striking, with the famous Longs Peak she had read about hikers ascending, above them all.

"Welcome, travelers!"

Isabella turned to see a stocky man on a horse, waving and riding towards them. He reined in between Mr. Rogers and Mr. Downer and clapped Mr. Rogers on the back. "Platt! Good to see you again." He turned sideways and shook Mr. Downer's hand. "I hope you're staying longer this time, Sylvester."

Before the men could respond, he paced his horse backwards a few feet, turned toward Isabella and beamed. "But what I'm *really* looking forward to, is meeting our new visitor. *Pnawnd da.* That's 'Good afternoon' in Welsh. I'm Griff Evans. Pleased to make your acquaintance. You can call me Griff."

Isabella smiled and held out her hand. "I'm Miss Isabella Lucy Bird. I hope I may stay at your lodging while I visit Estes Park."

Griff leaned forward and firmly shook her hand. "Certainly, Miss Bird, as long as you wish. We always find room even if some of the men have to sleep on the floor. Isn't that right, Platt?"

Mr. Rogers smiled and nodded. "Sure is, Griff."

Griff turned towards Mr. Downer. "You boys hungry, Sylvester?"

"You bet we are, Griff."

Griff turned back to Isabella. "Miss Bird, you like beef and home-grown potatoes and fresh-made bread and home-churned butter and plenty of milk?"

Isabella nodded. "Sounds perfect."

Griff eyes shone. "Good. That's good. 'Cause that's what you're going to get tonight for supper and probably tomorrow night and probably the next night and the night after that!"

Isabella smiled. She didn't know what to say.

Griff started chuckling. "But don't worry, Miss Bird. Sometimes we throw in some venison or trout to make things interesting." Griff slapped his leg and laughed louder.

Griff paced forward a few feet with his horse while motioning with his hand. "Follow me, Miss Bird. Ellie should have supper on the table soon."

Isabella surprised herself by blurting out. "Griff, call me Isabella."

"That's how I like it, Isabella, everybody friends."

Toward dusk Isabella sat on a bench in Griff Evans's house and softly sighed with contentment. She had made it to Estes Park, a place that was not only beautiful, but also appeared to have no flies. Well, maybe one or two, but barely any. Not only that, all the Evanses had made her feel most welcome, even though she and the two men were three unexpected mouths to feed.

Ellie, Griff's wife, was also of Welsh descent, and though she matched him in his short height, was slim and much calmer and quieter. They had three kids, the boys muscular like their father but not as stocky. Isabella watched as Charlie, who had proudly told her he was nine years of age, wolfed down his food with intense concentration. Caroline, the eldest at fifteen, spent more time helping her mother than eating, and William, the youngest at seven, kept being reminded to stop petting Sport, their dog, and get back to eating. It was William who had broken the ice when she first arrived by excitedly asking curious questions about her riding outfit which she had happily answered.

They were a large group to feed. Besides Misters Downer and Rogers, there were several other young men who wanted to hunt or planned on prospecting. A middle-aged couple, Charles and Dorothy Gayer, had come to improve Charles's health, though Isabella wasn't sure yet what ailed him. Mr. and Mrs. Rudolph, who had been hired by Griff to help with the chores, also joined the gathering. Supper proved filling and satisfying.

Griff brought out a fiddle while Ellie and Caroline started clearing the table, and the group began singing a lively, little ditty. Well, everybody but Charlie, who was on his third helping of food, and Isabella. She was just so tired. Between not getting much sleep the previous night and the long day's travel, she could barely maintain a conversation.

But she smiled and pleasantly nodded to those around her and that seemed to be enough for now. After a good night's rest, she was sure she would be her usual sociable self.

She soon hoped to check out her sleeping arrangements. What a luxury that Griff was giving her a cabin of her own. She loved to travel but missed having her privacy sometimes. All in all, things were looking up.

The song ended, and Griff turned to Isabella. "Any idea of what you'd like to do during your stay here?"

"Would it be possible to hike up Longs Peak?"

Griff started to answer, but Sport diverted him, breaking away from William and rushing to the door, eagerly whining and wagging his tail. Isabella watched as the door slammed open, revealing Mr. James Nugent, growling like a bear with his arms raised over his head as if he was about to attack. Isabella was appalled a grown man was acting so . . . imprudent and . . . barbaric.

Charlie dropped his fork, and William shouted, "Mountain Jim!"

The two launched themselves on top of him, Charlie clinging to his back monkey-style, and little William hanging onto the side of his leg as if he were a baby opossum. More commotion ensued as Ring and Sport started growling and tussling at his feet for attention. He dragged himself, with Charlie and William still attached, over to the table in front of Caroline. Isabella couldn't believe the chaos Mr. Nugent was creating, and on purpose! Playing with children on occasion was fine, but this was beyond the limit of appropriateness.

Mr. Nugent bellowed, "Boys, you got me again. Caroline, you're looking particularly lovely today." Caroline blushed. He then glanced over at Isabella, and she realized she was staring with her mouth open. She quickly shut it.

Charlie jumped off and went back to his food while William switched his attention to Ring, tightly hugging him before chortling, "Jim, you wouldn't have said that a few hours ago. Caroline fell in the mud."

Charlie broke away from eating and got a mischievous expression on his face, eyes crinkling at the corners while he grinned. "Yeah, she looked like a pig!"

Caroline glared at Charlie, bit her lower lip and made a fist before giving him a hard shove.

Mr. Nugent sat down on the bench and said, "Caroline could be completely covered in mud and still attract a million suitors."

Caroline turned shyly toward him and said, "I don't have any suitors."

Mr. Nugent mockingly placed his hands over his chest and said, "You wound me. What about me?"

Ellie spoke up, "Jim, would you like some supper?"

"Just a slice of your fine bread would be welcome."

Isabella watched as Mr. Nugent took the attention away from Griff. It seemed he had made friends with many of the other guests already, especially the young hunters, and nearly all had some question to ask him. A brief debate ensued between the men as to whether Ring or Sport was the better hunting dog.

Isabella studied Mr. Nugent more closely. He had looked positively beastly, walking out of his crude log cabin today in his dirty buckskins, scuffed boots, and long straggly hair. The last thing she had expected was his rather refined manner of speech. She watched as he flirted some more with Caroline. She was definitely stunning; not the type of female who needed a certain hairstyle or just the right color of clothes to be beautiful. Years ago, Isabella figured, her own younger self probably would have resented Caroline just for her looks.

Mr. Nugent turned slightly, briefly exposing the scarred side of his face. Upon first meeting him, Isabella had been shocked by his disfigurement but quickly determined to not show her reaction out of sympathy towards his feelings. But after she had talked to him for a few minutes, she had concluded his scarring wasn't so ghastly—just mainly a closed right eye—and she had found it rather easy to ignore by the time she departed.

Isabella guessed he was in his late thirties or early forties. She discreetly studied him some more and realized that with his straight nose and strong chin he was actually good-looking with a classically handsome face like a Roman statue in one of Hennie's history books. She could imagine the attention he would attract if he dressed decently. But considering their age difference and the fact that Caroline could probably have her choice of husbands in the future, Isabella figured the flirting between the two had to be purely innocent.

Isabella startled slightly as Mr. Nugent addressed her, "Miss Bird, you look deep in thought."

"You did catch me woolgathering."

"I'm sure you're weary from your travels." He looked meaningfully over at Griff who jumped up from his place on the bench and said, "Och, sorry. I should have thought to show you to your cabin sooner."

Jim smiled. "That's right, Griff, you should have thought about it sooner. You are the lodge owner, aren't you?"

Griff playfully cuffed him in the back of the head. "You be quiet, Irishman. I'd like to see the kind of guesthouse you would run."

Jim watched a few minutes later as Griff escorted Miss Bird to her cabin. He shook his head. Miss Bird was certainly no sort of distraction for him. She had sat as boring as could be the whole time he was inside Griff's tonight. His mule Sassy would have been more entertaining.

Jim heard the peculiar screeching of a mountain lion. It didn't sound too close. He glanced again through the window. Apparently Miss Bird had heard the noise also. She quickly took off for her cabin, jumped onto the porch and slammed the door shut. Griff bent over laughing, knocked and went inside her cabin. Shortly thereafter a glow appeared in her window. Griff must have lit the fireplace for her. He watched as Griff left her cabin and made his way back to the main house.

Jim tightened the cinch on his horse a short while later, preparing to head home, and glanced up as Miss Bird threw the door back open, ran onto her porch, turned around, and with her hand over her eyes, tried to peer back into her cabin.

Jim quietly guided his horse over to her. "May I be of assistance?"

Miss Bird jumped a foot off the porch and threw her hands in the air. Upon landing, she grasped her chest with her hands and said, "Goodness, I didn't hear you approach."

He couldn't quite hold her gaze. "Sorry, didn't mean to startle you."

She straightened her shoulders, trying to compose herself before stating, "I thought I heard some noises under my cabin. It sounded like quite a few animals."

"Oh, that's the skunks."

She looked at him astonished. "You mean you know about them? Does Griff also know about them?"

"Of course, but there's nothing to be done unless we all want to take a chance of stinking to high heaven."

Miss Bird sighed. "Well, as long as they don't plan on entering my cabin, I suppose I'll get used to them."

She lingered on the porch, studying Jim a moment, and then frowned slightly.

Jim smiled. "You're still looking a bit puzzled, Miss Bird. Any more questions I can help you with?"

She removed the frown from her face. "No, no, not

really."

He tilted his head. "I sense there's something more."

"Oh, well, I wouldn't want to appear rude."

Jim smiled. "I'm sure you're incapable of that. I give you permission to query."

"All right." She frowned again slightly. "Then why do you dress like . . . uh, well . . . *like that*"—she slowly looked him up and down—"but are capable . . . well, at times . . . of speaking and acting as if you were *a perfect gentleman?*"

Jim chuckled; he found her amusing even though he knew he should be insulted. He glanced down at his old, but clean clothes. Hell, at least he was wearing his category-one clothes. "Oh, that's because both my parents had noble backgrounds."

Miss Bird gaped in surprise before remembering herself. She looked at him, skeptically. "I see."

"It's true. Both came from good Irish families. My father, as a second son, didn't inherit of course, and as was usual for second sons, entered the military. He was sent to Canada; my mother followed, and I was brought up there."

Jim tried to hold back a smile before adding, "What can I say? They did their best to raise a cultured and well-educated son, but the gentlemanly lessons didn't always stick."

She glanced sideways before muttering, "Indeed."

Jim snorted and she quickly looked back.

He was actually having fun with this woman. He cleared his throat and smiled. "Any more questions, Miss Bird?"

She bit back a smile. "No, no, nothing further. Have a good evening, Mr. Nugent." With that she turned, walked back into her cabin and shut the door.

Jim slowly rode home. Perhaps Miss Bird would be a bit of a diversion after all.

Chapter Nine

Jim left for several days of hunting and trapping while Isabella settled into her surroundings. She slept well, despite the skunks, and awoke one morning to a beautiful, cloudless sky and marveled at the scenery out her cabin window. A couple coyote youngsters dashed in and out of the shrubbery lining the nearby river before racing off. As ever, Longs Peak stood majestically in the distance. Isabella stretched, feeling remarkably better, her back no longer aching. After getting dressed she headed over to the main house for breakfast.

Ellie was making bread, and Isabella offered her assistance with the breakfast preparations. She had learned in America that it was quite unexceptional for gentlewomen to help with work. It hardly seemed to matter to Americans whether one had an aristocratic background. A person's wealth mattered, but not really his or her title. She suspected most Americans didn't even know the difference between a baron and a duke. She briefly wondered what her noble ancestors would have thought of her, with her shirtsleeves rolled up, no less, joining in the toil. It certainly would have disappointed her aristocratic 'de Byrd' ancestors, no matter how distant the relation now was. But even her current second cousins, the Archbishop of Canterbury and the Bishop of Winchester, would raise eyebrows. Isabella had done a little cooking while growing up, mainly for the novelty of it, but suspected she would learn a lot more about the art while staying here.

Griff walked in, carrying some milk. "Isabella, I trust you slept well. Would you like to do some horseback riding today?"

"Where did you have in mind to go?"

Griff hesitated a moment, then smiled. "I was hoping you might like to help with some cattle work I need done. I'm shorthanded and need to move a group out of a nearby canyon. It's close by so it shouldn't be too hard."

Cattle work? Well, she did want to get outside, and she knew she had the necessary riding skills so she pleasantly answered, "Why not?"

After breakfast she donned her special riding outfit and headed out to the yard. She took a deep breath, enjoying the crisp mountain air with a slight scent of pine. A gust of wind scattered fallen yellow aspen leaves at her feet as she walked over to where Griff was holding the bridle to the horse he had saddled for her to ride. "I think you'll like this mare. She's steady and reliable, but can be alert and quick when she needs to be."

"I can ride most any horse, Griff."

He grinned. "That's good to hear because some days the horses can be hard to gather, and we don't always ride the one we would like to."

Mr. Rudolph merely nodded a greeting as he joined them on horseback a moment later, and the three rode over to the canyon. Griff entertained her, joking throughout the morning, but Mr. Rudolph was disappointingly solemn and serious. She learned he was a Civil War veteran and suspected his experiences had dampened his spirits.

Isabella found she was a natural at cattle work. She quickly caught on to "reading" the cattle, figuring out how hard to "push" the cattle with her horse—as in how close and from which angle to get to a cattle's hindquarter to guide it in the direction she wanted.

Toward noon Griff complimented her on a job well-done and said he hoped she would help him again.

"Certainly, I'm enjoying this." She looked at him eagerly. "Sometime I would like to learn how to rope them."

"All in good time, Isabella. That takes a while to learn well."

Isabella glanced around at the surrounding mountains. "I was wondering, Griff, do you think one day we could hike up Longs Peak?"

Griff shook his head. "I don't know; September is late in the year to be considering that. It's not a place you want to be caught at in bad weather."

"I have such a glorious view of the mountain from my cabin. It's hard to resist not wanting to explore it."

"Well, let's see what the weather brings us the next few days, and maybe we can do something about it."

Later that evening there was more music with even the kids singing in harmony. Isabella wasn't surprised considering how the Welsh were known for their musical abilities.

The next few days progressed in a similar manner, with Isabella helping with breakfast, then riding with Griff and Mr. Rudolph to work the cattle. As far as Isabella was concerned, only a chance to hike Longs Peak could make things better. So at the end of each day it became her habit to ask Griff what he thought about it. For three days he told her that she'd better not consider it. But on the fourth day, after they'd finished more cattle work, Griff answered, "Since the weather's been fairly settled and mild, I suppose we could try it."

"That's brilliant!"

Griff chuckled. "Race you home."

They both kicked their mounts and took off.

Jim looked down over the valley and saw Griff's spread. It had been a successful hunting trip, and he was in a good mood. He thought he would stop in for a visit. A movement caught his eye. He recognized Griff galloping toward home with someone trailing only slightly behind. He focused more intently. Was that really Miss Bird? But who else wore such a ridiculous outfit? He could see she was laughing, her hair escaping from her bun in back. Humph. She rode well. He guided his mule toward Griff's.

Jim entered the main house and immediately sensed the excitement filling the room. All the guests seemed to be talking at once. Miss Bird glanced up from her conversation at the large table and smiled. "Mr. Nugent, Griff is guiding me up Longs Peak!"

Before Jim could respond she was back to talking with the other guests and the Evans family at the table. Jim sat down at the end of one of the benches facing the table. He was struck by a couple thoughts almost immediately.

The first was, *Miss Bird* is climbing Longs Peak? Not that a woman hiking the mountain was so spectacular anymore, times were changing, and a few women had already ascended the mountain in the last couple years—the lecturer Anna Dickinson just in the last month with a group of men. But hadn't Miss Bird said she was here for her health? Yet Jim had just seen her galloping a horse, and now she was going to do a vigorous hike? Jim shrugged; her illness must not be too serious.

But it was the second thought that Jim contemplated longer. *Mr. Nugent, Griff is guiding me. . . .* So Griff was on a first name basis, but he was still Mr. Nugent. It didn't sit well with him somehow. But on the other hand, she had spent more time with Griff, and nobody could deny he certainly was friendly.

Miss Bird abruptly stopped talking and looked lively across the table. "Dorothy, can I take a peek at your drawing? Is that the one you're doing for me to send to Hennie?"

Jim watched as Dorothy clutched the pad she had been sketching on, closer to her chest. "When I'm finished, dearie."

Her husband Charles shook his head. "That drives me crazy when you do that, Dorothy. Nobody wants to wait."

Isabella smiled. "That's all right, Charles. I'm sure it will be worth the suspense."

Charles nodded. "Probably so. By the way, Isabella, that concoction you gave me a few days ago seems to be doing the trick. I'm breathing better every day."

Jim watched as Miss Bird smiled complacently. "After all the doctors I've seen, I like to think I've picked up a thing or two about healing. I basically combined several of my elixirs. You're welcome to more if you wish. I've barely needed any remedies since I've come to Estes Park."

Jim nodded to himself. So the Gayers were Charles and Dorothy. It figured Miss Bird had made quick friends with the high-minded couple. Jim also liked them.

Charles was a retired history professor who could always be counted on for interesting conversation. With his wise and kind face, Jim was certain he was the person a stranger would approach on the street for directions.

His wife Dorothy was pretty and had few gray hairs as her husband, making it hard to determine her age. Dorothy had formal art training and usually carried a pencil and sketch pad around with her at all times. She had given Jim one of her sketches already even though they had only been at Griff's guest house for a few weeks. But it was more than Dorothy's pleasant manners and generous heart that Jim enjoyed so much. Right from the beginning of their acquaintance, Dorothy had treated him with true respect. She had never seemed to view him as just a ruffian, engaging him in honest, sincere conversation from the first—such as asking his views on the rapidly dwindling buffalo population on the plains—and then listening to his answers as if they were important to her. Jim had relished that about getting to know her. Yeah, he was on a first-name basis with the Gayers as well.

The Rudolphs both stood up from the table.

Miss Bird asked, "Mr. Rudolph, are you checking that sick steer again?"

He nodded and headed towards the door while his wife walked over to a bowl on a nearby table and punched down the dough that had risen.

Jim watched as Miss Bird's eyes lit up. "I can't wait for some of your fresh bread out of the oven, Mrs. Rudolph."

Mrs. Rudolph smiled back. "I add just the right dash of sugar whose secret amount I learned from one of my friends."

Jim scratched his chin. Now that made sense. He, also, rarely called the Rudolphs by their first name. Mr. Rudolph was too taciturn and his wife too much in everybody's business to want to make friends with either, no matter how long they had been working here.

Jim looked towards the door as Rogers and Downer walked in while Miss Bird asked, "Mr. Downer, did you have success hunting? What about you, Mr. Rogers?"

They both shook their heads, and Jim watched as Miss Bird briefly arched her brows. Was she taking pleasure in their failure? And did she call them by their formal name because of some reason in her head concerning their age differences or was it because she didn't like them and wanted to keep a distance from them? Well, Jim didn't enjoy being grouped in with the Rudolphs, Mr. Downer, and Mr. Rogers and silently vowed he would get her to call him by his first name—in fact, the next appropriate time when just the two of them were together.

Jim decided to join in the conversation and asked Griff what route he was taking up Longs Peak. He frowned as he listened to Griff's proposed ascent. Jim told Griff which way he usually went instead, and Griff soundly rejected his suggestion.

Jim shook his head vigorously. "Griff, your way is simply asinine. Stop being so stubborn and take my advice."

Griff glared back. "Your way will take too long."

"It may take longer, but the views are better; and isn't that the point, Miss Bird?" He didn't wait for her to respond. "Griff, it's also probably safer than your route."

"How would you know? You've never gone my way."

Jim glanced over another time at Miss Bird sitting at the table. He was almost a little envious that Griff would be guiding her up Longs Peak. Nah, he had better things to do with his time. But then again, there was just something about her. He turned back to Griff. "If I went your route with all those twists and turns, I'd end up lost."

"Spoken like a true idiot."

Jim again peeked over at Miss Bird. Why did he do that so much? Who cared whether she heard Griff insulting him?

Dorothy interjected, "I've got a warm blanket Isabella can use for the hike."

Miss Bird grumbled, "If they ever stop arguing about which way to go."

Dorothy assured her, "Don't fret a moment about it. They debate issues all the time."

Miss Bird shook her head. "Dorothy, you're a diplomat. I'd hardly call this debating."

Jim turned toward Dorothy. "I'll lend Miss Bird one of my fur robes. It'll be warmer."

Griff sputtered, "Och, we don't need your help. I've got it covered."

Jim turned back to Griff. "What horse will she be riding? It'd better be a steady mount."

"Probably Honeypie, not that it's your concern."

"Birdie would be better."

"As if an Irishman could ever teach a thing about horseflesh to a Welshman."

"That and more!"

Jim heard Miss Bird groan and watched her head drop onto the table.

The following morning at the main house Isabella drank a cup of coffee and thought about what she needed to do to prepare for her hike up Longs Peak. They planned on leaving early the next day, would spend the night on the mountain and return the following day—"they" being Isabella, Griff, and now, disappointingly, Misters Downer and Rogers. The two had returned, after briefly trying more hunting last night, and declared they wanted to hike up the mountain with them also.

Well, she couldn't go just with Griff. That wouldn't be proper, a married man and a single woman spending the night together. But then, it wasn't really proper for two men either to be acting as chaperones.

Isabella tapped her finger on the table. But on the other hand, the previous women hikers also had gone with groups of men.

She began biting her nail. She just wasn't sure what was appropriate under these circumstances. As if on cue, the gossipy Mrs. Rudolph said, "So I guess Mr. Downer and Mr. Rogers will be joining you, Miss Bird."

"Yes, would you like to come?"

"Heavens, no. Not my cup of tea."

No, spreading a scandal was her favorite brew.

Isabella finally caught herself from fretting. For goodness sake, at her age she should be able to do what she wanted. It wasn't as if she was some young maiden. Her already good reputation should be able to handle any untoward gossip this hike might produce.

Isabella watched as Mr. Downer and Mr. Rogers

started heading out the door to check on cattle with Mr. Rudolph.

Isabella stopped them by asking, "Don't you need today to prepare for the hike?"

Mr. Downer answered, "Not really, we're experienced at this kind of thing, Miss Bird."

By noon Isabella felt she had done everything she could to prepare for the hike including packing a satchel of food to bring along and sewing repairs to her riding outfit. She walked from her cabin over to the main house and after entering, asked Griff, "How early do you think we'll leave?"

Before Griff could answer, a grim Mr. Rudolph appeared in the doorway and announced, "The yearlings are acting sluggish."

Misters Downer and Rogers followed inside and slumped onto the benches, saying nothing.

Griff shook his head. "I'll ride over to the yearling pasture with you this afternoon and check on them. The owners are not going to be very happy with me if I lose too many of their cattle even if some of the things that can bring these young ones down are not my fault." He rubbed his forehead. "Just another thing I need to get done in Denver—talking to the cattle owners."

Isabella blew out a long breath. She knew there was no way Griff could take her to Longs Peak now.

Griff looked over at Isabella. "I'm sorry, but tomorrow's going to be tough to get away—"

She held up her hand and interrupted him before he could continue. "No need to apologize. I understand completely, truly I do."

There was a pause in the conversation until Isabella ventured, "What about Mr. Nugent? Do you think he would consider taking us?"

Mr. Nugent obviously knew the way. He had made that

perfectly clear yesterday. But, also, when she secretly thought about it, she couldn't deny that she was intrigued by the man. He couldn't be dismissed as just an uneducated boor. Perhaps the hike would be just a tad more interesting if Mr. Nugent acted as the guide.

Griff shrugged. "He might be busy or gone from home now."

Ellie intoned, "He's so nice. I'm sure if he can, he will."

Griff frowned a moment. "As long as he watches his drinking, I guess I have no problem with him taking you, Isabella."

Ellie looked thoughtful. "I haven't seen him drunk for a while now; have you?"

Griff shook his head. "Maybe not. But we don't know what he does when he's alone in his cabin."

Mrs. Rudolph spoke up, "The settlers around here are always happy to see him coming on that white mule of his. Remember when he brought several pounds of trout with him and gave some to everybody on the way to Denver? All the settlers around here are still talking about it."

Caroline turned to Isabella. "When our neighbor's daughter was sick, he rode to the doctor himself and brought the doctor back to help the Christners' baby."

Dorothy added, "He's really a sweet man, very knowledgeable."

Charles looked puzzled. "Sweet? What's so sweet about him? I doubt he'd appreciate being called that, Dorothy."

Ellie chimed in, "I agree with Dorothy; he's sweet."

Griff rolled his eyes. "Enough, ladies! We've heard it all before. Now who wants to head over to his place and ask him?"

Mr. Rogers answered, "Sylvester and I will once we grab a bite to eat."

Isabella offered, "I'll join you."

Mr. Downer replied, "Miss Bird, why don't you stay here? We can handle it."

Jim sat on a log in front of his cabin repairing one of his traps. He was using a trick with twisted, dried sinew to fix it that his trapper friend Wallace had taught him many years ago when they had both just been starting out at the Hudson Bay Company.

He paused in his work and stroked Ring's head who lay by his side. He thought about how pleasant it would be to have some of his good friends living nearby. His life could feel lonely at times.

His thoughts drifted to his friend Hugo Jaska. He recently had received a letter from him—actually, from his wife Lindsey whom Hugo had obviously cajoled again into doing the actual writing. Hugo's sons were growing up, and he wanted to send them to the best schools so they could receive the education that Hugo had not.

Jim brushed his hand through his hair. Hugo was such a good father. Would Jim be that dedicated a father? Hugo had teased him in the letter that it was more than high time to settle down. Perhaps he was right. Lately, Jim had been thinking more and more about it, especially what type of wife he would want. He knew he could never settle down with just a silly woman; he would want someone bright and intelligent, interested in all life has to offer, someone such as—well, Miss Bird. Jim chuckled, as if she ever had shown much interest in him! Quite the contrary, in fact.

Ring nuzzled Jim's hand, asking to be pet some more. Estes Park was starting to fill with other families, settling in the area. He had yet to meet the Macgregors who had placed a claim north of Griff's. Some of those guests at Griff's would probably end up staying in Estes Park. He wouldn't mind if the Gayers stayed on.

His thoughts wandered to some of Griff's other guests who had visited in the past. Jim frowned; he still didn't know whether anything was happening between Lord Dunraven and Griff.

Ring began barking, interrupting Jim from his thoughts. He saw Downer and Rogers approaching. Those were two he could do without. Well, perhaps they weren't so bad, just bothersome. Now Miss Bird would be enjoyable as a neighbor—Jim stopped. My God, did she ever stop popping into his thoughts?

Jim waited for Downer and Rogers to dismount before asking, "What brings you by today?"

"We were wondering if you were free the next few days to do some guiding up Longs Peak."

"Who's asking?"

"We are."

"Oh, uh . . . I'm busy."

"Well, also Miss Bird."

"I thought Griff was taking her."

"He can't—some problem with his cattle."

Jim scratched his chin, then said, "When did you want to leave?"

"Tomorrow, while the weather's still good."

"All right, I'll take you, but be ready early."

After they left, Jim walked over to his mule Sassy, then changed his mind and headed to his sleek Arabian mare. Miss Bird would appreciate this beautiful steed. Perhaps the horse might interest her even if he didn't at this point. He paused, putting his hands on his hips. Maybe he could change that. Jim smiled—it might even be entertaining, trying.

Chapter Ten

Isabella looked up ahead where Mr. Rogers and Mr. Downer were leading their group to Longs Peak—or rather, pretending to lead their group since she was sure they didn't know where they were going.

"I hope they get lost," she muttered to herself and then sighed. They were turning her into such a shrew. She just found the two men so irritating.

First, they had appeared late this morning, holding Mr. Nugent and her up, and she distinctly remembered hearing them saying yesterday that they didn't need any extra time to get ready. Next, what irked her, was that when they finally did show up, they acted as if Mr. Nugent was one of their best friends, and she hardly thought that was the case. Other than answering their occasional hunting questions when he was at Griff's place, Mr. Nugent never seemed to show much interest in them. Not that she should care one way or another how they acted toward him, but it still annoyed her. She supposed they wanted to brag to their friends that they knew him. He certainly was famous. There was something written about Rocky Mountain Jim in every newspaper she had read at Griff's, some paragraph about one of his local hunting exploits or short opinion articles written by the man himself.

Isabella looked over to where Mr. Nugent was riding

his horse. She didn't think she would ever figure him out. Not that she couldn't have predicted his outfit today. The filthy buckskin pants, mismatched boots, patched-together fur hat, and ripped waistcoat with a revolver sticking out of a pocket were completely expected. But to see him wearing that outfit, while riding one of the most beautiful horses Isabella had seen thus far in America, was baffling. What made it even more noteworthy was that he was such a superb horseman, right now reining his Arabian mare in tight circles, then pacing backwards, before performing another tight circle, demanding proper obedience from his horse.

Appearances aside, she had yet to be in his company when there was a topic of conversation in which the man couldn't join in and participate intelligently. Just this morning, while grabbing a cup of coffee before heading out, Isabella had walked in on Charles and Mr. Nugent discussing falconry, of all things, as apparently Gayer was an old Bavarian German name meaning bird of prey, and medieval Gayers had been falconers for nobility.

Mr. Nugent waved at Isabella and trotted over before stating, "I need more riding time. This horse is getting lazy."

Isabella smiled. "Well, get to it then. No time like the present."

Mr. Nugent galloped off and worked with the mare some more. She found she was fascinated watching him, at a distance that was. It would be unseemly, otherwise, to stare at him up close. Isabella shook her head. Not that she was actually staring at him, she was observing his equestrian skills, that's all.

Jim noticed the surrounding landscape was becoming more heavily covered with trees and cantered over to where Miss Bird was now riding before coming to an abrupt halt. "This bit of work has helped. She's already more responsive."

Miss Bird smiled amiably. "You look as if you've been riding all your life."

"My father taught me."

Just then Downer turned around and shouted, "Jim, are we heading in the right direction?"

"You're doing fine. Just keep going." He waved his hand forward and chuckled.

"What's so entertaining?"

"If I just can keep them moving ahead I might not talk to them the whole day!"

"You're terrible, Mr. Nugent." Her eyes sparkled with amusement.

He grinned. "Then it wouldn't be any hardship if you didn't talk to them, either?"

"Honestly, no."

"Well, then, let's enjoy the day together."

He looked over at Miss Bird in her bizarre riding outfit. Griff had loaned her some sturdy boots that were way too large for her feet. He shook his head and smiled. The boots made the outfit even more absurd looking.

He cleared his throat. Now that he had suggested they ride together, he couldn't think of a thing to say. After an awkward moment, he was grateful when she broke the silence. "I heard the first women to climb Longs Peak were just in the last couple years."

He nodded. "Well, actually, the first were probably Indian women, considering the Ute and Arapaho lived around here for years before us. The Arapaho used to climb Longs Peak for eagle feathers."

"Where are the Indians now?"

"Reservations, when they choose to stay on them. There's talk of trying to change the braves, who grew up being warriors and hunters, into farmers. I doubt they'll agree when there's still plenty of game to feed their families in the surrounding area. I hear many only report to the agency for their staple of rations, such as sugar and flour, which they have become used to eating. Slaughtering all those buffalo on the Colorado plains, however, is going to force many Indians eventually to live off of rations alone. Hopefully the crooked agents will be caught or the Indians could end up starving on those reservations."

She nodded thoughtfully. "Quite so."

He searched for something to add. "The Ute have a smart chief by the name of Ouray. I hear he speaks several languages including English. He went to Washington last year for land negotiations, but the treaty the Utes signed this year so miners can prospect on their prior territory has cost them some of their best grounds. I'm sure not all the Ute tribes are happy about it, and there'll be trouble ahead."

She was quiet a moment, then replied, "It seems to me that the Indians have not been treated well at all in this country."

He nodded. "There's still a lot of unrest. They fight the settlers and still have age-old battles amongst themselves, though Estes Park itself has not had any significant Indian trouble for several years now."

He couldn't think of anything more to add. Another awkward silence.

"Um . . . I never asked who or what is an Estes."

Jim inwardly groaned. He hoped the whole day wasn't going to be this stiff conversation.

"Estes was the original settler."

"Where does he live? I haven't met him yet."

"He and his family left. Your cabin is on the original homestead. They only stayed about five or six years."

She looked baffled. "That seems rather strange to name an area for someone who didn't stick around."

"There are worse names it could have been called. Talk to Byers, the editor of the *Rocky Mountain News*, if you don't approve. He named the area."

"I like it when Indian names are used. Cheyenne is a dirty frontier town, but the name is almost . . . melodic."

Jim caught himself from chuckling and attempted to look serious. "I take it Cheyenne was not to your liking."

"Certainly not. Rough shacks and crude people."

"Miss Bird, you just need to get in the spirit of things when you're there." He arched his brows. "Have a little party."

She frowned. "And I suppose you have no problem doing that, Mr. Nugent."

He grinned. "Call me Jim, and in answer to your question, not at all." He stretched and added, "I didn't eat enough breakfast. I'm so hungry right now I could eat a bear."

"Mr. Nugent, if you did that you'd end up as huge as Henry the Eighth."

Jim smiled to himself. He was going to get this woman to call him by his first name if it was the last thing he did today. "Isabella, call me Jim. Now, your Henry the Eighth would have known how to appreciate Cheyenne. I wouldn't mind inviting him to my little party if he were still alive."

She gasped. "Mr. Nugent, you've just insulted one of England's finest monarchs."

Jim laughed. "Okay, I'm not particular. Let's make it Peter the Great instead. I'd let him come to my little festivity."

She narrowed her eyes. "That Russian destroyed every elegant London manor he stayed at with his drunken behavior."

He chuckled. "I know."

She stuck out her chin. "Why don't you invite one of your own patriots, such as John Adams, while you're at it?"

He scratched his neck. "Nah, John Adams was a stick in the mud. His cousin Sam, possibly. Now, good old Benny Franklin could come, but only if he invited some of his French girlfriends."

"That's outrageous! At least you seem to be well versed in your history."

Jim smiled. "I try, Isabella. I try."

The morning flew by. They continued to banter during their midday break, to the exclusion of Misters Downer and Rogers, on into the afternoon. Finally both became sleepy and quieter later in the day, but by now silent moments were no longer awkward.

Toward dusk Jim instructed the group to make camp near a group of sturdy spruce trees that provided some shelter from the blustery wind. While eating, Downer asked Jim about his scarred face, and he told the details of his bear attack.

Isabella shook her head. "Lucky you survived."

Jim looked over at her. "Actually, it's nothing compared to what some men have gone through. You know the story about Mountain Man Hugh Glass?"

"No, another bear attack?"

"Yeah, only his fellow trappers left him behind for dead with no horse or gun, and when he came to he made his way, barely crawling at times, to the nearest fort, a couple hundred miles away. He wanted to kill the trappers when he finally caught up with them."

Rogers asked, "Did he?"

"No, he forgave them. One of those trappers was a young Kit Carson. And I'm still dumbfounded about that woman up in Montana years ago."

"What woman?" Downer asked.

"I forget her name, but she was traveling by wagon through the Montana Territory with just her father and two brothers when they left her one day to do some buffalo hunting. They never returned, and she had to make it on her own."

Isabella shuddered. "Goodness, what did she do?"

"She made a shelter out of logs and sod and spent the winter there by herself. The snow practically buried her. When spring came some Indians found her and were so amazed she had survived the winter by herself that they didn't kill her, but took her to a nearby fort. Don't know what happened to her then."

He added, "She was lucky. A lot of the Indians up north aren't so friendly, never really have been. Over fifty years ago trapper John Colter was captured by some Indians and told they would let him go if he won a footrace against the fastest braves in their tribe. He had to do it naked and barefoot, of course. But he survived after killing the one Indian who caught up with him and then managing to hide. He also eventually made it to a fort a couple hundred miles away."

Isabella shook her head. "It's a wonder the West was settled at all."

Jim smiled at Isabella and started singing, "Oh, there once was a trapper, who put on his capper, better to look dapper, so the maid'd be on his lapper."

He pointed to his lap and raised his eyebrows. Isabella shook her head, reprovingly.

"Well, if you don't like that, how about some poetry?"

Rogers frowned. "By whom?"

Jim smiled. "One of my own masterpieces."

He stood and composed a piece quickly. He had no intention of sharing his best poetry with the overconfident college boys. He bellowed in the most dramatic voice he could muster,

> "Oh, as I look at the moon over yonder,
> It makes me want to ponder,
> If the fair maiden was mine,
> wouldn't it be a wonder,
> The heavens would rejoice so loud, it'd sound like thunder."

A coyote howled in the distance to the unexpected noise, and Ring perked up his ears. Jim caught Rogers smirking at Downer while Isabella sat grinning. Jim watched as the two men grabbed their bedrolls and spread them far enough away from Jim not to hear him.

He turned back to Isabella. "I was wondering what it would take to get rid of them."

She chuckled then looked at him seriously. "Were you involved in any Indian attacks yourself?"

He sat down a few feet away from her and stretched out his legs. "When I was a scout for the army, sure."

"No, I mean just you."

He stared at her a moment. He didn't tell people what happened to Wallace and himself; it just wasn't a story he liked to share. But there was something about this woman that made him want to tell her. Her and nobody else.

He began, "When I worked for the trapping company I had a good buddy. Oh, and you'll like this—his name was Wallace, as in the Wallace clan, as in William Wallace, grand defender of Scotland."

"Don't tell me he claimed him as his ancestor. William Wallace lived over five hundred years ago."

He smiled. "Well, I would have liked to see you try to tell him that. Anyways, Wallace and I started out together as two new hires for the trapping company." He shook his head. "Our first week we didn't know what we had gotten ourselves into. Neither one of us had figured on trapping being so hard. It was bad enough wading in freezing streams for hours, laying traps, but just hideous when you had to go back for the drowned beaver. Wallace told me he wasn't sure what smelled worse, the stinking furs or some of the men. You could always tell the more experienced men, though, because besides stinking, even if they were only in their twenties, the grueling life left them looking like old men—"

Isabella broke in, "You don't. I mean, you don't look like an old man. You look . . . well, handsome, as I'm sure you must realize." Even though the campfire light was dim, Jim could see her suddenly blushing.

There was an awkward pause. Jim was shocked. This scarred face was *handsome* to her? He couldn't help but feeling pleased. He bit back a smile and shrugged. "I guess everybody ages differently."

He waved his hand dismissively to get pass the embarrassing moment. "Anyways, the experienced trappers would refer to us as 'boy' or 'kid,' but that stopped once we distinguished ourselves among the men. Wallace was some kind of genius. He could fix just about anything, and believe me, things always needed repair with our rough lifestyle. And I became valued—"

Isabella held up her hand and interrupted, "No, let me guess." She looked him up and down, hesitated, and then said, "I know. You became known as the trapper to go to for clothes mending and cleaning." She started giggling.

It was a pleasing sound and made her look years younger. Jim smiled. "All right, Miss Fancypants. I'll admit I'm wearing some of my category-two clothes, but I needed to so I would stay warm this trip. I'd like to see you stay clean and tidy working as a trapper."

She stopped laughing and looked at him puzzled. "Your category-two clothes?"

He shook his head. "Never mind. I'll tell you about that sometime later. No, what I became skilled at was sign language and learning Indian words, which was particularly handy when it came time for trading. But Wallace and I were quite a pair at first, I couldn't fix anything, and he couldn't learn a foreign language if it killed him, but we helped each other out and became tighter friends. But what really made us close was, after working for about a month, we started getting a little cocky, and we told Hugo Jaska, our Booshway—"

She shook her head bewildered. "Your what?"

"Our boss, that we wanted to explore for beavers on our own. Hugo agreed but told us to leave the horses and go on foot. Well, we ended up getting lost. Wallace was like some male dog sniffing around his new territory, having to check out what was behind every set of rocks and trees. So we'd hike together for a while, then separate, then again rejoin each other. But when we rejoined each other, we would talk up a storm."

Isabella perked up. "What kind of things did you two men talk about?"

Jim smiled. "Were you hoping for something scandalous, Miss Bird?"

She looked indignant. "Of course not, I'm just interested in your conversation."

"Uh-huh. Well, we spent a good part of the time complaining about the other men who were a prickly minefield of personalities, to say the least." He smiled. "But I always loved hearing Wallace's grand schemes for making money and then settling on a homestead with his girlfriend Karla. He could go on about her forever. The problem was, we talked so much that we neglected the most basic rule of exploring."

Isabella frowned. "What basic rule? I've never heard of any basic rule." She fussed with straightening her bloomer trousers.

He cocked his head back in surprise. "With all the travelling you've done, Isabella? Keep checking behind you, and take note of landmarks so you can find your way back. Well, anyways, Wallace took off to explore one more set of rocks way off in the distance and never returned. He simply vanished. I looked everywhere for him, and after about an hour, I was so turned around myself I didn't know where I was going."

She looked up. "Were you scared?"

Jim hesitated. Yeah, of course he was, but did he want to admit that to her? Maybe she would think him weak. Jim shook his head slightly. No, this was a woman who would understand. So Jim answered honestly, "You bet. I had never been so truly lost before. It became cloudy and snowy so I had no sense of direction, nothing to help guide me."

"What happened?"

"Oh, we eventually found each other by shouting for one another, but had to spend one endless, miserable, cold night together listening to the wolves howling. We didn't dare build a fire not knowing who else might be around. Finally, the sky started lightening in the East, giving us some sense of direction, and we found a stream that luckily ran by the camp. It was humiliating, to say the least, but I remember Hugo just shook his head and told us to get back to work. Anyways, after that experience, Wallace and I should have been best friends for life." Jim looked at the ground.

"Should have been?"

Jim looked up and smiled softly at Isabella. She had caught that. She really listened carefully to him. "Yeah. So months later Hugo asked us to get some meat."

"Why you two?"

Jim raised his chin smugly. "He knew Wallace and I were obviously the best marksmen."

She smiled. "If you do say so yourself."

He threw a small twig at her. "Yes, if I do say so myself, and stop interrupting, Isabella, or I'll never get the story told."

She crossed her arms. "By the way, I never gave you leave to use my familiar name."

"Your what?"

"My familiar name."

"You mean Isabella? For the love of God! We're spending the next couple days together. You're stubborn, Isabella. How many people have told you that?"

Isabella uncrossed her arms and studied her hand. "Maybe a few. Oh, all right, but call me Miss Bird when other people are around."

Jim shook his head, incredulously. "Why should I do

that?"

Isabella shook her head as if she couldn't believe he had just asked that. "Clearly, because we're both single, people with think if we use our first name with each other that there's more going on between the two of us than there is."

Jim mockingly clasped his chest. "Oh, heaven forbid!"

Isabella frowned. "Just do as I say, all right?"

He looked skyward and then continued. "Anyways, where was I? So Wallace and I headed out and spotted a deer entering this densely wooded forest. We hobbled our horses and decided to separate. When we were about thirty feet apart, Wallace had the clearer shot and signaled that he would take the deer. His shot was true, and the deer stumbled and fell. I shouted, 'Well-done,' and Wallace waved back."

Jim paused and took a deep breath. "It was the last time I ever spoke to him."

Isabella remained quiet and held his gaze several long seconds.

He continued. "As if from nowhere, an arrow hit Wallace in the neck. Blood instantly started pouring out. Another whizzed by, barely missing me. I tried to take a shot, but I couldn't see through the dense forest where I should be aiming. Both of us took off at a run, but I saw Wallace quickly overcome by about five Indians shrieking up a storm."

She gasped. "What did you do?"

Jim hung his head, then looked intently back at Isabella. He was going to tell her the whole truth. "I kept running . . . to find adequate cover. Maybe then I could try to help Wallace. . . . I guess I thought I needed some cover to shoot from."

Isabella frowned and nodded. "I understand. Go on."

Jim cleared his throat. "But as I was dodging and jumping over fallen trees, I heard Wallace's gargled scream and honestly thought then only about saving myself."

Isabella reached over from where she was sitting and briefly squeezed his hand. "As anyone would have done." She straightened and looked at him with concern.

Jim barely nodded. "So I kept running, but my side was cramping and I paused. That was when I heard the Indians trying to catch up to me."

She brushed her hand over her head grabbing her bun. "Good Lord, what happened next?"

"I saw three large trees that had fallen on top of one another, providing a hiding spot. I slowed, did my best to quickly cover my trail and slipped in deep under the trunks. The forest became quiet then, and I remember hoping the Indians had given up on me. But sure enough, one came close by. Luckily he didn't see me and left. I waited what seemed like hours before leaving that place. I slowly made my way back to check on Wallace, hoping he had survived."

Isabella shook her head. "But he hadn't."

"No." Jim remembered gagging at the gruesome sight of Wallace hacked in the head. Isabella didn't need to hear all the details.

He resumed the story. "I started back to camp, but at the edge of the forest I rested, crouching down in a clump of bushes. The birds stopped singing. I heard footsteps, a soft rustling of leaves. I peered through the branches. There was an Indian standing right in front of the bushes, his knife in his hand with his back to me."

"Not more trouble."

"Yep. The Indian must have heard me slightly shifting because he suddenly tensed. I saw no other Indians, so I rose up, covered his mouth with my left hand, and . . ." Jim wavered before continuing, not sure if he should tell her.

But Isabella practically cried out, "And what?"

Jim frowned, then motioned with his hand. "I sliced across his neck."

Isabella covered her mouth with her hands and said nothing. Jim sighed. Well now she knew without any doubt what he was capable of doing.

"I dragged the Indian back into the bushes." He paused, absorbing all the painful memories. "I remember feeling no sense of triumph; in fact, the death sickened me. I had been involved in minor Indian skirmishes before, but always with the rest of the company. This was the first human life I had taken. And when I turned the Indian over I realized how young he was, and it sickened me even more." He swallowed. "At dark I finally made it back to camp."

He frowned and became quiet again. He remembered going straight to Hugo, who told him to get some rest, that they would get Wallace in the morning. But he didn't listen to Hugo and started drinking. The men let him get drunk after learning about his day. One tried to reminisce about Wallace—*You'd think he was William Wallace's son, the way he went on about him.* The other men had laughed softly. Furious, Jim had grabbed the man by the throat but was restrained by the other men, who guided him back to his bedroll. The next day Hugo told him: *You can't find a better gentleman sober, but when you drink, you're out of control.*

Jim looked up at Isabella, who thoughtfully stared back at him. What was she thinking? Was she completely disgusted with him now? He experienced a sudden sharp feeling of disappointment over what he might have lost by telling her the whole story.

He continued. "After all these years I can't help thinking, what if I had done something different? Taken a better shot. Gotten back to Wallace sooner. Maybe he would still be alive."

Isabella got up and sat down next to him, looping her arm through his. "You did the best you could, and that's all any of us can do. You're lucky to be alive. I would guess at least half the mountain men who headed out West never returned. Wallace must have known the dangers."

He nodded, relieved by what she had just said. "I don't usually talk about this."

"I'm sorry I made you recall the memories."

"Oddly enough, I found I wanted to tell you."

Isabella unlooped her arm and turned to face him as if taking in the full meaning of what he had just said. "But these recollections hurt you, and I'd never want to do that intentionally."

He gazed back at her. "I know. But perhaps having someone to talk to about them helps heal the pain."

They stared at each other a moment. Jim wondered what was happening between them. Did she also feel this sense of closeness?

"What are you thinking about right now, Isabella?"

She looked away briefly and then, with wonder in her voice, said, "For some reason I'm finding I'm curious about all sorts of things about you."

"Like what?"

"What were your parents like? What were you like as a kid? Why did you become a trapper?"

Jim smiled softly. "My parents. Well, my mother was pretty and always stylishly dressed. She could busy herself finding things to do all day long, but at the end of the day you could never figure out what she had actually accomplished. My father was definitely stricter than she was. I was an only child, and my mother doted on me."

Isabella smiled warmly. "You mean you were spoiled rotten."

He chuckled. "Well, if I wasn't skipping school to wander in the woods, I was only making a token effort at learning my lessons. Then after school my first stop was always to the blacksmith."

She shook her head confused. "The blacksmith?"

"Sure. The blacksmith always had the best stories from people who were traveling through town and needed his repairs. Everyone thought he was one mean brute, but I somehow managed to tame him."

She briefly looked skyward. "Why am I not surprised?"

Jim shrugged. "For some reason he took a liking to me and never seemed to mind answering all my questions."

"Then I bet you were off to the woods."

"Not yet. From the blacksmith's I would saunter by the millinery and give a wave and a wink to the ladies inside. Then I usually moseyed over to Old Man Gilbert's porch to pat his big dog, then a game of tops with the little kids in the street before a stop inside the general store. If I was lucky the old widow was inside. She'd buy me a candy stick and give me some of her homemade ginger cookies if I offered to carry her groceries home. *Then* it was squirrel hunting in the woods."

Isabella shook her head while smiling.

"What about you, Isabella? What were you like as a kid?"

Isabella sat more erect and crossed her arms. "I was always perfectly behaved. Never gave my parents a bit of concern."

Jim snorted. "I bet."

"Anyways, don't change the subject. How old were you when you left home?"

"Late teens. My father wanted me to enter the military as he had, but the strict rules and discipline, definitely, were not to my liking. I wanted to travel the world, but I couldn't figure out how I would support myself. Then one day an agent with the Hudson Bay Company came to town." Jim smirked. "What a glorified version of the pleasures of traveling, the camaraderie, and, of course, the great potential for profits and wealth I heard that day."

"What did your parents think about you joining?"

"They really opposed the idea. My mother could only imagine all the dangers involved, with wild animals and

Indians, and my father was concerned with my making money. This was the late 1840s, not the 1820s, and the beaver were becoming trapped out by then. Also, hat styles were changing and there just wasn't the same demand for beaver. But I figured there were other valuable animals to hunt and trap."

Isabella frowned. "So you left against their wishes?"

"Not for a year or so. It took a sorrow over a girl to give me the final push to leave home."

"Who was—?" She didn't finish the question. Jim was relieved. He didn't want to talk about another woman with Isabella right now.

He quickly continued. "The problem was my parents remained opposed to the idea of me becoming a trapper. My father just refused to support what he considered a bunch of foolishness. So I left saddened with this big rift between my parents and me."

Isabella shook her head. "I was always close to my parents. I'm sorry to hear that you weren't at this important time in your life."

Jim ruefully nodded. "If you only knew. With no money from my father to pay for a horse and trapping equipment, I had to start as an 'engage,' or hired hand. All my necessities were supplied by the company. In exchange, any furs or hides I brought in belonged to them. I quickly learned that there was a hierarchy among the trappers, and the elite were the free trappers who owned their own equipment, kept all profits for themselves, made their own rules, and lived life on their own terms. I had to follow the company rules. In some ways, I was living a life no better than a slave. The experienced men told me I had sold my soul to the company."

Isabella indignantly said, "I'm completely opposed to slavery in any form. I come from a line of abolitionists." She sat straighter. "Why, I'm a proud relation of Wilberforce, the 'Liberator.'"

Jim frowned. "Who?" He pursed his lips pretending seriousness, then asked, "Is this someone I would want to invite to my little party in Cheyenne?"

She tried not to smile. "Certainly not. I'll have you know William Wilberforce was a leading English abolitionist. He led the parliamentary campaign against the British slave trade for years until the passage of the Slave Trade Act of 1807."

"Oh, I forgot. The English eliminated the abomination of slavery long before the Americans."

"That's right. There's plenty you Americans can learn from the English if you'll only listen."

Jim smiled. "Oh, I'm listening, Isabella. Believe me, I'm listening. Especially when the words are coming from a pretty Englishwoman such as yourself."

Looking flustered a moment, Isabella quickly composed herself and stated, "I know I'm not pretty . . . attractive maybe . . . but only in a certain light."

Jim frowned. "That's not so, Isabella. First off, you're pretty on the inside, and that's where it counts the most. And secondly, you're pretty on the outside, but only when you smile—definitely not when you scowl at me."

Isabella stood and shook her head though she was unable to hold back a smile. "I think I've heard enough for one evening. I'm going to bed. See you in the morning."

Jim grinned. "I'm looking forward to it, Isabella. I really am."

Isabella headed over to the nearby cluster of spruce trees where she spread a blanket over a mound of soft needles. Jim ordered Ring to stay beside her for the night.

"You speak to him as if he's human."

"He understands. Ring, go."

Ring curled up next to Isabella, but stared longingly back at him.

Jim fell asleep quickly, but the blustery wind and dropping cold temperatures high on the mountain awoke him several hours later. He looked over at Isabella. Her back was turned to him, but he could see she was awake, fidgeting with her covers. He felt an unexpected concern of protectiveness toward her. He longed to walk over and join her next to Ring. He didn't dare, knowing it would make her feel uncomfortable. He wondered how a woman could have such courage traveling around the world by herself. She had said it was for her health. He still hadn't asked her any of the details. He had learned today that she wanted to write about her travels. She hoped the letters she wrote to her sister would help her remember the details later. He suspected there was probably a lot of the reality that would be changed in the writing, and a lot of the writing that would be changed in the publishing.

He heard some coyotes howling and felt for his revolver lying next to him. He realized he hadn't seen a gun on Isabella. He shuddered at the thought of something dangerous happening to her, helpless without a weapon. Maybe she had a gun in some hidden pocket in that crazy riding outfit of hers. He would have to ask her in the morning. He was beginning to like that getup. Actually, he was becoming fond of more than just her clothes. He smiled to himself and slowly drifted back to sleep.

The next morning Jim and Isabella gazed at the beautiful colors reflecting off the pond far below them. They had never looked so vivid, and he had been to this campsite many times before. He treasured sharing this exquisite view with her. What would it be like to have such a woman beside him always? When Isabella glimpsed over at him, he looked away quickly and muttered, "The wind causes my eye to tear sometimes."

He saw Downer and Rogers playfully punching each other in the arms about thirty feet from where he was standing. "Guess they have trouble appreciating the beauty around them."

She followed his line of sight and smirked. "Guess so."

The group mounted up and headed out shortly thereafter, Downer and Rogers leading again. Jim asked Isabella where she kept her derringer.

"Oh, I don't have a gun."

"You mean you didn't bring one for this trip?" He could understand that considering she probably felt he would keep her safe.

"No, I never carry a gun. I wouldn't know what to do with it."

"What? Are you crazy? That's one of the most foolish things I've heard in a long while. Are you even aware of the possible dangers you face as a woman traveling alone?"

She laughed at his concern. He stared at her wide-eyed for a moment and shook his head.

He asked, "Did you bring any change of shoes? Those boots Griff gave you are really too big."

"I know, my feet are sliding around in them when I try to walk. I didn't realize how difficult it would be and didn't bring any others. Oh, well. Beggars can't be choosers. Do you think we'll see an eagle's nest on the summit of Longs Peak today?"

"If not, I'll take you on another hike up Eagle Cliff Mountain where there usually are some."

Isabella smiled. "I'd really like that. When could we go?"

"Maybe next week. You'll want some rest after today's hike."

Jim wondered whether it was the fact that she would see an eagle's nest or that they would be doing something together again that she liked. He added, "And while we're up there, I'll show you how to shoot a gun."

Isabella playfully said, "I'd never shoot an eagle. Why, they're magnificent. How could you consider doing such a thing?"

He lifted a corner of his mouth. "I have no intention of

letting you and a gun anywhere near an eagle. It will be target practice only."

"Well, I'll think about it. But I have another question."

Jim smiled. "Don't you always?"

"Was that army explorer, Major Stephen Long, the first white man to climb Longs Peak when he discovered it?"

"No, he never climbed Longs Peak, and Captain Zebulon Pike never climbed Pikes Peak."

"How odd. I think a naming committee should be formed to review the selection of names chosen thus far."

"And who should head this committee? You?"

"Why not?"

An hour flew by again, and they reached the spot called the lava beds which was actually a field of boulders and large rocks. They hobbled their horses at the base, being no longer of any use on the rough terrain.

Isabella looked at Jim. "The lava beds look challenging. Maybe I should just stay here and watch you climb."

"I'll help you over the toughest rocks."

Rogers asked, "Where are we headed next?"

"Do you see that notch in the rocks up there that looks like a keyhole? That's where we're climbing to next. From there we'll make a turn and head up to the summit."

Downer briefly glanced at Rogers, then announced, "Jim, we'll climb these rocks by ourselves, ahead of Miss Bird and you, and then meet you two at the notch."

Isabella, Jim, and Ring started climbing, but it became clear that even the smallest rocks were a problem for Isabella because of her cumbersome boots.

They stopped to catch their breath, and Jim spoke up, "I know Griff meant well, but those boots are making things worse."

"Wait a minute. What's that? Aren't those a pair of boots?"

Jim looked over to where Isabella was pointing and saw a patch of leather sticking out from underneath a rock. "It can't be."

They climbed a few more rocks and found the pair. Jim handed them to her. "Incredible. Here, try them on."

Isabella took off Griff's boots and slipped on the new pair. Her eyes lit up. "They're definitely ladies' boots. They're not a perfect fit, but close."

Jim shook his head. "Your luck is amazing. They must have been left from one of the previous women hikers."

Isabella smiled. "Maybe I should become a gambler."

"If so, I'm your partner. Are you planning on writing about this hike in your travelogue?"

Isabella looked at him incredulously. "Of course I am."

"Then, may I give you some writing advice?"

"Sure. Hennie usually helps me with my writing, but I'm all ears."

"Don't put in your travelogue that you found those boots. Nobody's ever going to believe you."

Isabella frowned. "But you just said, they're probably from one of the previous women hikers."

Jim shook his head. "But why would a woman leave something so valuable behind?"

Isabella pondered a moment. "Well, maybe she sat down to change shoes and forgot them she was so exhausted. I'm pretty tired myself right now."

Jim waved his hand. "It doesn't sound credible. It really doesn't. Well, do what you want. Forget I mentioned it."

"No, no. I appreciate your advice. I'm just not going to take it this time."

They began again, Isabella huffing and puffing, lagging frequently behind, until Jim took her elbow to help her climb. They tried to follow a path around the larger rocks, but it was still tiring climbing the smaller ones. A light snow briefly fell, making the rocks more slippery and even harder to climb.

It seemed to take nearly all of her breath just to make it the rest of the way to the notch where Downer and Rogers were waiting. They had a spectacular view for hundreds of miles of the surrounding Continental Divide.

"This view . . . makes . . . the whole hike . . . worthwhile," Isabella said, panting.

They turned when they heard Ring whimpering.

"He can't make it . . . around that rock." Isabella paused. "I should stay behind . . . and wait with him. I'm so tired already."

Jim shook his head. "Nonsense. You can make it the rest of the way up if we take a little break here. Besides, Ring has done this hike with me before. He knows to wait for me here until I climb back down."

Rogers, casually leaning against a rock with his ankles crossed, asked, "Miss Bird, how long until you think you'll be ready to start climbing again?"

Downer snickered.

Isabella glared at them, and Jim answered, "Give her a few minutes and we'll all head directly up that path."

The path proved icy, and Isabella slipped more than the men, even with the new boots. She eventually sat down on a rock and declared, "You go ahead. . . . I'll wait for all of you . . . here."

Jim answered, "No, you can do this. What I think we'll do is descend a little and try climbing a safer route."

Downer protested, "But that's going to take so much longer. I really don't want to be caught up there in the dark trying to get back down."

Rogers added, "I don't, either."

Rogers then leaned toward Jim as if in confidence. "Probably was foolish to bring a woman. She could prove a danger to us all, holding things up."

Isabella frowned.

Jim smirked and shook his head at the men.

"Unbelievable. You honestly think I'm doing this guiding for you men? I wouldn't have bothered if not for the chance to bring a woman."

Downer and Rogers stood speechless a moment, gaping at the thought, while Isabella grinned.

After descending a couple hundred feet, they began to climb a safer route. Downer and Rogers were a good fifty feet ahead of Jim and Isabella on the ascent. Jim watched Isabella a short while struggle to get a foot-hold at an especially high set of rocks with her diminutive frame. He looked up ahead. In fact she was never going to be able to climb the next *two* sets of rocks without more help.

"Isabella, remember how Griff's sons Charlie and William climbed on top of me when I pretended to be a bear?"

Isabella nodded. "You mean when Charlie acted as if he were a monkey and William, an opossum? Don't get me wrong. I really adore all of Griff's children, but the way you and the boys acted that night—"

Jim cut her off. "Forget about discussing our behavior right now. I only mention it because I'm going to need you to climb on me like a monkey and then like an opossum."

Isabella put her hands on her hips. "You have got to be kidding."

Jim cupped his mouth and shouted, "Sylvester, Platt, come back down here. We need you." He motioned with his hand to encourage them.

Isabella grabbed his arm. "Wait a minute. What are you doing?"

Jim couldn't tell what Rogers and Downer said to each other, but they started climbing back towards him. "You'll see. Just follow my directions."

Isabella shook her head. "I really don't know about this."

"Well, I do, so just obey. Pretend I'm one of your

parents—you know the ones you are always so obedient towards."

Isabella sighed. "They both died in the last ten years."

"I'm sorry to hear that, truly I am, but just tell me this—how did they die? Did you kill them with worry? 'Cause I'm beginning to know how that feels."

Isabella huffed.

Jim watched as Downer and Rogers lithely scampered down the rest of the way towards them. "What's up, Jim?"

"When I say 'now' you each pull on one of Miss Bird's shoulders from that rock you're standing on above me." He turned toward Isabella and ordered, "Climb on me like Charlie."

Isabella looked horrified and whispered to him, "You mean *as a monkey?*"

Jim nodded.

"Oh, no. Out of the question."

"No, it's not. What better use to make out of your special riding outfit. That split skirt and trousers won't show a thing."

Isabella stomped her foot. "That's not the only issue!"

"It is right now."

Rogers whined, "Are we going to do this or not?"

Jim arched his brows. "Well, Miss Bird."

Isabella groaned, "Oh, all right."

Jim crouched down and she haltingly and lightly climbed onto his back.

He ordered, "Hold on tighter with your legs and grab my neck."

She followed through with his command. Jim enjoyed the feel of close contact with Isabella even though he knew she was probably blushing the shade of a ripe cherry. He couldn't tell since he couldn't see her face.

After juggling a bit, Jim managed to push himself upright and stand next to the rock atop which Rogers and Downer were standing. "Now! Pull her up by her shoulders."

Making loud obvious grunts the whole time, the two pulled her up. When they finished, they glared a moment at Isabella, who was trying to straighten her riding outfit.

Rogers asked, "Is that all, Jim?"

"No, after I climb up there, we're going to need your help with the next even higher set of rocks."

Downer rolled his eyes at Rogers. Jim was glad Isabella was still adjusting her clothes and didn't notice. He climbed the rock himself and then asked Isabella, "Are you ready?"

Isabella looked in pain, briefly scrunching her eyes. "What now?"

Jim ordered Downer and Rogers up the next set of rocks. Once there, he told them to grab *his* shoulders this time on signal. He leaned with his back against the tall rock facing Isabella.

"When I tell you to, Miss Bird, grab my legs the way William did."

Isabella shook both hands. "Oooh, no . . . *as an opossum*?" The last word came out as a squeak.

"Okay, boys, pull my shoulders up."

The men worked this time without grunting. When Jim was a couple feet off the ground, he yelled, "Grab on now, Miss Bird."

She obeyed and again Downer and Rogers started grunting. When Jim was up and over the rock enough that he could sit on it, he bent forward and grasped Isabella under her shoulders and with a heave yanked her up the rest of the way. She landed with an "Oomph!" sprawled on top of Jim. He stared into her eyes only inches from his own.

She slowly smiled; he slowly smiled back. Jim couldn't remember a time he had felt more happy and blissful—like rapture and euphoria rolled into one. As if the clouds which had been gathering the last couple hours were breaking apart; the wind which had been blowing all day was suddenly hushing; and the tiny jagged pebbles which had been jabbing into his back were magically disappearing. He relished this feeling and lightly stroked his hand down her back.

"Can we go now?"

Jim closed his eye for a moment, disappointed he wasn't alone with Isabella. He opened his eye and then angled his head backwards. Isabella quickly scampered off him as he said, "Yes, Sylvester. I'll meet you guys at the summit. I should be able to help Miss Bird the rest of the way myself. None of the rocks look as steep as these last two sets."

An hour later Downer and Rogers were thirty feet ahead as Isabella gingerly sat down on a rock and took a break. She looked up at the sky and then at Jim. "I'm honestly going to die."

Jim shook his head. "I won't let you."

"Oh, don't get me wrong. I know I'm not going to die from exhaustion, nor from exposure to the bitter winds and cold. Not from thirst either, though I could really use a drink of water right about now."

Jim handed her the water canteen. "What is it then?"

"I'm going to die of embarrassment. How ignorant and foolish could I have been to think I could make a hike like this? I'm too weak and out of shape. I feel like a sack of lard being pulled, hoisted, and pushed up over these giant rocks."

She leaned toward Jim and turned her voice into a whisper, "God forbid, I even needed Downer's and Rogers's help."

Jim chuckled and looked away. He enjoyed helping her. A lot. Probably too much. On this current stretch of the hike, if he wasn't pushing up her nicely rounded rear, he was pulling her front up the length of his, then catching her against him again.

Isabella interrupted his thoughts, "I regret every piece of candy and pastry I've ever eaten in my entire life."

"You're light as a feather."

"Oh, please."

What a woman. She had fortitude. A lesser one would have given up long ago. Of course, she needed an occasional word of encouragement from him, but it was clear she was trying her hardest.

"Jim, do you hear me?"

Jim. Not Mr. Nugent. He looked back at her. "Yes, Isabella?"

"Perhaps I should wait right here."

"You're not quitting now. We're almost at the summit."

An hour later Jim watched her gaze out at the view. Downer and Rogers coughed and hacked nearby having made the climb too swiftly.

She turned to him and sighed. "It's even more spectacular than I imagined."

Jim smiled. "You *are* a lucky person, Isabella. The weather up here turns cloudy and rainy or snowy in the afternoons, even in the summer. The worst is to be on the summit in thunderstorms with the lightning striking at will. I've never seen it as bright and clear as it is right now. The view is remarkable; maybe we're seeing Pikes Peak a hundred miles away. Too bad there's no eagle's nest though."

"But we can see one next week, right?"

"Certainly. How long are you staying in Estes Park? We can do more than that if you wish."

Isabella smiled. "When I make these big excursions I've learned never to make concrete plans ahead of time. Some places end up appealing to me more than others. How much money I have left, also is a factor. But surely I should leave Estes Park before the weather turns too wintery. And perhaps I should see other parts of Colorado, such as Pikes Peak, before I head back to Scotland."

Gazing intently at her, he asked, "So you can spend a few more weeks here in Estes Park if you desire?"

Isabella grinned. "Yes—"

"Oh no, oh no, oh no!" Downer rushed over to Jim and stood clenching his fists. "I just coughed up blood."

"It happens. It'll clear. Sometimes it's nothing more than your nose bleeding from the arid air irritating your nostrils and then you swallowing—"

"Not to me. I've got to leave." Downer took a few quick steps away, then turned back around. "Now!"

Rogers walked over and took an authoritative stance, hands on hips. "Jim, seems the prudent thing to do. We'll take the quicker route down and meet you at the base of the lava fields."

"Whatever you prefer."

After watching the two depart, Isabella asked, "Do you think I can make it down without their help?"

Jim smiled. "Is, I got ya."

Isabella placed her hands on her hips. "I never gave you leave to change my familiar name from Isabella to Is."

Jim shook his head. "There you go, getting stubborn again."

They took their time descending. They had no choice. Isabella was exhausted and at her last bit of strength. They sat down for a break when they reached Ring. He promptly jumped all over Jim, trying to lick his face.

"Ring, sit down. You'd think he hadn't seen me for a year."

Isabella sat down, leaned backward over a rock and stared at the sky. "I'm too tired to make any comment."

"What about a question? You always have one of those."

"Oh, be quiet."

Jim laughed.

When they finally joined Downer and Rogers, Jim saw that the men had the horses saddled and were talking about heading home. He carried Isabella the last few yards and placed her gently on top of her horse. He knew she was never going to make it all the way home that night. They would need to stop again at the grouping of spruce trees.

"Gentlemen, I need a rest tonight. I can't head back until tomorrow." Jim waited for them to argue, but they both looked done in themselves.

"Fine," Rogers muttered.

Jim had to lift Isabella off her horse when they reached the spruce trees. She dropped to the ground and said she couldn't walk a foot more. He quickly made a bed for her out of the blankets and gave her some cheese and bread. She fell asleep before the fire was even started. After the men ate, they fell asleep as well, all feet toward the fire.

In the middle of the night Jim sat smoking and watched as Isabella stirred. She noticed Ring by her side and began to stroke his head. She looked over at Jim but kept quiet. He put out his cigar and motioned with his finger. "Is, come closer."

Isabella held back a smile. "Why should I?"

"You're a million miles from the fire." *And from me*, he thought. She didn't move. He frowned. "Are you all right? Need I carry you?"

"No, I can make it." She slowly got up and stiffly walked over, but still sat down a few feet away from Jim. Ring followed, curling up at her side again.

"Is, come next to me so I can warm you."

She shook her head.

"Don't be ridiculous. We've already spent a night together, and I've had my hands all over you."

"You're contorting the facts." She looked over at Downer and Rogers, snoring loudly, and scooted over.

Jim, on her right, placed his arm around her shoulders, and Ring, on her left, placed his head on her lap.

"Well, now I'm between my two favorite males in the world."

Jim looked over at Downer and frowned.

"Mr. Nugent and Mr. Ring."

Jim smiled and chuckled, so pleased he wanted to hear it again. "So I'm one of your favorite males."

Isabella's face took on a serious expression. "Well, actually, Ring is my favorite male, you're a distant second."

Jim gaped. "What does Ring possess that I don't have?"

Isabella tapped her chin. "Well, let me see." She pointed her finger in the air and smiled. "He gives me unconditional approval . . . and he's quiet. He's not a drinker, doesn't attend wild parties, and I haven't once heard him call me stubborn."

Jim smiled. "Oh, very amusing. Did you enjoy yourself today?"

"Oh, yes. But I'm sure you didn't, with all the hauling you ended up doing."

Jim looked at her earnestly. "I did."

She shook her head. "I don't believe you."

He placed his right hand over his chest. "I swear there is no one in the entire world I would have rather done the hike with."

Isabella looked up and studied his face. He gazed back and smiled softly.

She looked down, picked up a small pebble and rubbed it between her fingers before dropping it. "You know I think I actually believe you."

Jim reached for her hand with his right one and placed both in his lap. Isabella snuggled a little closer and sighed in contentment. They quietly stared into the fire.

"Is, I should have asked you something before we started yesterday."

"What?"

"You said you came to Estes Park for your health. You seemed so vigorous I didn't think to ask you beforehand. I hope the hike didn't do any harm."

"Oh, not at all. I've been feeling great since coming here."

He looked her up and down, trying to assess what might be wrong. Clearly flustered, she turned so she was facing Jim more, forcing him to let go of her hand and to drop his arm from around her shoulders. Ring was nudged by her movement, got up, and snuggled in between the two of them.

Jim started petting his head. "What exactly is the matter with your health, if I might ask?"

Isabella sighed and started pulling on a loose thread on her skirt. "I get headaches."

"Headaches? You came to Colorado for headaches?"

She looked up. "Headaches, and kind of a numb feeling in my arms and legs, and I'm so fatigued sometimes that I don't want to get out of bed."

Jim frowned. "Have you seen a doctor?"

"Oh, believe me, many."

"What did they say is the matter?"

Isabella sighed. "They can't find anything wrong."

"What do you mean?"

"Well, the truth is that I only feel sick when I'm home. I feel fine when I travel. My doctor was the first one to suggest that I get away and see if that helped."

Jim paused. "You mean it's all in your head?"

Isabella looked down and started fussing again with the loose thread. She finally yanked the thread off with a sharp pull and threw it on the ground. She looked up at Jim. "I hate to admit it, but probably so."

She looked thoughtful a moment, then said, "Sometimes I think the potions I'm taking to make me better are actually causing some of my problems. You see I usually don't seem to need as much of them when I'm traveling, and maybe taking less, is actually what is helping. I really don't know what the matter is."

"What are you taking?"

She waved her hand. "Oh, the usual. Alcoholic remedies and the like." She looked down again and sighed. "I'm rather ashamed about it all."

"Don't be."

She raised her head and studied him a long moment. "Life can be hard."

"I know."

She half-smiled. "You probably think my life was all roses growing up . . . but it wasn't."

He frowned. "How so?"

"My father was a pastor and a good man, but he strictly believed that no work should be done on Sundays. He preached accordingly." She paused and took a deep breath. "He was forced to resign at one parish and stoned out of another for his views." She shook her head. "Such cruelty. I remember being so hurt for my father and so intensely embarrassed myself."

"How old were you?"

"Just entering womanhood."

"Ah, a sensitive time."

"Yes. If I wasn't feeling chagrined about what happened to my father, I was becoming abashed about my illness when no specific cause could be found."

"Is, if those were the only things I felt ashamed about, I'd be a happy man."

She pleated her brows. "What do you mean?"

"There are things I've done that I now deeply regret."

"Why did you do them?"

Jim shook his head. "A bad temper. Drinking got the best of me."

"I've never seen you in a foul mood."

"I'm usually not. I didn't always have a volatile temper either. I was once an average, ordinary person."

"*That* I can't quite believe."

Jim smiled softly before rubbing his mouth, getting somber again at the memories that were assailing him. "The drinking was at its worst after I quit trapping and got a job as a scout. It was a heady time for me. I started getting known as a fierce Indian fighter." He paused. "Real fierce, considering the Indians were mainly old men and innocent women and children."

Isabella frowned and shook her head. "That's terrible."

Jim sighed. "I know. Afterward I would get so disgusted with myself and the men with me that I'd drink myself into a stupor. But if someone else dared criticize me, I'd threaten to shoot him or just beat him mercilessly."

Jim stared into the fire. What was it about this woman that made him talk about these things?

"When did you quit and come to Estes Park?"

"Not for a while. The Civil War was a bad time for me also. More violence, a lot of it unnecessary, more drinking." He looked away.

"It's hard for me to imagine you doing anything such as that. Not after today."

He turned back. "Is, you're good for me. I want to be better around you." He reached for her hand again and kissed the back of it, not caring that she felt his wet cheek.

Isabella gazed into his face, then turned her hand and slowly wiped away his tear. She stared into his face a moment more, swallowed, then looked down as she placed her hand back into her lap.

"Is . . ." She raised her head, and Jim stared into her shimmering eyes and gently smiled. With trembling lips, she smiled back.

He adored this woman. She was bright, funny and kind. Sometimes she seemed to understand him better than he understood himself. What was she thinking right now? Did it make her tearful just because he was sad himself?

"Hepme."

They turned their heads to see Downer, mumbling in his sleep. Jim inwardly swore. Not again. But as he tried to reassure Isabella that Downer was still fast asleep, she stood and briskly brushed the dirt from her skirt. "Well, I should get to bed."

Jim shook his head in disappointment. He would have enjoyed talking to her longer. "But, Is, come closer to the fire for warmth at least."

She nodded and pulled her bedding nearer to the flames before lying down and shutting her eyes.

Jim felt closer to her now than he would have ever thought possible. He chewed the corner of his lip. Of course, nothing could ever come of it. They were from such dissimilar worlds, and she would be leaving in a few weeks.

He shook his head. He could just imagine the cleaned-up version she would write her sister about the hike. She might even want to distance herself from him. People tended to do that after exposing their secrets.

But Jim found himself smiling in the end. Because while she remained in Estes Park, he, for one, planned on getting to know her even better.

Chapter Eleven

They arrived back home around noon the next day, and Isabella rested for a couple of days. Jim hunted and checked his traps but didn't stop in at Griff's. He wanted to see Isabella again, but hesitated about dropping in. Almost predictably she had acted a little distant and formal on the ride home. Perhaps he had told her too much, shown his feelings too openly. But after three days he missed her enough to suffer any possible rebuke and wanted to see whether she had recovered from the hike.

He opened Griff's door, and Charlie's face lit up as he shouted, "Mountain Jim! You're back!"

While Sport and Ring wrestled at his feet, William ran up to Jim, and asked, "Where've you been? Did you catch a grizzly?"

"Not this time. I need your help for that." He tweaked William's nose.

Dorothy spoke up next, "It sounds as if you had quite an adventure. Isabella has been singing your praises ever since."

Jim scanned the room and saw Isabella sitting on a bench in the corner. With a slight smile, she looked up from her sewing. Jim grinned back.

Dorothy added, "Oh, Sylvester and Platt headed back to college, but before Sylvester left, he said to tell you that his cough had cleared."

Still looking at Isabella, Jim deadpanned, "I was worried."

He saw Isabella choke back a laugh and walked over to her. "Scoot over, Miss Bird. There's room for two on that bench. How are you doing?"

"Just fine, Mr. Nugent."

It was a tight fit, and Jim moved his arm on top of the bench behind Isabella's back. She pretended not to notice and returned to her sewing, but moved slightly into his arm.

"Griff, I see you're back from Denver."

"Yeah, had some business to attend to."

Jim stiffened. Such as business with Lord Dunraven, for instance? "Anything special?"

"Nothing in particular but I brought my niece back with me."

Jim looked across the room. "Mary, I didn't see you at first. Would have given you a special welcome. How long has it been since your last visit? At least a couple months."

Mary smiled. "I'm helping Aunt Ellie pack up for the winter." Her eyes strayed over to Mr. Buchanan, a frequent guest who came for the hunting. Mr. Buchanan smiled warmly back at her. Jim glanced over at Isabella. Buchanan had it easy. Courting a woman such as Isabella would be tough.

Isabella looked up from her sewing. "Ellie, do you and the kids stay the whole winter in Denver?"

"We usually leave Estes Park in the fall and return in the spring unless the winter's a mild one, then we return earlier. But don't worry; you're welcome to stay here as long as you wish. The Rudolphs spend most of the winter here, and Griff, of course, will be back frequently to check on things."

"How soon will you be leaving?"

Ellie turned to Griff. "What do you think? Considering it's the first week of October, the temperatures have been rather mild; it's just been windy with a little rain, though it's snowing already on the mountain tops."

"It'll be a couple days at least. I've got a few more things to take care of here before I can take you there." Griff clapped his hands together. "But while we're here, who wants music?"

William jumped up and down. "I do!"

Griff brought out his fiddle and started playing a lively tune. Jim noticed Isabella tapping her foot.

"Miss Bird, how about a little dancing?"

Isabella's eyes widened. Before she could refuse, Jim stood, grabbed her arm, and pulled her up. He started to lead her around the small floor in a country dance.

Charles turned to Dorothy. "My dear?"

The couple joined in, and soon benches and tables were moved aside to make room for the others.

When the tune ended there were shouts for more, and the dancing continued. Jim began to twirl Isabella, and she laughed with glee.

After another tune, Griff put down his fiddle and shouted, "Clear the floor."

He performed a jig on his own, everyone clapping their hands in encouragement. When the dancing finally stopped, they all took their seats again.

Isabella, flushed with exertion, hair escaping her bun, reached up to tuck the stray hairs back. "I must look a mess."

Jim whispered to her, "A lovely mess. Isabella, don't. I like your hair down."

Isabella stayed her hand and her cheeks turned pinker. She whispered back, "You shouldn't say such things."

"Why not? It's the truth." Jim started laughing. "You're blushing."

"I am not." Her cheeks turned even redder as she quickly tucked her hair back into place. "Mr. Nugent, I don't know how you manage to do it."

"Do what?"

"Force me to lose all sense of decorum and dignity."

"Is, nobody could force you to do anything." He leaned in to whisper, "Face it, you're a savage beast at heart. Rrrrr. Just what is your ancestry?"

"Not baboons, like yours."

Jim laughed. "God, I missed you the last few days. Did you miss me?"

"No."

"Not even a little?"

"No."

"I'm crushed."

"No, you're not. Now go sit over by Mary and give her your special welcome."

"You're jealous."

"Certainly not. You must be the most arrogant—"

"What are you two talking about?"

Isabella looked up at Griff and answered, "Nothing."

Jim chuckled, and Isabella bit back a smile.

A few days later, with the family packed, Isabella approached Griff. "Could you cash this promissory note for me in Denver?"

"It would be my pleasure."

"How long do you expect to be gone?"

"A few days. I'll bring the mail back with your money."

Isabella nodded. "It'll be nice to get some news from my sister Hennie. I plan to use the money for a horse and more warm clothes before I visit Pikes Peak. Well, have a good trip. We'll look forward to seeing you soon."

Griff smiled. "Don't get into any trouble while I'm gone, Isabella."

Isabella smiled back. "Never, Griff."

He studied her a moment. "Irishmen can be wild; find yourself an unmarried, solid and steady Welshman."

"Well, Griff, I really adore the twinkle in your son's Charlie's eyes, and of course William's forthright manner, but I think it will still be a few years before they are interested in courting me."

Griff slapped his leg and laughed heartily. "I like you, Isabella. I have from the start."

The next day Isabella sat on the front porch of her cabin and savored her independence. She was free to do as she pleased. She looked around at the tree-covered hills and took a deep breath, enjoying the scent of ponderosa pines. It was quiet at the homestead. She already missed the Evanses' noise and chaos.

"Be ready early tomorrow."

"Aaah!" She jumped out of her chair, clutched her chest and glared at Jim riding his mule. "Do you always sneak up on people like that?"

"No, just you. Woolgathering again?"

She ignored the question. "Be ready for what?"

"I'm taking you to Eagle Cliff Mountain. Eagle nests, target practice?"

She placed her hands on her hips. "Yes, to the eagle nests; no, to the target practice."

"Nope, if you want one you have to do the other. Is, come on, you need to know how to shoot a gun in this kind of country."

Isabella looked skyward before dropping her head back down. "Very well. You show me the eagle's nests, and I'll shoot a gun."

Jim shook his head. "Somehow I thought it would take longer to convince you. You having that problem with stubbornness and all."

Isabella bit back a smile. "Maybe it's because I don't have a stubborn problem *and all*. Was that the only reason you came over here, to invite me?"

"I missed you and wanted to spend some time with you

again. Let's start over. I'll scare you and this time you be your normal self and take longer for me to convince you."

Isabella chuckled. "You're really impossible *and all.*"

Aaareee!

Isabella furtively looked around. "There's that noise again. I can't figure out what it is? It sounds as if nails are scratching a chalkboard or a sleigh is skidding to a stop on rocky ice."

Aaarrraaa! Eeerrraaa! Isabella flinched.

Jim laughed. "Why, Is, hasn't anybody told you yet what that is?"

She looked at him askance. "No, what?"

"It's the sound of love."

She rolled her eyes. "I should have known I couldn't count on you for a straight answer."

Jim smiled. "I jest not. It's mating season for the elks, and the males bugle a call to attract the females. Maybe I could get some pointers from them on courting difficult women."

Isabella smiled back. "Oh, you do that. Make sure you add it to your arsenal of wooing weapons. I'm sure it will make you very successful."

He arched his brow and smiled. "You think?"

"Absolutely. Now if you have nothing more ridiculous to say, I'll see you tomorrow."

"Aaarrreee. You bet, Is."

The next morning Jim showed up early as promised, riding his beautiful mare. Isabella jumped out of her porch chair and rapidly walked toward him.

Grinning widely, she announced, "I'm ready. I got one of Griff's horses already saddled."

Jim smiled back. "Excellent, Is. I'm happy to see you too."

Isabella smiled smugly. "But how do you know if I'm more excited about seeing you or the eagles?"

He scoffed, "Is, of course me. Why wouldn't you be?"

Isabella just shook her head.

After packing some food and a blanket behind her saddle, they headed out. They rode quietly south along the Thompson River until they reached a narrow valley surrounded by mountains. Jim pointed at Longs Peak in the distance. "Do you think it looks more like a beaver is climbing its side, or the prow of a ship? I've heard both."

"I have also heard both and have actually put some thought into that question. I've decided definitely a beaver; in some places you can see it all the way from its head to its tail."

"We hiked it just in time. A lot of snow came a day later up there."

They turned west and started to climb Eagle Cliff Mountain. The wind whipped around them, making conversation difficult as the narrow valley acted like a tunnel. When they reached about a third of the way up, they stopped by a tall set of granite rocks which acted as a shelter from the gusts. They dismounted, sat down and leaned back, looking out on the surrounding scenery.

Jim pointed to a nearby pine tree and whispered, "Look over there."

Isabella looked but saw nothing special. "What?"

"Shhh."

A few seconds later Jim said, "I can see you don't know the first thing about watching birds. It flew away. I've never seen one like that before. I'll have to write Gertie."

"Who's Gertie?"

"A brilliant lady, probably the smartest lady I know."

"Oh, *do* tell."

"What's wrong?"

Isabella clipped, "Nothing. What could possibly be wrong?"

"I thought I detected a note of skepticism in your voice

a moment ago."

Isabella frowned. "Oh, my goodness. Just tell me who she is and get on with it."

Jim shrugged, puzzled by her tone. "She's a lady my partner Hugo and I guided part of the way back East, after she decided she didn't want to settle in Wyoming after all."

"Is this the Hugo who was your boss at the trapping company?"

"Yeah, we left the company and became partners for a while."

"So she went with just you two men over miles and miles of country?"

"No, we guided her and her husband George, after they couldn't make a go of it in Wyoming."

"If she was so *smart*, why couldn't they make a go of it?"

Jim bit back a smile. Something was really bothering Isabella. "George was an artist and really just wanted to paint landscapes, but of course couldn't make a living doing just that. So they decided to return to Boston and open a bookstore. Hugo and I guided them part of the way back. Gertie basically runs the bookstore and is the brains behind it while George still paints."

"Oh, she's the *brains* behind the bookstore. But what does this have to do with *that bird?*"

Jim smiled. "Lordy, you sound riled up."

Isabella frowned. "Do you take pleasure in irritating me?"

Jim laughed. "Yeah, truthfully, sometimes I do. But what is it that's bothering you so much?"

Isabella held up her hand. "Fine. I wasn't going to say anything, but since you asked. The truth is, as opposed to most women, my sister Hennie and I are proud of our book learning. Our parents encouraged us to learn more than just the typical reading, writing, and embroidery. Why, we had tutors not only in the classics, but the sciences as well.

Hennie's even attended ladies' classes at the University of Edinburgh. She's probably the smartest woman on the whole planet!"

Jim blinked. "Am I to get this right that you're upset because I said Gertie was brilliant and probably the smartest woman I know?"

"Hennie's smarter, I'm sure of it."

Jim bent over laughing. When he raised his head again, he said, "I know, why don't we make a test? We'll send questions to Hennie and Gert and see which one answers the questions first and the most accurately." Jim smiled. "Would that make you happy?"

Isabella crossed her arms. "Don't be absurd. And you still haven't told me what this convoluted story has to do with that bird."

"Gertie's a great bird and nature-lover. When we stopped at night, Gertie would sit with her huge, shaggy dog named Suki, get out her journal and write about what she had seen that day while George would sketch. They were fun to be around and I liked them." Jim shrugged. "Gertie got me to pay more attention to my surroundings. We now have an arrangement where I write to her if I see something unusual in nature, and she writes to me if there is a book she thinks I might want to buy."

Still sounding perturbed, Isabella asked, "Why would they ever think to move to Wyoming in the first place?"

"Oh, the West has all types, but Gertie likes to think of herself as a modern woman. She thought the West gave women more freedom. She has some crazy notions—such as giving women the right to vote. George had grown up on a farm and thought he might like to raise cattle, but they quickly dropped the idea once they came west and saw all the difficulties involved."

Jim smiled. "Ready to get going now that you've scared away all the birds?"

Isabella paused before answering, "All right. But

there'd better be a few birds still left to view, as in eagles and their nests, or I'm not shooting that gun."

"You still sound annoyed."

"I'm not."

"Well then, let's mount back up."

They stood and took a few steps toward their horses before Isabella stopped and covered her face with her hands. "I'm sorry. I'm so sorry. My peevish and rude behavior is so inexcusable." She dropped her head and sighed loudly.

Jim hugged her lightly as she buried her face in his chest, crushing her bonnet. He patted her back. "Is, it's all right."

She dropped her hands from her face and looked up at him, shaking her head. "No, it's not. I don't know what's wrong with me when I'm around you. My emotions are up, down, front, back and then sideways."

He grabbed both her shoulders and looked intently into her face. "You know what I think?"

Isabella pouted. "What?"

"You have a sister that you love and miss—"

Isabella looked down. "Well, actually, sometimes even Hennie can irritate me—"

"—*and* you're a bright woman yourself."

Isabella looked up contentedly.

"What I said pricked your pride and maybe hurt you a little."

Isabella frowned.

"I shouldn't have laughed."

Isabella bit back a smile. "I guess it was kind of funny."

Jim smiled softly, then looked away a moment before returning her gaze. "Is, there's a happiness deep inside me when I'm around you. I'm enjoying the feeling. It makes me kind of . . . well, giddy."

Isabella smiled. "Silly, you mean."

"All right, silly. Now let's see those eagles." He motioned with his hand for her to follow.

They walked a few feet before Isabella excitedly blurted, "Jim!"

He turned back around.

"I just thought of a great question to put on our Gert versus Hennie contest!"

Jim smiled and resumed walking. "What?"

Isabella followed. "How about who climbed Pikes Peak and Longs Peak first. See, it's a trick question . . ."

Within an hour they reached the summit and again dismounted. The wind was steady and brisk. Isabella's bonnet went flying, and her hair started escaping her bun. She shook it free while Jim retrieved her hat. "Don't bother putting this back on until it's less windy."

"I realize that. Besides, it's just the two of us. I'm sure my lack of proper head attire does not offend *your* sensibilities." Isabella smiled.

Jim stared at her but said nothing.

She looked back at him. "What? What are you looking at?" She rubbed her chin. "Is there breakfast on my face?"

"You look younger . . . and happier than the first day I met you." Jim paused. "Guess it's because of me."

"What?" Isabella looked at him surprised, then gradually narrowed her eyes and crossed her arms. "You really are quite conceited, you know that? If I do look different it's because of all the fresh air."

Jim smiled. "Whatever you say, Is."

They climbed a group of rocks and sat down, side by side, legs bent over the edge. They surveyed the grass-covered valley below, surrounded by snow-capped mountains. The Thompson River was a narrow ribbon winding through the meadow. Elk were grazing, but appeared only as moving specks from so far above.

Isabella looked west and saw a bird, circling in the air,

then swooping downward. "Look at the hawk."

"No, it's too big. That's one of the eagles that probably nests up here."

They saw another one, circling.

Isabella looped her arm through Jim's. "Oh, I love this."

"I do, too."

She turned and smiled up at him. He warmly smiled back, and their gazes held a moment before returning again to the eagles.

"Jim, where do you think their nests are?"

"There used to be some on that group of rocks over yonder. But I haven't been up here for a while."

"I'm not sure if we should disturb them."

"I agree. This is enough for me if you're satisfied."

"I am." They continued watching, but the wind became excessively gusty and nippy. Isabella shivered. Jim put his arm around her and she snuggled closer. "Seen enough?"

She smiled. "Yes, thanks for taking me. What's next?"

"Target practice."

Isabella groaned. "I was hoping you were going to say dinner. I packed a pie, you know."

"Bribery won't work. We're doing target practice next." He looked at her curiously. "Who made the pie?"

"I did. My first one."

He mocked a shocked response. "You can cook?"

She shoved him with her elbow. "When I put my mind to it. But it seems a lot of effort for little reward. You work and work and then it's eaten in a few minutes."

"Ah, spoken like a woman aspiring for the crown of Best Homemaker."

"I never aspired to any such thing."

"Really? I never would have known. What do you aspire to, Is?"

"I don't really want to say."

He steadily gazed at her. "Tell me. I want to know."

"Well, if this travelogue I'm working on sells, I'd like to keep writing. Maybe make a real job out of it just as men do. I mean the money could be used for so many good causes such as helping the poor."

"Why did you not want to tell me that?"

"Because women aren't supposed to want careers."

Jim nodded. "I hope you do it, though. I personally don't have a problem with women having careers the way men do. I'm just not sure how I feel about them voting. They need to understand the issues first and not just follow their husbands. But that's really noble if you give some of your earnings to the poor—"

She interrupted excitedly, "Actually, one of the best things I ever did . . ." She paused.

"What?"

"No. It might sound as if I'm bragging."

"Come on, Is. We tell each other things, don't we?"

Isabella smiled smugly. "Well, actually, once I convinced this shipping baron to allow passage on his vessels so the poor crofters in the Scottish Western Highlands could immigrate to Canada."

Jim laughed. "I would have liked to witness that conversation. The poor man didn't have a chance at refusing you, I am sure."

Isabella grinned. "I was quite convincing, I must admit. I've also written articles in *The Leisure Hour* concerning the need for schools that not only teach, but feed and clothe the children as well. I also am very proud of that."

Jim smiled softly. "Is, didn't I tell you about you being pretty on the inside and out?"

Her cheeks turned pink before she looked away.

He touched her chin and pulled her face back. "Don't get bashful on me now." Jim smiled. "We're having one of our sensitive and touching moments. You can write about it in your travelogue."

Her lips curved. "As if I would. And we don't need any more sensitive and touching moments. We've had enough already." She playfully pinched his arm.

"Ouch. Can I see some of your writing?"

Isabella crossed her arms. "I'll think about it. Look, let's get this gun shooting over with so we can eat. I want to try my pie."

A half hour later, sheltered behind large rocks, Isabella took aim at a tree. Jim stood behind her. She turned around, holding the gun. "What do I do if the gun backfires?"

"Christ Almighty, never point a loaded gun at someone. It can go off unexpectedly."

Isabella turned back around.

"That's better. It's not going to backfire. That gun never does, but if it did, duck."

"Duck? Are you serious?"

"Stop stalling."

Isabella held her arms out, holding the gun in front of her, lining up the sites while squinting before finally squeezing the trigger.

The bullet hit the target. Jim tilted his head and stared, mouth open.

"There. I did it. Can we eat now?"

"I'm glad you're not my jilted lover. How'd you do that?"

"It must be a hidden talent. But I'm not shooting anymore because I hit the target. Here's your gun."

He took it and watched her walk in the direction of their horses.

She turned back around. "Come on. Aren't you hungry?"

"I could eat a bear."

"Do you always feel as if you could eat a bear?"

Jim shrugged, then said, "Let's go over there to eat. I want to show you a different view."

They walked their horses to a secluded group of trees and spread out their blanket. They nibbled on some cheese and bread and drank from Jim's canteen.

"When are you unpacking your pie?"

"Now. You try the first piece."

"What kind is it?"

"Dried berries." She handed him a portion.

Jim took a bite and swallowed while Isabella looked on intently. "Well?"

"It's very good, and I've had some of the best baking in the world."

"Let me see." She took a bite. "Mmm. This is great."

Jim smiled. "If you do say so yourself."

Isabella smiled back. "If I do say so myself."

Jim lay down on his back, yawned, and closed his eye. "I'm a bit sleepy. I could take a nap."

After a moment, Isabella reclined next to him, surprising him at first. He peeked and realized she had made sure she wasn't touching him with any part of her body, her arms stiffly laying by her side. She stared up at the tree branches above before stating, "I'm drowsy, too, but I don't think I can fall asleep."

Jim took her right hand in his left. "Try for a few minutes."

Isabella let go of his hand and fidgeted with the blanket underneath them. Jim rose up slightly, bent his right arm behind his head, and lay back down. "Is, rest your head on my left shoulder for a pillow."

She looked over at Jim, cautiously. He could almost see the thoughts churning inside her head. This was really pushing the appropriate limits in her mind and he knew it. *Come on, Is, you can do it,* he almost wanted to say. She frowned slightly, then took a deep breath and swallowed as if she was venturing into some unknown scary territory. With another loud exhale, she lay down and curled a tad into him as he wrapped his left arm around her. After moving around slightly to adjust her position, she quieted. After a few minutes Jim realized by her breathing that she had fallen asleep and he drifted off himself.

They awoke when Jim started to turn in his sleep. Isabella gave a slight gasp, obviously realizing where exactly she had so easily and comfortably fallen asleep. Jim smiled to himself. They sat up and Isabella said, "I can't believe it. How long did I sleep?"

Jim looked up at the sky. "An hour, I guess."

She started to pack up their remaining food. "We need to get back. People will begin to wonder."

"Wait. Just a little longer."

She stopped her packing and hesitated a moment, staring at Jim. She then wrapped her arms around her bent knees.

"Is, you ever been madly in love?"

Her eyes widened. "Is there anything you consider too much to ask? That's a rather personal question." She looked down at the blanket and started smoothing the fabric. She sighed. "Maybe once."

"What happened?"

"I met him in my twenties. My father introduced me to him. In many ways he was perfect for me. You see, he held the same religious and abolitionist views as my father. The problem was, I discovered he drank too much."

She briefly looked up at Jim as if to see his reaction. He exhaled loudly, but didn't say anything so she continued fiddling with the blanket. "He proposed and I admit I was tempted at first, but deep down I knew there could never be a union between us. It ended badly, and it hurt, though I'm not sure either one of us was madly in love. I vowed never again to get involved with any whiskey fiend." She paused before saying, "Shortly after that, my father encouraged me to travel on my first trip to America."

"Where did you go?"

"Mainly East Coast."

She hesitated, then looked up at him again before asking, "What about you? Have you been madly in love? You said you had experienced a great sorrow before you left home. What happened?"

Jim thought about Salme and asked, "You want to hear the short or long version?"

"In between."

Jim contemplated what he wanted to tell Isabella. His feelings had felt very raw at the time. He didn't usually give details of what happened to friends who asked about Salme, his first love. But Isabella felt more than just a mere friend at this point. Jim smiled gently. "I remember very well the first day I met her."

"How old were you?"

"Sixteen or seventeen. I was on my way to church with my parents, thinking about how I was going to sneak out in the afternoon and do some hunting. My mother was chatting away, but got my attention when she said there was a new family attending church from someplace exotic. Imagine that!"

"Where were they from?"

"Estonia. Do you know where that is?"

"It's a Baltic country across from Finland. Not really exotic."

"I know. Anyways, later I was sitting in the church, and the Estonians showed up. There was nothing at all remarkable about the parents, but the sons were huge. These really tall, blue-eyed, blond giants."

"How tall?"

"Easily over six feet. But then their daughter entered the church, and she was really stunning. All the men and even the women stared at her."

"How did she look?"

"Blond, blue eyes, sweet face."

Isabella frowned slightly. "That tells me nothing. Many women appear that way. What made her so special?"

Isabella looked away and tucked her hair behind her ear.

"Is, sometimes you make it hard to tell a story, asking all these questions." Jim briefly gazed skyward. "All right, let's see. It was her smile, I guess. Her lips curled up a certain way."

Isabella turned her head back and watched Jim try to do an imitation.

Isabella bit her inside cheek. "Like a speckled trout?"

"No."

"You're right. More like a largemouth bass." Isabella giggled.

Jim smiled. "No, not like a fish. Never mind. I liked her looks. Can we move on?"

"No. I want to hear more about how she looked."

Jim shook his head exasperated. "Is, I don't know. Delicate, I guess. Delicate facial features. Curly hair, high cheekbones, full figure."

Isabella looked down. "Oh."

Jim lifted her chin and looked at her. "Not too thin the way some petite women can be."

Isabella smiled slightly as she looked away. "Oh . . . um, what was her name?"

"Salme Sundbach."

She looked back. "Did Selma like you?"

"Salme. Probably not at first. I made an ass of myself the next Sunday."

"What'd you do to Saaalme? Tell her she was stubborn?"

"No, I only say that to woman who are actually stubborn. What happened was that I concocted this scheme to sit next to her in church. When my parents and I arrived, I told them to go on in because I wanted to talk to some of my friends before the service. After a few minutes I saw her arrive with her family, and I thought that if the pew next to my parents was filled already, I could casually slip in next to her. So I waited just a minute or so after she arrived, and then I started walking confidently down the aisle. I saw the seat next to her was still not filled and figured, 'Here's my chance.' But my foot got caught on one of the pews and I tumbled forward, just barely managing to catch myself before landing on the pew in front of her. Her brothers snickered, of course. I turned around and Salme smiled. That smile just hooked me. So full of mischief—her eyes actually twinkled."

"Show me how they looked."

"No. No more fish jokes. You'll just have to imagine."

"What happened next?"

"Nothing, actually. For the next year I barely saw her. Salme's family didn't go to church regularly, and I only caught her occasionally in town when she and her mother went shopping. We hardly talked at all. But I was smitten for sure. I wanted to know what she was doing all the time, and I wanted to tell her about me . . . you know, like someone in love."

Isabella frowned slightly and didn't say anything.

Jim continued. "After a year of only watching and barely talking to her, I was ready to make a bolder move. So I headed over to her house. My knees were so weak and my palms so sweaty that I just stood a few moments in front of her door to try to get my bearings. I finally knocked, and her mother opened the door with this strained look on her face. I knew something was wrong."

"What was it?"

"It turned out that Salme was sick, something in her lungs. She died within a week. I was absolutely crushed."

"But . . ." Isabella hesitated. "You barely knew her. I'm not sure I understand."

"I know. Looking back at it now I'm not sure I do either, but at the time it was a great tragedy. I wanted to get away and ended up joining the fur company." Jim paused. "Well, you know the rest."

Jim stared out at the view. Isabella reached for his

hand. He squeezed hers gently. "That's another story I don't usually tell for obvious reasons." He looked back at her. "How do you get me to tell all these stories?"

"Because I'm such a good listener, never interrupting."

Jim smiled. "I'm sure that's it."

"We'd better get going. After all, you've got a letter about a bird to write."

They returned slowly. When they got closer to Griff's lodge, but were still beyond sight of it, Isabella told Jim to hold up. She dismounted and handed him her reins. When she started pinning her hair back in a bun, Jim said, "Figures. Is, you're completely predictable."

Isabella paused and looked up. "And you're not."

"Why, thank you."

Isabella shook her head.

A few days later, after working on his trapping, Jim walked into Griff's to find Dorothy and Isabella drinking coffee. "Good morning, everybody."

Isabella smiled. "Good morning, Mr. Nugent."

"What does everybody have planned today?"

Dorothy spoke up, "Charles is taking me horseback riding. He's trying to teach me to ride better. I can't say I'm improving."

Jim puffed out a breath. "Most of Griff's horses here are worthless. You need to step up to a better horse. See how responsive it is, then you'll improve. Why don't you try my Arabian mare? I rode her over here today, and I can help give you lessons."

Isabella stood and blurted out, "But you've never given me a chance—" She sat back down, blushing, and quickly took a sip of her coffee.

Dorothy looked at Jim. "I think your mare is a bit too spirited for me. But thank you for offering."

Jim turned to Isabella. "Miss Bird, you'll join us, won't you?"

"Sure. I can ride one of the *hags*."

Jim chuckled. "Would you care to trade horses for the day?"

"You'll ride my hag?"

"It's an offer for today only."

An hour later Jim watched Isabella and Dorothy riding side by side about thirty feet ahead of Charles and him. They were ignoring the beautiful scenery along the Fall River, chatting away. The last couple days Jim had thought of nothing but how soon he could see Isabella again; so right after breakfast he had headed over to Griff's to see what she was doing. Isabella was special, she made him think of a better life, and a year ago he hadn't even dared hope. Just what did he want from her?

He wondered if it was too late to turn his life around. The local settlers seemed to thrive on exaggerated stories about his past; they didn't really know what the truthful ones were or not. He knew his reputation as a ruffian would be hard to alter. The excessive drinking, though, he could change and in fact had already curbed. He hadn't shown up at Griff's tipsy for months. He would never stop drinking altogether, but he had slowed down.

Charles broke into his thoughts. "Jim, look at those interesting rock formations over there."

"That's Old Man Mountain."

"I want Dorothy to see this. Look at those two, yak, yak, yak." Charles raised his voice. "Dorothy, hold up. You're missing the sights."

Dorothy and Isabella turned around and waited for Jim and Charles to catch up.

Dorothy looked at Charles. "I'm perfectly capable of talking and observing at the same time. The colors here are spectacular. So clear and bright. Look at the river. It's not just blue. It's a million shades of blue."

Jim looked over at the river and turned back to

Dorothy. "You look at things with an artist's eye."

"Even though I enjoy doing portraits more, I wish I had brought my oils to try my hand at landscape painting. It would be interesting to attempt getting the shading just right."

Charles intoned, "But, Dorothy, did you notice those rocks over there on that mountain?"

"Oh, I see what you mean. They're in different shapes, as if they were benches and chairs and even beds!"

Jim stroked his horse's neck. "That mountain is famous for having those. Indians went on vision quests there."

Charles scratched his head. "Indian history is not my particular area of interest, but it seems to me I read about vision quests once. Isn't that where Indians fast for days and then try to have dreams that foretell the future for them or their tribe?"

"Something like that. Anybody want to climb it?"

"No, no, no," Dorothy said at the same time that Isabella said, "Yes!"

"We can hike partway; we don't have to climb all the way to the top."

"No, you and Isabella go on. I'd get too dizzy," Dorothy said.

Charles turned to Jim. "Dorothy's afraid of heights."

"Then how did she make it to Estes Park?"

"She closed her eyes most of the way."

Jim tried not to laugh.

Dorothy explained, "But I loved the views once I got here. I just like them from the ground. Even being up on a horse sometimes gets to me. Jim, I thought you knew that."

Isabella spoke up, "Dorothy, we don't have to climb it. Let's keep riding."

"Well, actually, Charles and I don't usually ride longer than this anyway. We'll head back on our own."

Charles reached over and shook Jim's hand. "You

heard the boss. We'll see you back at Griff's."

An hour later, taking a break from climbing, Jim lay on his back and looked up at the sky. Isabella sat on a rock next to him. "What are you doing?"

"Shhh. I'm trying to have a vision quest."

"That's going to be pretty hard, considering you need to fast for days, and you can eat a bear every day."

"Well, maybe you don't need to fast to have a vision. What I need to find is a tribe I can join that doesn't require fasting."

Isabella shook her head. "I doubt any Indian tribe will have you."

Jim looked over at Isabella. "Why's that?"

"Generally speaking, I would say Indian tribes don't let you join them when you've fought against them."

"You've got a point. Now come here next to me and watch the clouds go by."

With amusement in her eyes, Isabella retorted, "I can see them just fine from here."

Jim raised his finger in the air. "Ah, but you can see them better from here."

"I don't think so. You're lower than me."

"But you need my help interpreting their shapes, and I can only do that while lying down."

Isabella arched her brows. "Oh, really. What do you see right now?"

"A sassy woman." Jim motioned with his hands.

Isabella cocked her head back, quizzically. "What are you doing now?"

"I'm trying to speak to you in sign language."

Isabella nodded. "Oh, that's right. You know sign language. It helped you when trading with the Indians."

"Yep, also came in handy as a scout. I was placed in charge of the other Indian scouts."

"What did you just signal to me?"

"'Come next to me.'"

Isabella leaned forward. "Will you teach me some sign language?"

"If you sit next to me."

She briefly hesitated. "All right."

Jim sat up and made room for her on the rock. "What do you want to learn?"

"Hmmm, let me see. I know. How do you say, 'You are my friend'?"

Jim said slowly, "You . . . are . . . my . . . friend."

She gave him a shove. "I mean how do you *sign* 'you are my friend,' and you knew it."

He demonstrated, and she tried it herself, almost getting it right.

"Here, let me show you." He took her fingers and arms and guided her correctly, but then he took her hand and gazed in her eyes a moment before softly saying, "Is, you are my friend."

With a catch in her voice, Isabella answered, "And you are mine."

"Why the sad face?"

She looked down. "I'm not sure. I guess I'm sad about leaving in a few weeks. Maybe sooner if the weather gets bad."

"Why don't you consider staying?"

Isabella shook her head. "It's out of the question."

"Well then, I guess that Indian tribe that I join will have to teach me how to do a dance that keeps the weather nice. You know, the opposite of a rain dance."

Isabella looked up and smiled. "I think this Indian tribe is getting harder and harder to find all the time."

Jim smiled back. "I'll look, don't you worry."

Chapter Twelve

When they arrived back at Griff's from Old Man Mountain, one of the new guests hailed Jim and asked him about the best hunting spots. Jim told Isabella that he would take care of the horses and turned his attention to the hunter. Isabella headed toward her cabin. She knew Jim would answer the hunter without really giving an answer. Griff did the same thing. They both guarded their hunting secrets.

She stepped on her porch and turned around before entering her cabin. She saw Jim was watching her from the corral, and she waved good-bye to him before opening her door. She frowned; he was leaving for the next three days to do more hunting and trapping and hadn't made any new plans to see her when he got back. She had hoped he would have suggested another ride together, or at least that he would come by when he returned. Perhaps he had meant to, but the hunter had interrupted their arrival. Isabella shook her head. This was silly; of course she would see him again.

The next day Isabella went for a walk and marveled at her surroundings. She'd never seen colors look so bright or birds singing so sweetly. It was as if the world had suddenly awoken from a deep sleep and wanted to show off its splendor. She delighted in this feeling of wonder. When she returned from her walk, she helped with some of the chores and laughed and joked around with the others. She felt happy and looked forward to seeing Jim when he returned.

The second day Jim was gone, Isabella started feeling restless and couldn't keep herself occupied with any one thing for very long. One minute she would fret about when she would see Jim again, and in the next, she would scold herself for doing so. She joined the other guests at the main house and speculated why it was taking Griff so long to get back from Denver with their mail.

The third day Isabella tried convincing herself it didn't matter whether she ever again saw Jim. She had enjoyed her time with him, but he was just a friend, after all. If he didn't want to see her again, that would be all right with her. She had other things to do with her time . . . such as counting her cash. A guest had arrived announcing that the financial panic in the East was spreading west. Banks in the East weren't cashing checks, even their own. Some businesses and railroads had already gone under. The recession hadn't hit the West full blown yet, but it was a worry. Banks had over-speculated on railroads and mining interests that hadn't paid off. She found she still had enough to get by for a few more weeks even if Griff didn't bring back any money for her. She would need to save on luxuries, though, such as buying a horse and saddle for a trip to Pikes Peak. Isabella and all the guests anxiously awaited Griff and the mailbag that would surely contain newspapers explaining more about the panic.

The fourth day Jim was gone, Isabella awoke depressed. She knew he must have returned the previous day, but he hadn't stopped by. She missed him even if he didn't miss her. Well, she vowed, she wasn't going to concern herself anymore with his affairs, but repeatedly looked out the window to see whether he was coming. She joined the other guests at the main house, but simply slumped in a chair, unable to join in their conversation which was still about where Griff and the mailbag were—Isabella suddenly sat bolt upright. Of course, she should have thought of this earlier. Somebody should ride down the road toward Longmont, past Jim's cabin, and see whether Griff was coming down the road. Everybody wanted to know where he and the mail were, and that was what she was going to find out.

Jim heard Ring barking and looked up from his work. He saw Isabella approaching and smiled. He had arrived the previous night exhausted and gone right to bed. Early this morning he had started working on his hides and cleaning his traps and guns. He had planned on seeing her this evening if he got enough work done today. Her coming here now was much better.

He rose from his bench, and said, "Is, welcome. Nice to see you."

She fidgeted with her reins. "When did you get back?"

"Last night. I was looking forward to seeing you today."

"Oh."

"Is, get down. Come on in and we can have some coffee together."

She didn't dismount. "Have you seen Griff? We're all wondering where he's been. He should be bringing the mail back with him."

Jim looked at her a moment before answering, "No, I haven't seen him."

She sat more erect. "That's why I came. I want to look and see whether Griff is coming down the road."

What difference did it make if she saw Griff coming? Griff was either on his way or not. He decided not to argue the point. If she wanted to pretend that was why she was here, then he would too. She had never visited him on her own, and he quickly decided he needed to treat the situation carefully. One false move on his part and she would probably run away. Now that she was at his cabin he wanted to keep her here a while.

Jim slowly walked toward her. "Let me help you down. You can check for Griff after a cup of coffee."

She didn't answer, but allowed his help in dismounting.

"The coffee should still be warm. Come on in and I'll get you a cup."

Jim walked into his cabin and Isabella followed, but stayed near the open door. She looked around, but said nothing at first.

Jim smiled. "How have you been? Keeping busy?"

She nodded. "Yes, I've gone on walks and helped with chores. Did you have a good hunting trip?"

"Yes, very successful."

There was a pause in the conversation, and Jim searched for something to say. He was used to them having easy conversation, and this renewed awkwardness didn't sit well with him. They were beyond formal acquaintances at this point. The wind shifted directions and blew in through the doorway. He wanted to close the door but didn't dare. Her being alone inside his cabin was the peak of impropriety. She would run for sure.

Jim knew his cabin was a crowded mess. Trapping equipment was scattered in one pile while books were strewn in another. Hides and blankets were haphazardly stacked in one corner while his rifles randomly leaned against another. Pots and pans were heaped on the table, and his bed was unmade. But he wasn't ashamed of his cabin. He had built it himself, and it was snug and warm—when the door was closed. Right now he slightly shivered. Covered by the roof, his cabin was often cooler than the bright outdoors until he got a fire going and *closed* the door.

He saw her staring at the far wall. She gazed at the sketch he had hanging there and walked toward it. She read the signature in the corner: "George Weisz. That's Gertie's husband, I remember." She added, "I like the drawing. Where is it from?"

"He drew it in Wyoming."

She walked a few feet over and fingered a beaded bag he had hanging on a peg. "This is lovely. Did you trade for it?"

"No. It was a present."

She turned back around. "From whom?"

Jim stretched his back slightly. "Uh, I'm kind of beat from working so hard the last few days. Let me sit down. Why don't you join me at the table and drink some coffee while I tell you."

She hesitated a moment, but took a seat at the small table and Jim sat down opposite her, pouring each of them a cup. "It was the first time I traveled to Park Hill—that's what they used to call this area. Hugo Jaska and I had made some money selling buffalo hides in Denver and had celebrated heavily. But we had heard some guy talking at one of the saloons about how great this area was, and we wanted to check it out."

"What did the guy say about it?"

"It was supposed to have some of the best views in the West. Plenty of large game. Kit Carson had apparently traveled first through the area."

Jim paused and took a sip of coffee. "Hugo and I had seen our fair share of mountain scenery, but we'd never seen anything such as this. It was as if all the gods in all the worlds decided to have a contest—who could come up with the most beautiful view—and Estes Park was the winner."

Isabella sat upright in her chair. "There's only one God."

He shrugged. "So you believe. But just pretend. It was as if some deity personally supervised the landscape arrangement around here, placing the snow-capped mountains and the meadows below just perfectly right. You would think you had seen the most beautiful sight, walk a little farther, and then see another even more exquisite."

"I know; I've never seen anyplace more stunning. But let's get back to this 'god' contest."

"What about it?"

"If a group of gods had a contest, what would be the prize? They probably already have everything they want."

"Is, sometimes it amazes me how your mind works."

Isabella raised both her hands in the air. "You're the one who came up with this contest."

"All right, let me think." Jim scratched his chin. "Love, that would be the prize."

Isabella puckered her brow. "Love? If they're a God, everybody already loves them."

"That's worshipful love. But let's say God is just like an ordinary guy with his own personality. He'd want passionate love just as everybody else. Someone to love him just for himself."

Isabella stared at him.

"Good. I've rendered you speechless. In any case, after seeing this location I knew if I ever settled down, Park Hill would be the place. Park Hill felt like home, and I had never had that feeling before. But back then, I was far from wanting to settle in one place permanently. I didn't come back here until after the war."

"So what happened next?"

"Hugo and I decided to make camp for the night by the Big Thompson River. A rain started falling steadily, and the celebrating in Denver caught up with us, so we turned in early, dead to the world. But several hours later Hugo started shouting that the river was flooding. We gathered our things and headed up to drier ground, but then we heard this faint screaming."

"Who was it?"

"We couldn't tell at first. Finally we saw this person bobbing in the river. And let me tell you, that river was running fast and furious. I ran to the river's edge and grabbed this dead pine trunk and shoved it into the water. This petite form angled toward it, grabbed the other end, and as I pulled, the body twisted around and I realized, surprisingly, that I was saving a woman."

"A grown woman."

"Yeah, Stand Up Woman."

"Stand Up Woman?"

"Yeah, that's what we found out her name was after we brought her to our camp, made a fire and gave her dry clothes to change into."

Isabella crossed her arms. "What kind of name is Stand Up Woman? Even for an Indian, it sounds kind of strange."

"I'm thinking it's a good one. You know, she probably stands up to things, defends herself. I can just imagine what your Indian name would be."

Isabella narrowed her eyes, but couldn't hold back a smile. "What's that supposed to mean?"

Jim laughed. "Oh, nothing."

Isabella raised her chin. "My name would be . . . Woman of Many Talents."

"Stubborn Sassy Mouth, more like."

Isabella playfully kicked his leg under the table.

Jim scooted back a smidge. "Anyways, we found out she was a Ute. Her young son had been caught in the flooding river, and she had gone in after him."

"Did you find him?"

"No."

Isabella shook her head. "That's so unfortunate."

"I know. But the next morning, when we realized she had a badly sprained ankle, we knew we needed to take her back to her people ourselves. Actually, Stand Up Woman was from someplace far away. She had been staying at a temporary camp close to us with just her family. Her husband had left her and her son to do some hunting before the river disaster had happened."

"So he hadn't been around to help."

"That's right."

Isabella sighed. "You said the river looked treacherous. I don't know if I would have had the courage to jump in after the child even if he was my son. I'm afraid I might have reasoned that I wouldn't be able to save him. I'm not the strongest swimmer."

Jim shook his head. "I would have jumped right in, especially for my son. And you, with all the courage and kindness in you, wouldn't have hesitated one iota either. Oh, maybe you might have run along the shore for a bit to see if you could grab him from the side, but eventually you would have jumped also."

Isabella looked at Jim a moment, and then said as if just making a discovery, "You would make a good father. I think you would protect your children well. Griff's kids certainly like you."

Jim smiled, incredibly pleased she had just said that.

He couldn't think of anything she could have uttered that would have been more complimentary. Of course, she meant if he didn't drink excessively and led a stable existence, but still, it was huge praise on her part. He hesitated a moment, knowing what he wanted to ask, but realizing it was an extremely personal question.

He studied her face. "Do you ever yearn for children, Isabella? You would make an excellent mother." The room suddenly seemed exceptionally quiet as if the whole world waited for her answer.

With a sigh, Isabella answered, "I did at one time."

Jim frowned. "At one time?"

Cheeks reddening, Isabella confided, "I mean it's not too late but . . . it is too late." She looked away. "I'd be too old a mother for a newborn."

After a moment she looked back at Jim. "Maybe I could adopt an older child, but I'd want to be married first."

Softly, intensely, Jim said, "Yes."

On no more than a breath of air, Isabella asked, "Yes what?"

Jim cleared his throat. "Yes, you could always adopt."

She didn't say anything further for a moment, then asked, "Do you? I mean do you yearn for children sometimes?"

Jim frowned and whispered, "Yes." He raised his voice slightly. "I didn't always, but I do now."

Isabella nodded slowly. "I see."

She looked down and started slowly brushing the wrinkles from her skirt. "Well . . . I hope you get them." She looked back up. "My, oh my, how did we start talking about this? Isn't this supposed to be a conversation about how you got that beaded purse?"

Jim cleared his throat again. "Right. Where was I?"

"Uh . . . you're returning Stand Up Woman back to her camp."

Jim nodded. "Precisely. So we knew we had to help her return since she had that injured leg, but we were plenty nervous about taking her back. If her camp was flooded, maybe we would need to keep her for a while. And if her husband caught up with us unawares, he might think we had kidnapped her."

"And kill you?"

Jim shrugged. "Maybe. Anyways, we found her campsite. All was serene, no sign of her husband. We dismounted and helped Stand Up Woman down. Suddenly her husband appears, bow and arrow in hand, ready to let loose. Luckily Stand Up Woman starts waving her hands and shouting, and he slowly drops his arrow and places her behind him. I signal that we're leaving, and her husband nods and lets us go." Jim took another sip of coffee. "We thought that was it."

"Wasn't it?"

"No. Several days later, after elk hunting, we returned to our campsite and found the clothes we had loaned neatly folded on the ground and next to them were two intricately beaded pouches, a small knife with a carved handle, and some pemmican."

She rose and touched the beaded purse again. "Who got the knife?"

"We tossed a coin. Hugo got it."

Isabella nodded. "I probably should get going. Everybody might wonder if something happened to me."

"I'll walk with you up the hill behind the cabin. You can get a good look from there to see if Griff is coming."

Her eyes widened. "Oh, right . . . thanks. That's why I came."

Jim smiled. "I know."

After they confirmed Griff was nowhere in sight, Jim helped her mount her horse.

Isabella asked, "Will you be coming by this evening?"

"No, I think I have too much work around here to do. But you should check tomorrow morning whether Griff is coming. I'm sure everybody would appreciate that."

Isabella smiled. "Yes, you're right. I think I should."

The next morning when she came by, she dismounted on her own and knocked on the door. Jim was inside, estimating how much he could expect when he sold his furs. He walked to the door and held it open for her, smiling widely. "Is, you're back. I was hoping I'd see you today."

She smiled back. "Good morning, Jim. Have you seen Griff?"

"No, haven't seen him. How are you today?"

She shook her head. "I'd like to hear from Hennie. It's been so long since I've received a letter from her."

After she walked through, Jim closed the door halfway, keeping it partially open. "Want some coffee?"

She took the cup he handed her and looked at the table with his pen and paper out. "Did I disturb you?"

"You're always welcome. I was just checking some figures. I plan to sell my hides in Denver soon."

"What about the financial panic? Maybe you shouldn't go until it's over."

"I have other business while I'm there."

"How soon are you leaving?"

"Probably in the next couple weeks. I'll stay a few days and come back."

Isabella looked at the plank flooring. "Oh, I see."

"Would you like to come with me? Have you seen Denver before?"

"No, I haven't." She excitedly looked up, but then sighed and shook her head. "Thanks, but no. It wouldn't look proper you escorting me in a big city. I mean here it's understandable because I need a guide to go on hikes and see the scenery. Anyway, I'll probably go to Denver soon myself when I do more traveling."

Jim wondered what she meant by more traveling, but let the subject drop for now. He gestured to the chair at the table and they both sat down. She looked at an open book of Tennyson poems on the corner of the table.

"You read poetry? Tennyson?"

"Not at first. But Hugo once bought a book of poems with his earnings to read by the campfire. With his limited education, he figured it would be easier to peruse than a whole novel. I picked up his book one night and have been reading poetry ever since."

She lifted the Tennyson and read a few verses while Jim resumed working on his figures. "This one's a favorite of mine."

He looked up. "Read to me while I work."

Jim couldn't really concentrate on adding, but pretended to work so she would keep reciting. He smiled when she put emphasis where she thought appropriate. He eyed her occasionally and wondered how he had ever thought her not his type. She looked up and smiled with satisfaction when she finished.

"Read another. Please?"

She took her time looking through the book before deciding. Jim stopped pretending he was working, and placing his chin in his hand, he rested his elbow on the table while he listened to her. Isabella tried to act as if she didn't notice, but smothered a smile every now and then in the middle of reading.

When she finished the second poem she looked up. "Do you have any poems you've written yourself?"

"A whole stack of them. Want to see?"

Isabella smiled. "Yes, I'm interested in what you wrote."

Jim got up and looked through a small trunk he kept in the corner. He brought the collection of poems back to the table. Jim smiled. "Most start with 'When I look at the moon over yonder.'"

Isabella smiled. "That was so amusing when you recited that poem. At first I wasn't sure if you were serious. Thank goodness, you weren't. I don't think I could respect a man who wrote such terrible poetry!"

She began reading his poems. He tapped the table with his finger, nervous whether she liked them.

She raised her head. "This one I particularly enjoy. It has wonderful imagery of the mountains. They *can* look frightening, being so solid and strong . . . and impervious."

"Is, do you write poetry?"

"No, at least not yet."

"But will you let me see some of your writing?"

Isabella nodded. "I will. I'll try to remember to bring over what I have written so far about our hike up Longs Peak."

Jim smiled. "I'd like to see that."

Isabella got up to leave. He joined her at the door.

"Wait a second; let me grab my coat. I'll walk with you up the hill again to see if Griff is coming."

They held hands while climbing.

The next morning Isabella looked at the fog outside her cabin and wondered if she should check if Griff was coming when she had such a limited view. After dawdling an hour, she finally decided she might as well, but turned back when she discovered she couldn't see a thing around Jim's cabin and he wasn't home. She felt disappointed at first that she had missed him, but realized he probably had thought she wasn't coming because of the weather. She shook her head. It had been foolish riding over in this fog.

That afternoon Isabella was sewing inside the main house with Dorothy and Mrs. Rudolph when she glanced out the window and saw that the skies had finally cleared. "It's beautiful outside again. Have you noticed how the weather changes so quickly? It rarely stays the same for a whole day."

Mrs. Rudolph smiled. "You must have heard this saying by now: 'If you don't like the weather in Colorado, wait five minutes.'"

Isabella grinned and put down her sewing. "It's too nice to stay inside. Who'd like to go for a ride?"

Mrs. Rudolph placed another stitch. "Not today, too much work still to do."

Dorothy shook her head. "I'll pass also."

Isabella stood. "This morning it was too foggy to see whether Griff was coming down the road. I think I'll head that way now."

Dorothy looked up at Isabella. "All right, dear, you have a nice ride."

After observing Isabella through the window, saddling her horse and riding out of the yard, Dorothy looked over at Mrs. Rudolph. They started giggling.

Mrs. Rudolph shook her head. "Does she think we don't know?"

"Well, she is anxious to get some mail as are the rest of us. That road just has an added benefit that it goes by Jim's." Dorothy picked up her sewing before adding, "But I know what you mean. I think she does have some strong feelings for him."

"Some *strong feelings*? She's fallen in love with the man."

Dorothy smiled. "Considering how charming he can be, that would be easy for any woman, but especially her since she's unattached."

"Do you think Jim has fallen in love with her?"

Dorothy shrugged. "If he has, I bet it's the first time in a long time."

"They're so different."

"But opposites can attract."

"Do you think she'd ever marry him?"

Dorothy paused, needle in hand. "I'm not sure. He's a good man, I know that, but he's had so rough a life." She continued sewing. "You realize, even though Isabella is older and has traveled all over the world, she's inexperienced and innocent in some ways."

Mrs. Rudolph cut a thread. "Meaning?"

"I'm not sure that she'd recognize it if she was in love with him. To her, she might only be checking to see if Griff is coming down the road."

Mrs. Rudolph shook her head and didn't respond.

Jim was sorting through his food supplies when Isabella knocked on his cabin door. He opened it. "I didn't expect to see you today."

"The fog cleared so I decided to see whether Griff was coming, but he wasn't."

"He will, you just have to be patient." He closed the door three-quarters of the way, still making sure it was partially open.

She looked over at the open satchels on the table and

asked, "What are you doing today?"

"I'm checking to see what I need to buy in Denver."

"Want me to help? I can make a list for you."

"No, but you can help me use up some of these odds and ends. I was planning on making bread with the leftover dried fruit and nuts. Why don't you stir while I figure out what to add to the bowl?"

Fifteen minutes later Isabella tapped the spoon on the side of the bowl. "I don't think I'd add so much of that lard. And are you sure those nuts haven't gone bad?"

Jim held up his hand. "Is, I've been cooking a long time. Trust me; I know what I'm doing."

"Well, that may be, but . . . Wait, what are you adding now?"

"A pinch of salt. Don't you know baked goods taste better with salt?"

"I'd hardly call that a pinch."

"Stop fussing."

She resumed stirring, and he added some cinnamon and nutmeg. "I've always liked lots of spices in bread. Beavers like spices, too."

She looked up. "You're kidding."

"Nope. To bait beaver traps you take castoreum from the caster glands of the beaver. But the best bait is castoreum mixed with nutmeg, cloves, and cinnamon."

"Who'd of thought? How much more do you plan on adding?"

"I think that will do it. Here—let's pour it in this cast-iron pan and bake it."

Isabella studied the pan he was holding. "I don't think I'd use that."

"What's wrong now?"

"It's too flat. Don't you have a loaf pan?"

"Does this place look like a bakery?"

"Well, I'd still use one a little deeper."

Jim held up his hand. "It'll be fine. Trust me."

After pouring and placing the pan to bake, he turned around and looked at Isabella, sitting at the table. She was watching him with a slight frown on her face.

"What are you thinking about now, Is?"

"Do you realize that if strangers walked in, they would think we were some old married couple?"

Jim shrugged. "Should I put on an apron to make it more realistic-looking?"

Isabella shook her head. "I'm serious. If they found out we weren't, can you imagine what it would do to my reputation?"

"Oh, I'd just marry you and save your reputation."

Isabella looked at the ceiling. "Just what I always wanted—some forced marriage."

Jim smiled. "I'd be happy to marry you."

She looked at him wide-eyed.

Jim stopped short. Not for the first time, he realized, the thought was crossing his mind, but he doubted she was thinking likewise. To cover his embarrassment he said, "Of course, you would need to learn to bake as well as I do first."

Isabella smiled and shook her head.

He needed to change the subject. "Uh . . . what do you want to do while we wait for the bread to finish?"

Isabella perked up. "I know. Tell me some more tricks of the trapping business."

Jim puffed out his cheeks. "Well, let's see." He glanced around the room and then saw some dough that had fallen on the floor when he had poured it into the pan. He picked it up and added some flour to make it stiffer before rolling it into a ball. "All right. Show me how you would dig a cache."

"A what?"

"When you have too many hides to carry and need to secretly store them, you dig a cache." He handed her the ball of dough. "Here, show me how you would dig your hole."

Isabella formed the ball into a bowl shape.

Jim pulled his chair from around the other side of the table and sat down next to her. "Not quite. See, what you would want to do, is shape the bowl with a small well on the bottom somewhat deeper."

Isabella reshaped the bowl. "Like this?"

Jim took the dough from her hand and examined her work. "That's right. Then you'd line the cache sides and bottom with sticks. That way, when it rains, the water collects in the very bottom and doesn't get the hides all wet."

She looked up into his face and smiled warmly. He smiled back. He had a sudden urge to give her a kiss. He took a deep breath. He needed to back off. She would run away for sure right now if he did that.

"What else?"

Jim scratched his chin. "All right. Tell me how to make a bull boat."

Isabella scrunched up her nose. "A boat to carry a bull?"

"No, Is." He tweaked her nose. "A bull boat is a boat trappers and Indians built made out of bent branches, usually willow, built into the shape of a bowl. The frame was then covered by a bull buffalo hide stretched over the framework so you could carry your furs and hides over water."

"But how did you keep it from sinking?"

"You sealed it with pine pitch, animal fat and charcoal. Now tell me, would you use the hide with or without the hair on it?"

Isabella pursed her lips in thought. "Hmmm."

He shook his head. She obviously didn't realize how kissable the expression made her look.

"Without the hair. The boat would glide faster."

"Nope. With the hair, to help seal the boat and also to

prevent the boat from spinning. Why would you keep the tails on the hide?"

Isabella smiled. "This is so fun. Let me think. . . . I got it. I got it. So you could tie the boats together."

Jim laughed. "Correct."

"Tell me another trick. I'm good at this."

"All right. One more. Where on a buffalo is the best place to aim and shoot so you have a hide to make into a bull boat."

Isabella pursed her lips again. Jim looked away, smiled and shook his head. The woman was a tease and had absolutely no idea. Whatsoever.

"Well, it must be the center. It's the easiest place to hit."

He turned back around. "Wrong."

"What? I like getting questions right."

Jim laughed. "So does everybody."

"Let me guess again. The head."

"Wrong."

"The rear?"

"No."

Isabella sighed loudly. "All right, tell me. I give up."

"The novice shoots for the center; the experienced hunter knows to shoot a few inches above the brisket just behind the shoulder."

Isabella put her hands on her hips. "That's not fair to give me a trick question."

Jim shook his head in bewilderment. "It's not a trick question. You just got it wrong . . ."

A half hour later Jim gave Isabella the first slice. "Well, how is it?"

She gingerly chewed and swallowed a bite. "It's . . ." She held back a smile. "It's . . ." She snorted, holding back a laugh.

She struggled to maintain a straight face. "It's . . . it's .

. . absolutely horrible. Is this . . . is this what you eat with your bear?!" She doubled over in a fit of laughter.

Jim glared at her. "Let me try it."

He took a bite, then grimaced and ran out the door. When she heard him spitting, she broke into peals of laughter again. He returned and sat down on the chair next to hers, but they couldn't look at each other without bursting into howls, putting their arms around each other for support. Eventually Isabella quieted, took a deep breath and pulled out from his arms, smiling.

Jim grinned back. "I'm not sure what happened. It usually turns out better."

Isabella wiped the tears from her eyes. "I should hope so. I don't know what got into me. I usually only laugh this hard when I'm with Hennie."

"Glad I could provide some entertainment for you."

Isabella grinned. "Believe me, you did."

Jim gazed into her eyes a moment. "Is . . ."

"What?" She stared intently back at him.

He paused. "What if . . ."

"What?" she softly asked.

"What if we were to . . .?"

"What?" She looked his face up and down.

Jim swallowed. If it was too soon to ask, she might not only go running, but never come back. He didn't want to take the chance. "What if we were to go trapping together tomorrow?" He inwardly groaned. That was the last thing he wanted to do with her, but he couldn't think of anything else to ask.

Isabella looked stunned a moment. "You mean lay traps? I don't know; I'm not sure if I actually want to do that."

Jim shook his head. "Uh, no. Forget I asked. We'll think of something else to do if Griff doesn't get back by tomorrow."

Isabella smiled. "All right."

The next day Jim was mounting his mule Sassy when Isabella showed up. "Perfect timing. Join me for a ride."

Isabella bobbed her head. "Where to?"

"Not far from here. I want to check out the beaver population in a nearby stream." Jim smiled. "In one spot you can get a good look at the road up ahead and see if Griff is coming."

Isabella smiled back innocently. "Oh, right. That would be a good idea."

He almost asked her, teasingly, how long she was going to keep up the ruse, but decided calling her on it might embarrass her so he kept quiet.

The outing took longer than Jim expected. When he didn't find many beaver in the first area, Isabella agreed to go with him to check out another region before heading back.

When they were about a mile from his cabin, Jim felt the first plop of rain hit his nose. Five minutes later a deluge poured down soaking each of them thoroughly. He looked over at Isabella. "Are you cold?"

"More wet than cold."

Jim nodded through the rain and urged Sassy to a faster pace. The rain let up for a few minutes, but the wind started blowing gustily, and eventually fine pellets of freezing rain began hitting his face. Sassy slipped on the frozen trail within a few minutes. He looked over at Isabella hunched down on her horse to keep warm. "We're almost there."

Isabella nodded.

By the time they reached his cabin Sassy's mane glistened with a coat of ice and Isabella was shivering.

"Is, you can't go back until you and your clothes dry out."

Isabella frowned. "But—"

Jim held up his hand. "I'm not debating this one with

you. You could get really sick."

Her frown deepened. "Sometimes you're bossy, aren't you?"

"Yep. Now get down."

Jim helped her dismount. After taking care of her horse and Sassy, they entered his cabin. He closed the door all the way.

"First we both need to get out of our clothes." Jim handed her a blanket. "I'll turn around while you take yours off; then you can do the same for me."

Isabella eyes widened. "I can't get undressed!"

Jim shook his head. "Well, you can't just stand around shivering in wet clothes. Look, get undressed down to your undergarments and wrap the blanket around your shoulders. I won't see a thing."

Isabella sighed loudly. "Oh, my Lord. I can't believe I've gotten myself into such a fix."

Jim smiled. "Believe it. Now hurry up. I want to get out of my wet clothes next."

"You mean just down to your undergarments, right?"

"Yep, I'll keep on my corset and bloomers."

Isabella snorted, then motioned with her finger for Jim to turn around. He could hear her repeatedly sighing as she took each garment of clothing off. When she was finished she told Jim he could get undressed now.

He peeled off his wet outer clothes. "All right. I'm done. You can turn around again."

"Do you have a blanket wrapped around your shoulders also?"

Jim chuckled. "No. I'm standing here buck naked."

Isabella gasped. "Put on a blanket. Put on a blanket."

Jim chuckled. "It's on, I was just kidding. You can turn around."

Isabella sneaked a quick peek first to assure herself, then turned around. Jim stoked the fire and arranged their wet clothes on a bench placed in front of the fireplace. He looked up and saw her standing and still shivering.

"Is, we're getting in the bed under the covers."

She looked at him, horrified. "We can't do that. It wouldn't be proper."

Jim sighed. "For God's sake, it's only the two of us. I won't tell anybody if you don't. I'll read to you while we wait for the clothes to dry."

She hesitated a moment, then slowly lifted the covers and slid into the bed. Jim grabbed a book off the shelf. "Scoot over."

She moved a couple inches and eyed him warily.

Jim shook his head. "Move over more. Come on, I won't bite."

Isabella scrunched her eyes closed and shook her head. "I can't *believe* I'm doing this."

He smiled. "I think it's kind of fun, don't you?"

She opened her eyes quickly. "You won't get fresh, will you?"

He bit back a smile. "You don't want me to?"

"Absolutely not. You keep that blanket wrapped around you at all times. You do have some clothes underneath it, don't you?"

"Yep. Wanna look?"

She screamed, "No!"

Jim chuckled.

Isabella frowned. "Stop laughing. This is a serious matter. My reputation is at stake."

"You're right. I'm sure if somebody walks in and sees us together that it will make a huge difference that we each have a blanket wrapped around ourselves while we lay in bed. Now scoot over some more."

She sighed loudly again but moved over. He slid in and pulled up his side of the covers. Isabella lay stiff next to him, holding the covers up to her chin, still shivering.

"I'm cold."

"Obviously. Why don't you let me hold you? Put your

head on my shoulder."

She frowned and eyed him suspiciously.

"It'll be all right, I promise." With his right hand holding the book, Jim nudged his left arm around her shoulders as she turned into him very slightly. She continued to clutch the covers tightly.

"This book's about a man sailing around the world. I'm halfway through it. I'll catch you up with the first part, and then we can continue where I left off."

"I suppose your friend Gertie sent it to you."

"Yep."

"I thought you'd read books about the West and mountain men."

"What would be the point? I've lived that life. Do you only read books about lippy, headstrong women?"

She elbowed him in the chest.

"Ouch."

"So what's happened so far?"

Jim explained and began reading to her. She stopped clutching the covers and gently placed her hand on his chest. Jim continued reading as if he didn't notice. He turned the page with both hands and crushed her against him.

"You're squeezing me."

Jim smiled. "You noticed."

He resumed reading and turned several more pages the same way without her commenting. At one point she chuckled at an amusing part. He leaned down and kissed the top of her head. She glanced up and smiled. Their eyes caught and held.

"Is, let me kiss you? Just once. I promise that's all."

She gave a slight nod and raised her face to his. He touched his lips softly to hers for a brief moment before she lowered her head to his shoulder.

"Is, I hope one day you'll give me a real kiss, but I'll take that for today."

Jim didn't continue reading and after a minute Isabella asked, "Do you think our clothes are dry yet?"

Jim slid out of bed, went over to the bench and felt the garments. "Not completely but probably close enough."

"Oh."

Jim turned around. "Maybe we should wait a little longer."

"Yes, you're probably right."

Steadily meeting her eyes, he asked, "You want to . . . read some more?"

Isabella hesitated, then sat up. "Um . . . no." She scooted to the side of the bed. "Um, maybe we could make some hot coffee before I go."

"That's fine."

They drank the coffee quietly, Isabella not meeting his gaze, frequently glancing around his cabin as if the objects were suddenly of special interest. When she finished her cup, she stood and looked at Jim. "Well, I better go."

Jim nodded and stood. Isabella smiled slightly and motioned with her finger for him to turn around. He smiled and obliged. Isabella went outside and waited by her horse as Jim finished dressing.

A few minutes later Isabella raised her foot to mount her horse, but suddenly stopped and turned to Jim, who was holding the reins. She went up on her toes and hugged him around the neck. "Thank you."

"You're welcome, sweetheart." But when he thought about it, he wasn't exactly sure what he was being thanked for.

Isabella returned later in the afternoon in a happy, almost giddy mood from Jim's and headed over to the main house to grab a bite to eat and chat with some of the other guests. An hour later she headed to her cabin and walked up onto her porch. She glanced up before entering her cabin and saw Dorothy and Charles walking toward the corral.

She asked them, "Going riding?"

Charles nodded. "Just for a bit."

Dorothy asked, "How's Jim doing?"

Isabella answered, "Oh, he's fine."

Isabella walked into her cabin, closed the door, and suddenly stopped. She dropped onto her bed. Oh, no. Dorothy had asked about Jim, not whether she had seen Griff coming down the road. Did she think she was spending time with Jim? Did everybody? She had said she was checking to see whether Griff was coming. Did they believe her? Oh, no, no! Did they think she was chasing after Jim? What must they think of her? What was this going to do to her reputation? What was she going to do?

Isabella got up, clenched her fists and started pacing. She was going to put some distance between Jim and her. That's what she needed to do. As soon as possible she should get away.

She rubbed her forehead. Pikes Peak. If she went to Pikes Peak, that would take care of the problem. She quickly got out her map of the Colorado Territory and studied it.

First she would need to travel southeast about fifty miles to Denver. Then she would head due south about seventy miles to Colorado Springs which was the town adjacent to Pikes Peak and the Garden of the Gods. From there she could return directly to Denver or maybe she would travel northwest of Colorado Springs a bit and see some of that region before she returned to Denver. From Denver, then maybe home to Scotland . . . she didn't really want to think about it now. She could make a decision later. Of course all these distances were as the bird flies and that hardly applied to this mountainous region.

She heard a wagon outside her cabin, looked out the window, and saw Griff. *Oh, thank God.* She opened her door and hurried over to him. "Welcome back. We all missed you."

"It took a little longer than I thought it would to drop off the family and get everything done. That business with the lord took a while."

"Who?"

"Oh, one of your fellow countrymen." He patted her on the back. "Nothing to concern yourself with."

"Did you bring back the mail?"

"Yes, but it's packed at the bottom of the wagon. Give me a few hours to get it out."

"Certainly. What about my note?"

"I need to talk to you about that." Griff stared at the ground a moment, kicking his heel in the dirt, then looked up. "I got in a real tight pinch and needed the money. The bank cashed the note, but the stores are hesitant to extend credit and want only cash during this financial crisis."

"Oh, but I wanted to go to Pikes Peak. I needed the money to buy a horse and saddle."

"I'll give you your choice of any of my horses, any saddle, anything you require. And when you return I promise I'll pay you back every penny. I have some money coming to me in the near future."

Isabella frowned and then sighed. "What can I say, but all right."

"You have nothing to worry about. I promise I'll do right by you. Try riding my horses the next few days. When you find one you like, you'll be ready to leave."

Griff had brought a keg back with him, and it was an especially lively evening among the men. Isabella watched Griff tell jokes and sing, but it struck her as a bit of false cheer. She caught an occasional sad expression on his face. It had been a little awkward discussing the money situation with him, but she had been gracious in accepting his explanation and fully expected to get the money due her in the future. Perhaps he missed his family, but she couldn't shake the feeling that there was something more going on.

She started to sort through the mail and placed it in

piles according to the recipient: a few for Dorothy, one for Mrs. Rudolph. She reached into the bag again and pulled out a letter for Jim. She peeked at the return address and saw it was from a woman, Lindsey Jaska. Her breath caught and her hand shook a little as she placed it in a pile for him. What was happening to her? How had she become so attached to him that she was jealous of another woman's attention? She stared out the window. Wait. Jaska. Jaska. That was Hugo's last name, wasn't it? She took a deep breath and finished sorting the mail, placing several more in a pile for Jim. She needed to get her emotions in order. The sooner she left for Pikes Peak, the better, but she owed Jim at least a word of farewell.

"Griff, I'll take these over to Mr. Nugent in the morning."

"That's not necessary since he usually comes by regularly."

"Uh . . . he told me that he's leaving for Denver soon, and I'm sure he would want these before he goes."

"Well, do as you wish. I'm sure he would appreciate it."

The following morning Jim looked up from chopping wood and watched Isabella ride toward his cabin.

"Good morning, Mr. Nugent."

He wasn't surprised with the "Mr. Nugent" again. The kiss had probably been too much for her even as brief as it was. She didn't dismount.

"Griff returned. Did you know?"

"Yes, I saw him briefly as he passed by. Did he apologize to you for taking so long to get back?"

"Oh, he said something about some business with some lord taking a while."

Jim frowned. "What business? Did he tell you?"

"No. Why, is it important?"

"Damn right it's important." He threw his ax onto the

wood pile, looked up and glowered at her. He took a deep breath. He needed to control his anger over hearing the news about Griff and *some lord*. It wasn't her fault after all that she was the bearer of potentially bad news.

Isabella frowned. "I'm tired of your swearing, and it's rude to subject me to it. But the reason I'm here is to bring you your mail and to tell you I'm leaving." With the last statement Isabella sat squarer on her mount.

"Leaving? Leaving to where?"

"I want to see Pikes Peak and maybe the Garden of the Gods and some other places."

Jim placed his hands on his hips. "What? Are you crazy? This time of year? That was weeks ago when you talked about it briefly. It's too late in the year to go now." He paused and shook his head. "I forbid you to go—" He stopped short. He couldn't believe he had just said something so domineering. He knew she wouldn't like it.

Her eyes widened and she shot right back at him, "I'm a grown woman. You can't forbid me anything."

He rubbed his forehead. "You're right, but listen to reason."

She asked curtly, "What?"

"Let's start with the weather. It could snow, and a large amount, anytime from now on. You know Longs Peak was covered the day after we climbed it. You could get caught in a major storm and freeze to death."

"I'm not stupid, Mr. Nugent. I plan to dress warmly."

"That might not be enough, Miss Bird. Then there's the Indian problem. Different tribes have been attacking and raiding all over this year. You know the stories. They're madder than hell at the way they've been treated, and they want revenge. It makes no difference that you're a woman. The Cheyenne and Arapaho certainly haven't forgotten Sand Creek."

Isabella sharpened her gaze. "I told you to stop swearing; and what's Sand Creek?"

"That idiot Chivington and his volunteer militia slaughtered over a hundred Indians, mostly women and children, even though the tribe had a flag of surrender raised. It occurred several years ago, and the militiamen were eventually condemned, but the Indians are still furious." He shook his head. "That's not to mention that you're a woman traveling alone, and there're plenty of rough outlaws and miners in Colorado."

With a forced smile, Isabella declared, "Mr. Nugent, I've managed to travel alone plenty of times before this. I think I can handle it."

"Look, wait until spring and I'll take you then."

Flinging her head skyward and with a short laugh of disbelief, Isabella looked back at him and said, "That's the last thing I need."

"Why? What's gotten into you?"

"Nothing! It hardly would appear proper for you to accompany me." She rolled her eyes and shook her head. "You just don't understand."

His voice rising, Jim blurted out, "You're not making any damn sense. You just told me this week that it was all right for me to guide you in the wilderness, just not a city. Make up your mind!"

Isabella narrowed her eyes. "If you swear one more time, I'm leaving. It's complicated. We're talking miles and miles of guiding, not just Estes Park. You and me alone—"

Jim roared, "Fine, Miss Bird. We'll ask Downer and Rogers to come with us again. They could act as chaperones!"

"Shouting's not going to change my mind. Besides, I can hardly wait until the springtime to go to Pikes Peak. Why, that would be months more of just us spending time together."

Unable to keep the exasperation out of his voice, Jim asked, "And that would be so bad?"

Isabella shouted, "No! I mean, yes! People might see us and start thinking I'm—" Isabella shook her head. "Stop irritating me. I don't want to talk about it. I just came by to tell you I was leaving, not to hear you swear at me and give me all sorts of reasons why I shouldn't make the trip. This is my life and I can go where I please!"

Jim raised his hands in surrender. "You're making a mistake, but I can see you won't listen. You're stubborn as hell, and it's going to get you into trouble this time."

Isabella reached into her pocket. "That's it. I'm leaving. Here, take your mail, Mr. Nugent."

He grabbed it from her. "Fine, but let me be clear: I'm not having any part of this stupidity. I'm leaving for Denver, and I'm not going to stick around to see you off."

Face rigid, Isabella said, "That's perfectly acceptable to me."

Jim could only shake his head.

She reined her horse to leave.

"Dammit. Wait a minute." He marched into his cabin and came back out holding a small gun. "Take this Sharps revolver and keep it with you. Don't argue with me about that."

She snatched it from his hand and rode off without another word.

Chapter Thirteen

The next morning Jim was still fuming. Certainly, Isabella aggravated him. But also, what was Griff doing with Dunraven? He took a sip of whiskey. After packing today, he would head for Denver tomorrow. First he needed to check one more trap.

An hour later, while riding Sassy, he glanced up and saw Griff on the trail ahead, drinking from a flask. Jim smirked; he wasn't the only one imbibing this morning.

He headed toward Griff and stopped a few feet away. "I need to talk to you."

"What about?" Griff slurred slightly.

"Dunraven."

"It's none of your business."

Lips set in a grim line, Jim said slowly, "I'm making it my business starting now."

Griff took another swig from his flask. "What do you want to know?"

"What's going on between the two of you?"

"He's been my guest."

"Don't bullshit me. I know he's been your guest. What dealings do you have with him?"

"It's private."

"Dunraven told me he was interested in property in Estes Park. I know that much. What more do you know?

Did you show him some choice piece of land?"

Griff sighed. "All right. I haven't told anybody yet and don't plan to for a while, but you'll find out anyway. I sold my property to him."

Jim stared at Griff. "Why would you do something so stupid?"

"It's simple. I have a family to feed."

Dripping with disbelief, Jim asked, "Between your hunting, cattle, and lodging businesses, are you going to tell me you haven't been making enough money?"

Griff looked away. "I have expenses, lots of them."

Jim shook his head. "Only a fool could have mismanaged his money the way you have."

Griff turned back and frowned. "Well, I have a better life than the moron I'm looking at right now."

"Trusting Dunraven is idiotic. Do you think your homestead is going to be enough for that rich bastard? He's going to want to take over Estes Park."

Griff shook his head and took a sip. "Not my concern anymore."

Jim eyed him speculatively. "You know something. What is it?"

"Nothing. And I have better things to do than talk to you. Get out of my way."

"Wait. Just one more thing. When are you leaving and Dunraven showing up?"

"I'm not leaving."

Jim frowned. "What do you mean?"

"I don't know when he'll be coming back, but I'm staying to help run things."

"Ha! Dunraven will be running you. What a miserable existence under his thumb."

Griff sighed. "If you must know, I'm not happy about my new circumstances either. But I'll make the best of it."

"Good luck with that." Jim reined Sassy around and with a kick, rode off. After a few minutes, he stopped and took another drink. He studied his flask. He couldn't blame the whiskey this time for making him furious; he hadn't drunk enough to make a difference. No, it was Griff who had sent him to the roof. Even if it was Griff's property to do with what he liked, couldn't Griff have seen before he made the sale, what he had potentially set in motion?

In the afternoon, Jim had trouble concentrating on packing. His mind was filled with thoughts either about Dunraven or Isabella. He could do nothing about Dunraven right now. Isabella was another matter.

He thought about riding over and trying to talk some sense into her, but he finally dismissed the idea. She was too independent and stubborn and probably wouldn't listen to him anyway. What had gotten into him, getting involved with such a stiff and unreasoning woman?

Later that evening, despite his swirling thoughts, he remembered to pack extra cash in case he had trouble getting money out of the bank. He retrieved some from his stash hidden under a floorboard of his cabin and secured it in his special money pouch.

He sat down at his table, took a sip of whiskey, and opened Lindsey and Hugo's letter. He had decided not to read it the previous evening. Letters from friends were too precious to read while he was in a foul mood. They needed to be saved for when he could more thoroughly enjoy them. He read the first paragraph and shook his head. Hugo had run into Reginald Whene on a sidewalk in Cleveland. Hugo asked Jim whether he remembered Reggie. Jim smiled. How could he ever forget that guiding trip? Reggie couldn't shoot a thing. He continued reading. Reggie had gotten married and his wife was expecting. Jim chuckled. A potential Reggie Junior was on the way. Reggie had asked for Jim's address. He thought he might like to hire Jim again on a hunting trip before his baby arrived. "That would be great!" he had told Hugo. Hugo had sold Reggie a very expensive hunting rifle.

Jim poured another shot and kept reading. Hugo and the family were doing well. They had bought a bigger house, and Hugo was thinking about expanding his business, maybe a second store. He asked whether Jim would ever be interested in moving there. Jim shook his head. Hugo still thought of him as the better man he once was. He stared at the letter. He didn't know exactly what kind of man he was now, yet he knew thoughts of settling down with a wife and family had recently occurred to him. Jim ran his hand through his hair. The excessive drinking Hugo would never accept. He had drunk too much today. Whiskey first thing in the morning was never a good thing. He needed to stop binge drinking altogether, but it had been an aggravating last couple of days. Jim rubbed his forehead. No excuse.

Jim lay down on his bed and rested his head on his arms. He would send a reply to Hugo from Denver. He knew he would never leave Estes Park even if he could once again live up to Hugo's expectations. He tried to fall asleep, but his mind churned and kept returning to Isabella. What an idiot he had been to spend so much time with her. That kind of woman would never change. Intimacy probably scared the living daylights out of her. He punched his pillow and repositioned his head. He was determined to put thoughts about her behind him and enjoy himself in Denver.

The next day Jim was pleased with himself. The ride to Denver was nearly complete, and he hadn't thought about that blasted woman once. Well, maybe for a short time to consider how annoying Isabella was, but that was all. He had more important things on his mind, such as Griff and Dunraven. She was finally behind him once and for all.

He reached Denver, found lodging, and went to his favorite saloon. He talked with some of the men he had known for years, spent time dancing with a few of the gals, and played some cards. He tried to enjoy it all with his usual gusto, but when he thought about it the next morning he realized that the evening had seemed a bit flat. The crowd just hadn't been that stimulating. The crude teasing and bawdy jokes had become tiresome after a while. The whole night had lacked something. He supposed the Dunraven business was depressing his mood.

After he finished breakfast, he headed to one of the many hide stores in Denver. He'd been selling to the same place for years, but left an hour later, disgusted. He had argued with the owner for a good part of that time, only to be given a small amount of money up front. The owner didn't want to take any chances during the financial crisis. If the hides and furs sold, Jim would be given more money later.

In the afternoon he went to the land office to make sure he knew all the laws pertaining to settlement in Estes Park. Right now a settler could claim squatter's rights, but once the area was surveyed, the homestead law would require improvements on the property—a dwelling of some sort or the land needed cultivation—for the settler to claim ownership. If a settler didn't want to live on the land for five years before claiming ownership, he could purchase the property from the government after six months for a reasonable sum.

After leaving the land office he passed by one of the finer Denver hotels and decided he would eat there that evening. Funny, but he felt like getting away from the coarse crowd with whom he had spent the previous night. He went to the barber for a shave and bath and decided to go shopping for clothing.

On his way over to the store, he saw a woman who looked like Isabella and did a double take. He didn't figure on seeing her in Denver but knew it was a possibility. It didn't matter to him one way or the other if he saw her.

After all, he was over her and had certainly had enough of her company. My God, he couldn't imagine anything more boring than spending time with her, and her highbrow attitude, in Denver.

A few minutes later, he walked into the general store and noted it didn't seem to have as many items, probably because the store was afraid to restock if business slowed during the financial panic. Jim looked around briefly and picked up an ordinary-looking shirt and pants to purchase, then hesitated, and put them back on the shelves.

He headed to the fine gentlemen's tailor shop next door instead. He supposed it wouldn't hurt to purchase an expensive suit and new boots in case he had to deal with Dunraven in the future. His mother's voice came to mind: "Clothes make the man." No, they didn't, but she and a lot of folks never seemed to understand that.

The tailor was more than happy for the business during this recession. Even though the financial panic had just hit Colorado recently, and the Territory was not seeing the full effects that the East was now experiencing—with banks and businesses closing and large numbers of people unemployed—a store selling finer goods was overstocked because people hesitated to make expensive purchases when they weren't sure how much money they would have a year from now.

Jim was pleased to receive a discount on a suit nearly finished that someone had ordered, but never claimed. It fit him with few alterations, and the tailor promised to complete it by day's end. Jim could wear it to dinner that night.

Later that evening Jim walked into the Big Nugget Hotel lobby and surveyed the plush surroundings. Gleaming hardwood floors, leather chairs, thick rugs, brass fixtures and crystal chandeliers all caught his attention. In his new boots and custom-tailored suit, he looked as if he belonged to the setting. His parents would have been proud. He turned to go into the restaurant, but was stopped short by a familiar voice.

"Mountain Jim! You old dog! I almost didn't recognize you!"

Jim turned back around and saw Billy Cody standing with his arms outstretched, waiting to give him a bear hug.

"Buffalo Bill! I see you bought another new buckskin outfit. I like the fringe." Jim walked into his arms and the two embraced, patting each other heartily on the back.

"What's with the fancy outfit, Jim? I thought I was the only one who liked to dress sharp around here."

Jim placed his thumbs under his lapels. "I thought it might come in handy when I want to make important business decisions."

Billy guffawed. "The day you quit huntin' and trappin' I'm turning in my spurs. But I'm here on business myself for a few days. I'm thinking about buying more land out West. Can't decide whether I like the Colorado Territory, Wyoming, or Nebraska the best. Might buy land in each!"

Jim smiled. "Want to get a bite to eat with me in the hotel restaurant?"

"You bet. You can treat also!"

Seated at the table, Jim lit a cigar while he waited for the food. Billy sipped his third shot.

Jim looked over at Billy with affection. "I was hoping I might run into you, Billy, while I was here in Denver."

Billy grinned. "Always nice to see you too, pal."

"I read something about you recently that I want to ask you about."

"Now, Jim, if it's about that acting on stage back East, I can explain. I'm just on a break from the theater right now, but I plan to do more—"

Jim held up his hand. "Actually, Billy, considering how colorful you can be, that didn't surprise me much when I heard about it. No, it's about Lord Dunraven and you spending time together."

Billy cocked his head. "The Earl?"

"Yeah. First off, why would you hunt with that slimy son of a gun?"

Billy shrugged. "Why not? He's a paying customer."

Jim frowned. "He's an ass."

Billy smiled. "A wealthy ass. What? You only guide people you like? Oh, he was sure of himself all right. But he was one damn excellent hunter, a true shot."

Brow quirked, Jim said, "Sorry to hear that. I like thinking only the worst about him." He leaned forward. "But did he talk to you about what he wants to do to this area? What his plans were?"

Billy frowned. "Not that I remember. What's got you in such a storm cloud?"

"I met him when he visited Estes Park several months ago. He said he was interested in buying some land there. I'm afraid he wants to take over the whole place, maybe make a private game preserve for just him and his buddies."

Billy shook his head. "Don't know anything about that."

"Too bad. I was hoping you might. I figure the more I know, the sooner I can try to stop any scheming he might plan."

Billy looked puzzled. "What you getting at?"

"I have no doubt he'll try to get the land for cheap on the sly."

With a rueful twist of his lips, Billy said, "Yeah, there are all sorts of ways to slip a fast one out West–especially when homesteading." Billy tipped his glass and motioned for the waiter to bring another. He looked at Jim. "Need one?"

Jim took a sip of his first shot. "No, I'm good."

"Hell, Jim, I remember nights when we were scouts

when you drank me under the table."

Jim smiled. "Still could I'm sure. Just don't have the same desire to tie one on so frequently."

Billy slapped his thigh. "Oh, my Lordy. You got a gal, don't you? She's roping ya in."

Jim smirked. "Nobody's roping me in, I can assure you. I'm just tired of the type of person I become when I drink too much."

Billy nodded thoughtfully. "Yeah, not everybody's a happy drunk."

"Anyways, what do you know about homesteading schemes?"

"Oh, there are all sorts of ways to scam the land office. They don't have enough agents to monitor claims, and some of the agents are crooked themselves. And what some homesteaders call their required improvements to the land are just plain comical."

Jim nodded. "I read some only put a few logs in a pile, and that's their cabin; and some just pile some brush together, and that's their fence."

Billy waved his hand expressively. "That's nothing, Jim. One group built a cabin on wheels and rolled it around to different claims depending on where the agent was checking things out. Another guy claimed he had built a cabin, but when the agent arrived it was only the size of a hat box!"

Jim shook his head. "A hundred and sixty acres can support a farming family back East, but can be a ridiculously small amount of land in this dry West. And right now one guy can stake claims to several parcels of land. All he needs to do is falsely change his name a few times and walk into a land office."

Billy slammed his glass on the table, sloshing some of the whiskey on the tablecloth. "That's damn right. Then there's the corruption when the land is sold. A rich bastard, say someone who wants all the land next to the railroad, can hire low-life men to stake false claims, then buy the land cheap from the government through these hired men."

Jim nodded thoughtfully. Dunraven could try that scheme to get the land inexpensively in Estes Park.

The food arrived. A baked potato with a thick steak, dripping off the edge of the plate, was placed in front of each of the men. Next a cut glass vase was carefully positioned in the center of the table; it was filled with some fancy, new vegetable called celery. The supercilious waiter straightened his cuffs before explaining that the celery was a luxury item shipped by train from back East where it was highly fashionable to serve at elegant tables.

Jim grabbed a stalk of the celery and took a tentative bite. It was crunchy but didn't really have much flavor. He shrugged; no accounting sometimes what Easterners liked.

He looked over at Billy who was grimacing after taking just one bite. Billy placed the remaining stalk, held on end by his thumb and forefinger, onto his plate. "Gad! Maybe the Colorado Territory should reconsider trying to become a state if this is what the rest of the nation thinks is great."

Jim smiled. "Oh, it will be a few more years before that happens. Guess we better eat up. If this financial panic hits Colorado as hard as it has already hit some places in the East, we might all be paupers."

"Those trains that so kindly brought us this delicious celery were over-speculated on by the bankers. Now the common folks suffer. Any banks in Denver closed yet?"

"Not that I've seen. But it's a definite worry."

Billy nodded, then grinned. "Enough serious talk. You met any interesting gals lately even if none have roped you in?"

Jim nodded. "Oh, yeah. Sure have. Billy, have you ever seen one of these crazy riding outfits for women with bloomers for trousers?"

When he was alone in his room much later that evening, Jim's thoughts turned again to Isabella. He was finding it harder to hold on to his anger toward her and was becoming more concerned about what she was getting herself into, traveling on her own to Pikes Peak. He probably should have gone with her whether she had wanted him to or not.

   The next day Jim went shopping to resupply his cabin with the necessities and also the few extras he enjoyed indulging in. Nuts, salt, cinnamon, and nutmeg all brought Isabella to mind. He started turning corners expectantly, feeling a little disappointed when he didn't see her. As the day went on he told himself repeatedly to stop thinking about her, but to no avail. By the evening he admitted to himself that he missed her. The following day, while riding back home, he realized that he not only missed her but he cared for her . . . a lot. He just hoped she returned safely from her trip so he could tell her.

Chapter Fourteen

A few days after Griff's return and her fight with Jim, Isabella found a horse to ride to Pikes Peak and said her farewells. She hoped the trip would kick the slight depression she had been feeling recently which was confusing for her in the first place. She was happy about getting away from that intolerable man, wasn't she? She never liked fighting with anyone, but James Nugent had deserved every harsh word she had uttered. The gall of the man trying to tell her what to do. And his temper . . . she had finally seen his temper. Oh, yes. She was much better off not getting involved with a man like that.

    She was greeted warmly by Ellie at her house in Denver and spent several days there before heading on to Pikes Peak. She regretted having to say her good-byes to Dorothy and Charles, who were already in Denver for the first leg of their trip home, but, oh, how nice it was to spend time with civilized men. The mayor and editor of the *Peak Mountain Press*, who knew about her from the regional newspaper articles that had explained her arrival in Colorado, were so pleasant, not at all the offensive type. Of course, there were a few rough characters in Denver, on the streets and coming out of bars, who made her think of Jim, but there were also plenty of gentlemen who knew how to treat a lady properly with all appropriate decorum.

No, she had definitely made a lucky escape by coming on this trip. Jim had confused her for a while, but now she knew her true feelings toward the man. He was a boorish beast who should never have treated her that way. He had turned her emotions upside down for a while, and she didn't need that kind of turmoil in her life. Her anger felt good. No, it felt great! It was much better than feeling any sort of attraction to that unbearable man.

For about a week Isabella did a good job of holding on to her anger, but it started to fade shortly after she left Denver for Pikes Peak. In Denver, she had kept busy staying with the Evans brood, meeting people and preparing for her trip—buying a warm coat, winter boots, and food supplies. It all helped keep her mind off Jim. Now, traveling by horseback on her own to Pikes Peak, she had too many hours alone with her thoughts. Maybe she shouldn't have refused to take the stagecoach as everybody and their cousin had urged.

Fine. She'd admit it: She could be stubborn. And truthfully? If she really was going to be honest with herself, she'd have to admit he had been right about a few things. The weather had turned blustery cold and snowy. The wind practically blew her off her feet at times. And there were rough-looking characters *everywhere* on the plains.

Perhaps she had been a little too harsh with him. He had only been trying to see to her safety. She had a reminder of that every time she felt the revolver in her pocket.

But her anger really faded at night, spending evenings in people's homes as improvised lodging along the way since there were no hotels for her to stay in. The company was never as fascinating as Jim. She couldn't stop herself from comparing every man she met with him. They just weren't as bright, funny and charming as him. In fact, she found not just the people, but everything else duller. The scenery south to Pikes Peak didn't excite her. Even Pikes Peak itself wasn't as spectacular as she had hoped. And the Garden of the Gods? Why, that described Estes Park, not someplace south of there.

A few days after seeing Pikes Peak, Isabella sat at a grubby dining table and looked across the dingy room of the Mountain View Tavern. This was the best lodging she had been able to find for the night in the region northwest of Colorado Springs. She tried consoling herself. She had only a few more nights to make it through before she would be back in Denver.

One of the patrons approached, a weather-beaten old man who spit tobacco on the floor before reaching her table. "You're that Englishwoman I heard about, ain't you? My pard said he read in the newspaper you've traveled all over the world, even wrote books and you're just a woman. Where you headed next?"

Isabella looked him over. She decided to give him an answer though it was none of his business. "Denver."

"Goin' by Colorado Springs? That's where I'm headin' next."

"No, I just came from there after seeing Pikes Peak. I'm taking a different route back to Denver."

"But that would mean you're traveling through the next mountain pass. Wouldn't do that, lady, not this time of year."

Isabella frowned. "I'm a seasoned traveler and like to make my own choices."

He chuckled. "You're snarly. Well, suit yerself. I tried to warn ya."

Isabella shook her head. Could she just make one decision on her own and not have everybody in the world give their opinion on the subject? She'd made it this far in Colorado, how much more difficult could a mountain pass be?

The next day Isabella looked across the expanse of endless snow at least two feet deep in some parts. Getting through the pass was taking forever. The horse Griff had given her, Birdie, was falling and slipping with nearly every step. She shivered, feeling the cold and wind cut through her coat and boots. If she just made it through, she vowed never to do anything so foolish again.

Isabella shook her head. She was scared witless—how else explain her talking to her horse. "Come on, Birdie. You've gotten me this far. I know you can make it."

Isabella dug in her heels. Birdie didn't move.

"Please, Birdie. I'm stupid and stubborn and I owe you, but can you just try a little longer?"

Birdie held her place. Isabella kicked hard and Birdie took another step. They fell in a drift of snow up to Isabella's nose and Birdie's head. It was puffy and dry and filled her mouth when she gasped. She spit it out and got off Birdie. Scooping snow out of the way as best she could, she pulled on Birdie's reins with hands gone stiff from the cold. Birdie resisted moving.

This was bad. As bad as things could get. If Birdie wouldn't budge, she would have to trudge through the snow on her own, and Birdie would probably perish. She didn't look forward to that prospect. She gave another hard tug on the rein. Birdie took a step. With another pull, Birdie walked until they were both standing in snow less deep. Isabella sank onto the nearest rock to catch her breath. The rock proved to be cold and icy as Isabella adjusted her position.

How was she ever going to make it? If only Jim were with her. He always made her feel safe. Isabella shook her head, as if Jim would ever have attempted this mountain pass in the first place. She tried to stand up, but sat back down as her clothes stuck to the rock. Yanking on her garments, she forced herself to rise, knowing she would freeze to death if she didn't keep moving. She looked at the sky and realized it must be in the afternoon already. Goodness, she didn't want to be in the pass with frigid night temperatures. And what would she do for food? She had a hard biscuit and some jerky, assuming she would be at some lodging for her supper tonight. She hadn't thought to bring any nourishment along for Birdie, foolishly thinking she would be out of the pass by now.

Several more deep drifts followed, making their pace painfully slow. Her legs buckled frequently from exhaustion. She wanted to just lie down and sleep but knew it was the last thing she should do. She might never wake up in this frigid cold.

Two hours and a mile later Isabella dropped her head and sighed in relief when she saw level plains up ahead of her. She could make it now. She just needed to forge ahead. One step at a time.

When she glanced up again, she caught a fleeting image of a man on horseback in the distance. The glare off the snow made it difficult to focus properly. Isabella placed her hand on her forehead to shade her eyes. The man was dressed in buckskins on a white horse or mule, leading another behind. Jim! He'd come to help her!

Isabella shrieked with joy, "Jim! Jim! I'm over here!"

Head down into the wind, she pulled Birdie's reins and stumbled ahead as fast as she could. She came to an abrupt halt when an unfamiliar voice announced, "Darlin', the name's Bill, not Jim."

Isabella looked up at the man twenty feet away, wearing a big floppy hat and toting so many guns and knives it looked as if he had robbed an entire army fort. Isabella gasped. A bandit!

What should she do? What should she do? She fumbled for the gun in her pocket, but it was twisted around in the fabric. She couldn't pull it out! Heavens, this man could harm her in a split second if he wished.

She took a deep breath and decided to pretend she was

calm and not threatened by him. "Uh, I thought you were Mountain Jim. He rides a white mule."

The man looked at her as if what she had just said was preposterous. "Why his saddle ain't near as fancy as mine."

Isabella looked at the flashy ornamentation. "You're right. How could I have been so foolish?"

The man smiled, revealing several blackened teeth. "No offense taken."

He studied her a moment. "You and your horse look tuckered out. Follow me, you can ride my spare horse for now."

Isabella straightened. "Please allow me to introduce myself. I'm Isabella Lucy Bird. I wouldn't want to impose on you . . . uh . . ."

"I figured who you were, the whole frontier is talkin' about ya. My name's Bill, but people around here call me Comanche Bill."

"How do you do, Mister, uh, Comanche—or should I say Bill? But your offer is too generous." She didn't know what to do: Take this man up on his offer, trail behind on his horse to some forsaken place where he could attack her savagely; or get that exasperating gun out of her pocket, no matter what it took, and make a stand refusing to go.

"Granny will get you warmed up. She lives close by."

Isabella decided not to debate the issue further. He had just said the one word that completely convinced her what to do. Even if Granny turned out to be the devil herself, she would follow just to get some *warmth*.

Comanche Bill kept up a one-sided conversation about the land, the animals, and the people of the surrounding area, requiring minimal responses from Isabella for which she was grateful.

Granny—no relation to Bill—proved to be a thin, leathery, tough old broad who lived in a cabin by herself on the edge of a small, nameless settlement. Granny served her some hot stew while Isabella sat on a chair in front of the fireplace with her feet almost in the flames.

Bill leaned over the table and devoured a bowl, talking to Granny with his mouth full half the time. He stood and belched after his last bite. "Granny that was go-oo-od as usual." He turned to Isabella. "Nice to make yer acquaintance, Miss Bird. You need any more help getting to Denver?"

Isabella smiled politely and raised her hand. "No, Bill. That's quite alright. I'll be fine on my own. But thank you for your help."

"Well, maybe I'll see you sometime again on the trail. Granny, you take care until I see you next."

Isabella watched as Bill tossed some coins on the table and walked out the door. She turned and asked Granny how he got his name.

"Killin' Indians, of course. His folks was massacred and his sister taken by Indians when she was only eleven. He's been searching for her ever since, killin' Indians ever' chance he gets."

Good Lord. Only a few more nights. She just needed to keep reminding herself of that.

"Uh, Granny. May I ask how you came to be living here in Colorado? I mean all by yourself?"

Granny put her hands on her hips and looked Isabella up and down. "If I may ask what you're doin' travelin' alone. It's a sight more dangerous than my living here by myself."

Isabella was taken aback, then thought about it. Perhaps Granny was right. Isabella cleared her throat. "I've travelled all over the world by myself. It helps my health. But you may be right. I didn't quite realize what I was getting myself into the last few days. How about you?"

Granny briefly scrunched up her mouth and nose before walking over to the window to look out. "Didn't always live alone. My man and I had a farm in Nebraska near Omaha. Did right well. But our son died getting kicked in the head by a horse and our daughter fell to sickness. Wasn't quite the same after that. My husband Pete just got up one morning and said, 'We're goin' to Colorado. See what riches we can find. We need a change.' That was in fifty-nine."

"So you headed to Pikes Peak?"

"Yeah, sold the farm and left. But it turned out most of the good stuff wasn't there but near Denver and Breckenridge and the like. We found out right quick it was easier makin' money peddling to the miners than mining ourselves. I started cookin' while Pete sold supplies. But when the Blue River diggins' began drying up and the Civil War came, the miners abandoned Breckenridge. There's probably only fifty people left in that town now. Pete and I also departed with our earnings and built this cabin. Thought maybe we'd try ranching next, but my man up and died on me too. I had enough money that I could have gone back to Nebraska where my brother is, but I couldn't find the will to leave. I get by with my savings, cookin', mendin', and doin' laundry for men like Bill." She turned back to look at Isabella. "I started gettin' called Granny by those men. Bet you think I'm real old but I ain't. I'm only five to ten years older than you."

Isabella's eyes widened.

"That surprises you? This West just wears a person down, women especially. If you're not doing the household chores, you're helping outside, baking so much you turn into a shriveled old fruit. At night you're so tired you're stooped over and unable to keep your head up to get the sock darning done."

Isabella nodded. "I've heard how people age out here."

Granny smiled and arched her brows. "Didn't stop me from getting a marriage proposal last year though. But I told him my Pete was the only man for me."

Isabella frowned. "But aren't you scared being out here alone?"

"Yeah, some of the time. I'd say more lonely than scared. Besides I can shoot a rifle and I got my shotgun. Women do get lonesome out here, though, for other women to chinwag with, especially if they're out on the plains with just their kinfolk. Look at me talkin' to you so. It's been a while since I seen a woman to chat with."

Isabella nodded.

"But I tell you what, 'Miss Travels-By-Herself.'" She pointed her finger at Isabella.

"What?"

"You find yerself a good man like Pete was, and you don't let him go. Pete was one of a kind and I miss him."

Isabella swallowed and nodded. Jim was one of kind also and she more than missed him.

The next day she stopped to eat at a crudely-made lodging establishment of sorts. She dismounted, completed arrangements for her horse with a dirty-faced youngster, then entered the large shack and quickly looked around. Coarse men leered at her in a worrying way. No, she would rather take her chances out in the open than sleep here that night. But for now, she needed something to eat. She took off her hat and gloves, placed them on an isolated table in the corner, and sat, waiting for the innkeeper to take her order.

The innkeeper, wearing a grease-smudged apron, approached, wiping a filthy arm across his nose before taking her order. She requested some coffee, bread and cheese, figuring those would probably be the safest items to consume. She didn't dare take a chance with anything else.

Across the room an Englishman she hadn't noticed at first was holding court with some other men, speaking with an obvious exaggerated drawl. Why did some of her fellow countrymen act so pretentious? Didn't they realize that the affectation that was often unremarkable in England was unacceptable in America?

The Englishman broke off his conversation and walked toward her. "I thought I just heard an English accent when you ordered. Allow me to introduce myself. Lord Dunraven." He bowed slightly, then pursed his lips in a most peculiar manner, waiting for her response. How did he do that? She wished Jim was there. She'd like to see him try to mimic *this* expression the way he had attempted to imitate Salme's smile.

She nodded her head slightly. "I'm Isabella Lucy Bird."

"Ah, the Englishwoman traveler making her way all alone, recent voyager of the Pacific, skilled rider—have I left anything out that the local journalists haven't covered? You're almost as famous as I am in these primitive surroundings."

Was he famous? For what?

He sniffed and added, "It seems establishments such as this are sometimes the best these Americans can manage. Too bad they won the war. Should have stayed a colony."

"This place aside, I rather like some of the American ways. Why are you in this country if the place offends you so?"

"The hunting. I'm planning a game preserve for select friends and myself to enjoy." He tapped his strange lips with his finger, and his face took on a determined expression.

She wanted to laugh. He certainly thought he was someone special. If only Hennie could see this pompous Lord Dundreary. They would be bent over in a fit.

The innkeeper returned with her coffee and placed it on the table. There was a layer of oily residue and some unidentifiable slime floating on the top. Isabella sighed. The lord looked down at the cup and smiled smugly. "I'll be entertaining Englishmen properly once I have my place set up."

"I'm sure you will. If you'll excuse me, I need to check

on my horse before my food arrives."

"Certainly." He bowed and walked back to his gathering.

Isabella had an uncomfortable feeling about the man. She got the impression nothing got in the way of what this lord wanted. She was glad he had left her alone.

Isabella checked to see that her horse had been fed and watered then returned to her table and ate some stale bread and foul-tasting cheese. She was tired of this little adventure, tired of the people, and just wanted to get home. Funny how she thought of Estes Park as her home. Hennie would be horrified. *What? No library? You call that culture? Just a bunch of mountains to look at? Yep, mountains and Jim.*

But Isabella started having second thoughts about returning to Estes Park once she reached Denver again. She knew she shouldn't try to travel back to Scotland until Griff gave her the money he owed her. Not that she couldn't probably make it all the way back to her homeland with what she had, but it would be tight, and if anything untoward should happen she might be completely broke on her journey home. Besides, she knew she could stay at Ellie and Griff's place in Denver indefinitely. Her belongings that she had left at Estes Park could be brought to her by way of another traveler. Jim's gun could be given back to him when Griff saw him next.

Anyway what was the use of seeing Jim again? They were worlds apart in so many ways. And yet . . . she missed him. She wanted to see him again. Finally she told the Evans household that she planned to stay the remainder of her trip in Estes Park, and after not being questioned why, she left with Muggins Gulch her first planned stop in the settlement.

Chapter Fifteen

When Jim returned from Denver to Muggins Gulch, he tried to keep as busy as possible to get his mind off Isabella. He was so worried about her traveling on her own. He knew he might never see her again. Even if she did make it back safe and sound to Denver from Pikes Peak, she might not necessarily return to Estes Park since she had already seen the area. The only reason he could figure for her to come back was if she shared the same feelings for him that he had for her. He now realized that he was in love with her. He probably had been for a while, but hadn't wanted to admit it. Not that she wasn't worthy of his love, it was more the near impossibility of their situation. It would take a lot of compromising on both their parts to make it work between the two of them. He would be willing, but would she?

He wavered back and forth about whether he should leave Estes Park and try to find her. He knew she must be somewhere between Denver and Pikes Peak—that is, if no harm had come to her. He could probably find her in a few days just by listening to the rumor mill.

But when he found her, then what? Would she welcome his company? He didn't believe she was that concerned about the impropriety of the two of them traveling together. She might still be mad at him, though.

He had let his temper get away from him that day they had fought. It wasn't only that she had been so aggravating; he also had been furious hearing from her about Griff and Dunraven's business and had probably taken some of that anger out on her.

But did she miss him the way he missed her? Did she love him? When he thought about their time together, he felt her actions spoke of love. She had come to see him so many times on her own. But if she did love him, would she ever admit it to him—or even to herself? He knew he wasn't the type of man she would choose to fall in love with, and she would probably fight any feelings she had toward him.

In the end he decided to stay in Estes Park. He would wait for her to come to him if she so chose. And if she did return, he would know that she must have feelings for him, that she cared for him and possibly loved him.

By the time three weeks had passed, Jim was beside himself with worry about whether Isabella had made it back safely from Pikes Peak. Word about her came to him from an unexpected source. A hunter Jim was guiding asked, "Have you heard about that crazy Englishwoman traveling in Colorado?"

His world seemed to skip a beat. He took a deep breath to steady himself. "She stayed a while here in Estes Park."

"Heard she was seen recently on a road heading toward Denver. The nutty woman was returning all by herself from a sightseeing trip to Pikes Peak." The man smirked. "Takes all kinds."

Jim didn't bother to respond but inwardly sighed in relief. Now he would wait to see whether she came back to Estes Park. He had agreed to act as a guide for another couple days, but then he would be free to spend time with Isabella if she returned.

Once Isabella decided to go back to Estes Park, she packed

up as quickly as possible and headed out. The trip seemed to take forever. She barely noticed the picturesque scenery, she was so anxious and impatient to return. She spent the night at the hotel in Longmont again and had trouble falling asleep. Estes Park had come to mean so much to her. She loved the views, the wildlife, and most especially the people. If she didn't have her own life and personal obligations back in Scotland, she could see herself happily settled there.

She left as early as possible the next morning. There were so many twists and turns climbing the hills and valleys leading to Estes Park that she didn't remember from her previous trip. Every time she rounded a corner she expected to see a familiar sight, but it frustratingly wouldn't happen. She told herself to calm down, but she couldn't manage it. She felt so happy and nervous that her arms practically tingled.

When at last she recognized a bend in the trail near Jim's cabin, she could barely keep mounted; she felt almost faint struggling for air. She was nearly there and she knew it. One more curve and she would see him.

She rode around a group of ponderosa pines and halted. Jim's cabin stood quiet, no smoke coming from his chimney and no signs of life. There was no one home. She felt crushed and dropped her head.

She rubbed her forehead and began to chide herself. How stupid could she have been, yearning to see him again so much? He was just her friend, not her passionate lover. Maybe he hadn't even thought about her. Maybe he hadn't missed her at all. She felt like a fool and sighed.

A moment later she heard barking and straightened. Could it be the one dog she most wanted to see? "Ring? Is that you?"

Ring appeared around a group of boulders and bounded over to her, jumping up to put his paws on her saddle. She warmly hugged him. "Where's Jim, you lovable dog? Show me Jim."

Ring started barking, then jumped down and raced through a path in the trees. She quickly followed and finally saw in the distance Jim and a man, riding horseback. Jim didn't see her at first, but then he looked up, stopped and stared. Without taking his gaze from her, he motioned to the man next to him and pointed toward his cabin. The man departed.

She watched Jim dismount and did the same. She took a few quick steps toward him but suddenly stopped in her tracks, doubts crashing in on her. What if he was still angry with her and didn't want to see her?

Jim could barely believe what he was seeing. After he'd spent weeks hoping to touch her again, Isabella was finally here. He wanted to give her a hug—and now! He walked toward her but stopped when she did. She looked nervous. She had come; she must want to see him. Why wasn't she running toward him? Wasn't she as anxious as he was for them to be together? Then it hit him: They had fought the last time they'd seen each other, and she didn't know his feelings toward her. He needed to talk to her, but she was too far away.

An idea came to him and Jim smiled. He held up his hands and started signaling: *You . . . are . . . my . . . friend.*

Isabella smiled brightly. He held open his arms. Nothing held her back from that moment. She ran toward him and hurled herself at him, grabbing him in a tight hug around his neck. It was the most wonderful feeling he could imagine.

"Is, you're back!" He lifted her up and swung her in a wide circle.

She started laughing and crying. He put her down and held her face in his hands. "You have no idea how much I missed you."

"I couldn't wait to see you again."

He kissed her forehead and grabbed her in another hug. "I don't know if I'm ever going to let you go."

She buried her face in his chest. "I thought about you all the time." Those few words were the best, most fantastic, remarkable, extraordinary words she could have said to him just then.

He stroked her hair. "You took years off my life worrying about you."

She looked up at him. "There's so much that happened I want to tell you."

He placed his hands on her shoulders. "Come back to my cabin and we'll talk." He grabbed her hand and started pulling her forward, but suddenly stopped and flung his head skyward. "Oh, hell!"

Isabella started chuckling. "Not even your swearing is getting me in a bad mood today. What's wrong?"

He turned back around. "That man I was with?"

"Yes?"

"I'm his hunting guide."

"So?"

"I'm guiding him tomorrow also, and he's staying with me."

Isabella smiled. "So what? Come back with me to Griff's place?"

"Griff's not there."

"I know. But the Rudolphs are, right?"

"No, they left yesterday."

Isabella frowned. "What? You mean I'm going to be there all alone?"

"No, there are two hunters who agreed to watch the place until Griff returned. I think you've met Mr. Buchanan. Mr. Althoff is there now also."

"Oh, that's a little awkward; I'm not sure what it will do to my reputation staying with two men all alone."

"You can stay with me. My hunter's leaving in a day. He can sleep at Griff's tonight."

"No, it wouldn't look proper. I mean, at least at Griff's I can have my own room."

"I don't think that makes much difference to gossipmongers, but we can debate your living arrangements later."

"I don't want to argue with you ever again. I felt horrible."

"Is, I shouldn't have lost my temper the way I did. I'm sorry. There was more to it than you know."

"Let's forget about it for now. Do you want to know what happened to me while I was away?"

Jim smiled. "Everything I warned you about came true."

"I can't imagine what you mean. The trip couldn't have gone smoother." Isabella raised her eyebrows and smiled back.

Jim snorted. "I bet."

They caught their horses but decided to walk at least part of the way back to Griff's. They strolled slowly, leaning into each other and laughing occasionally, holding their horses' reins in one hand and each other's hand in the other.

Chapter Sixteen

The next day Isabella settled into her surroundings. She finished unpacking, lightly cleaned the kitchen area of the main house where the men had made a bit of a mess, and did some much-needed sewing repair to her frayed garments. The previous night the two hunters at Griff's had been shocked to see her walk in the door. But they soon regained their composure, and she and the two men found out quickly they could get along well together; she would sleep in her previous cabin, the men would reside in the main house, but all of them would cook food together for shared meals there. Life was grand as far as Isabella was concerned. She looked forward to an easy, carefree few weeks before she left Estes Park again to return to her life in Scotland.

    Jim had asked her whether she would like to go on a horseback ride together after he finished his current guiding job, and she eagerly awaited seeing him again in the morning. Now that they had made up from their fight, she expected to have many pleasant days with him before she left for home after she received her money back from Griff. The worst was behind them, and she couldn't imagine what problems they could possibly have in the future. They now had a special friendship she was sure they both desired. She relished what days she had left to spend with him.

Meanwhile Jim kept busy guiding the hunter in their final day together. He couldn't wait to see Isabella in the morning. He tried to be pleasant but found he couldn't hide his irritation at being delayed from spending more time with her.

"Yes, yes, just take the shot," was all he could grumble when the man asked about a particular shooting position.

He had things he wanted to say to Isabella. She needed to know that he was in love with her, and he wanted to know how she felt.

The next morning Jim rode over to Griff's to pick Isabella up for their ride together. He heard laughing before he opened the door. He knocked and walked in.

"That's the most hilarious thing I've heard in a long while!" Isabella exclaimed to Mr. Buchanan and Mr. Althoff.

"I see you're all getting along famously," Jim said as he entered, envious to be part of the fun.

Isabella grinned. "Oh, Mr. Nugent, good morning. You didn't tell me how funny Mr. Althoff is! We've been enjoying ourselves immensely."

Jim looked at Buchanan first and frowned slightly. He hadn't noticed before how handsome the young man was. No wonder Griff's niece Mary was smitten. He looked over at Althoff next. Althoff smiled back with boyish enthusiasm. *Great. Just great.* The cheerful bunch.

He was jealous and he knew it. "Miss Bird, you ready for our ride?"

"Can't wait. It'll just take me a minute to get my coat on." She turned to the two men. "Would you like to come along? We're going riding this morning. We could all get to know each other better since we'll be spending time together."

Oh, no, no, no. She didn't just ask that!

Mr. Althoff spoke up, "Not this morning, Isabella.

We're going hunting. You enjoy yourself."

Isabella? Who did he think he was? Granted, there was a big age difference between these men and Isabella—she could almost be their mother—but still. Jim grabbed Isabella's hand and pulled her toward the door. "She'll see you when she gets back."

A short while later they rode along the Thompson River. Jim looked at Isabella. "There are some amazing cliffs up ahead I thought you should see."

"Sounds fine to me."

"Is, tell me something."

"What?"

Jim frowned. "Why is it all right for Althoff to call you Isabella, but I'm supposed to call you Miss Bird in front of everyone?"

Isabella fussed with pulling her bloomer trousers further down her leg. "Hmmm . . . I guess I'm becoming more American, equal rights for everybody and all that."

Jim scratched his chin. "That doesn't explain it."

Appearing slightly flustered, Isabella babbled, "Oh, all right. It's the age difference. I mean Mr. Altoff and I could never . . . I mean, you and I—"

Jim cocked his head. "The age difference, huh? Does that mean a man much older than you can address you as Isabella also?"

"Well, no. That's not quite right either. It's, uh . . . too complicated to explain."

Jim chuckled.

Isabella glanced at him. "What's so funny?"

"I like seeing you squirm."

She frowned. "Squirm? I've never squirmed in my life. What a ridiculous notion."

"Uh-huh." He laughed again.

"Have you seen any more interesting birds?"

"Changing the subject?"

She placed her hand on her hip. "Yes. Just tell me about your damn birds."

"Miss Bird, did you just swear?"

"If I did, it's clearly your horrible influence."

Jim chuckled. "Is, I really missed you."

Softening, Isabella asked, "You did? I missed you too."

An hour later Jim decided to stop along the riverbank where the surrounding cliffs provided a buffer from the wind and some privacy. He spread a blanket on the ground and wrapped another around the two of them as they sat down. "I've been thinking about something."

She looked up at him. "What?"

He looked down at her intently but said nothing.

"What? Tell me."

He took a deep breath. "Is, I'm in love with you." He waited for her to respond.

She stared at him, wide-eyed, mouth open, but said nothing.

Slightly disappointed by her reaction, he persevered, "I have been for a long time. I didn't realize it at first, but I think I've been in love with you since Longs Peak."

She frowned slightly before looking away. "I don't know what to say."

He pulled her chin gently back toward him. "Why not that you love me too?"

She shook her head. "I don't know how I feel. How could I? We don't even know each other."

He gaped. "How can you say that after all the time we've spent together?"

"Yes, we've spent time together, but I don't know everything about you."

Jim frowned. "I've told you things I've never divulged to anyone else."

She took a deep breath. "Yes, but you've held back some things."

He shook his head, puzzled. "Like what?"

She sat more stiffly. "I remember when we were on Longs Peak what you said."

"What?"

She stood up and held his gaze with an alarming intensity. "You said you committed some terrible acts during the war, but you didn't say what." She hesitated, shaking her head slightly as if searching for words. "You could be a murderer for all I know."

Jim got up and shook his head. "My God, now you want to talk about what I did during the war?"

Isabella frowned and didn't answer.

He sighed. "Fine, we'll talk about the war. But let's sit back down again."

Isabella placed herself a few feet away from Jim. "Can I have the blanket? I'm suddenly cold."

"Sure, take it." He wrapped it around her shoulders and lowered himself to the ground. "Is, this is hard for me to talk about. I'm not proud of what I did during the war. I should have just returned to trapping and hunting. I could have, you know. There were plenty of men out West during the Civil War who managed to stay out of the conflict."

"Why didn't you?"

"Because after working as a scout and Indian fighter, I was a drunken mess, going to saloons every night. My temper wasn't under control. I let little slights get to me, and one night I got furious at a man. He said he was a Yankee, and that was all it took for me to join some rebels."

Isabella gasped. "You were for the South? *Proslavery?*"

"Not really. I was a Northerner at heart. I wasn't proslavery, and I didn't really care about the South's secessionist ideas. I had just been part of the United States army as a scout. If I hadn't been on a long drunken binge, I never would have joined those men."

"What did they do?"

"Do you know anything about the Kansas border fighting?"

Isabella frowned. "Only a little. Kansas was antislavery and the neighboring states were not, right?"

"Correct. So the men would go on raids into Kansas to help supply the South. They weren't really part of any army. They were more like volunteer militias."

He paused and rubbed his mouth. "But things got out of hand. The plundering on both sides turned into indiscriminate murdering and stealing. Houses and businesses were burned down even if the owner hadn't taken a side. All it took was a rumor to justify the robbing and killing. So many innocent victims were hurt; men, boys, women and young children."

He shook his head. "I finally switched sides. I couldn't abide the leader of the southern brigand who was a man named William Quantrill. He was crazy as far as I was concerned. He kept his thirteen-year-old bride in camp if that tells you what kind of man he was."

"Thirteen years old? That's medieval."

Jim frowned. "Yeah. It was a really awful time. Lord knows I should have tried to stop what was going on around me, let alone been a participant. Liquor has a way of deadening you to reality. I have nightmares over it to this day."

Isabella sighed. "Now I wish you hadn't told me."

"Maybe it's for the better. Now you know the worst."

Isabella got up and walked a few feet away, then turned back to him and asked, "Why do you drink? Surely you see it does you no good."

Jim draped his hands between his knees and hung his head, before saying, "I've cut way back, but I don't know if I'll stop altogether."

She looked away. "I don't know what to say. I need time to think about all this." After several prolonged seconds she turned back around. "I knew some things about your temper and drinking issues before today, but the fact that you fought against abolitionists even if you did switch sides is . . . devastating. You know I come from a line of abolitionists."

He looked up at her. "Is, don't cut me out. Please don't do that. Can't you see we love each other?"

"I don't know if we can be friends—you know, special friends, let alone talk about love."

"*Special friends*? What does that mean?" Exasperated, Jim shook his head. "But I want more than friendship."

"Oh, why couldn't you have kept things simple between us? So what if you love me. I don't even want to think about whether I love you. Can't you see that a future between us would be so difficult?"

"Difficult but not impossible."

Isabella shook her head. "You're not thinking clearly."

Jim frowned and started to raise his voice. "And maybe the only thing you're thinking about is your reputation. Miss High and Mighty being seen with the ruffian, the desperado, the scoundrel!"

"Well, I will admit Hennie—" She caught herself.

"Go ahead. Finish your sentence. Your sister would never approve, and God forbid you disappoint Hennie."

Isabella clenched her fists. "Leave Hennie out of this."

He held up his hand. "You're right. It's between the two of us." He looked hard into her eyes. "I love you, Is. I can't be with you and not want to hold you and touch you."

With vehemence, she cried, "That's the last thing I want right now!"

Jim flinched, then composed himself and spoke softly, "Well, get this straight: I'm not going to stick around torturing myself, waiting for you to decide your feelings."

"What's that supposed to mean?"

"What I mean is . . ." He paused and stood up. "I'm going away. There's hunting and trapping I need to get done."

Isabella swallowed and frowned. "How long will you be gone?"

"Probably a couple weeks. If you're still here when I get back, we can talk then. If not, I'll know my answer."

It was a quiet ride back. When they arrived at Griff's Isabella dismounted quickly and turned back to Jim.

"Good-bye, Mr. Nugent."

Jim nodded with a tight smile. "Ah, I see we're back to Mr. Nugent, *Isabella*. Does nothing that we've experienced together the last few weeks mean anything to you? Are you actually as cold and unfeeling as you portrayed yourself today?"

Isabella gasped. "I'm unfeeling? I'm not the one who performed such brutalities during the war."

Jim looked at the ground. "No, you didn't." He raised his head. "And I wish to God I hadn't either."

Jim reined his horse around and didn't look back as he left.

Chapter Seventeen

The next day, Isabella swarmed through her cabin and the main house, attacking dirt and grime with a vengeance. She scrubbed pots and pans, wiped down tables and chairs, got on her hands and knees to tackle mud and stains off the floors, and washed towels and bed sheets. Anything to keep her mind off Jim. By the end of the day, she was exhausted but still fretting. He had done it again, turned her emotions upside down. Now what were they supposed to do? Go riding off together to some glorious future living happily ever after? After what she had learned? Even if she could eventually forgive him for his actions during the war, what about his temper and his drinking? What she should do is just tell him that she didn't love him and send him on his way. But she didn't really want to do that either. She cared for him; she would admit that to herself. She had enjoyed his company, certainly. But did she love him? Not only that, did she love him enough to put up with their huge differences? She didn't know and didn't really want to think about it. But despite her efforts not to, that day and the next were spent doing just that.

On the day after their talk, Jim packed up his equipment on Sassy and headed out to trap and hunt. He was worn out and drained, but attributed it to his conflict with Isabella. It wasn't as if her reaction was unexpected. He knew he had thrown a lot at her, and it would take a while for her to understand it all. At least she hadn't said that she didn't love him. He had to give her the time she needed to think things through. He hoped she could accept his past, or at least realize that he had moved on from it. He was a different man from the one who had participated in those vile acts during the war. He yearned now for something resembling a normal life, and he wanted Isabella by his side. By her actions he felt that she did love him, but that was different from her wanting to admit it. He would just have to wait for her to sort through all her emotions. But in the end he hoped she would realize they belonged together and should not just throw away a possibly happy future with each other.

The next day, a scratchy throat in the morning turned into a bothersome cough in the afternoon. By the evening his limbs were sore, and he had an ache in his chest. The pain was at the site of an old arrow wound that had occurred during his scouting days. Jim knew from experience that when that happened, he had no choice but to head back home and get in bed.

When he was nearing his cabin he ran into the jovial Mr. Althoff who asked, "Got any hunting advice? I'm not having much luck on my own."

Jim coughed and wheezed before answering, "Maybe another time. I'm feeling too poorly right now."

Mr. Althoff eyes widened. "My apologies. You do look sickly. Sorry to delay you."

The next day Isabella greeted Mr. Althoff with a cheery good morning. She was determined to enjoy her remaining time in Estes Park despite her issues with Jim. She poured a cup of coffee and sat down. "How's the hunting?"

"You'd think I'd never shot a prey before in my life. I ran into Mountain Jim on my way home last night and asked his advice."

Isabella hated that she felt a flutter inside at the mention of Jim's name. "He usually guards his secrets. What did he have to say?"

"Not much, he was feeling too sickly."

Isabella stood up. "He's ill? What's wrong?"

"He was coughing the short time I spent with him."

Isabella frowned. "Coughing. That doesn't sound good."

Mr. Althoff waved his hand dismissively. "I'm sure he'll be all right. I'm hungry. Let's make breakfast."

"Perhaps I shouldn't stick around this morning."

"Why not?"

Isabella grabbed her coat. "I should check on Mr. Nugent. He's all alone with nobody to look after him."

"Undoubtedly he can take care of himself."

"You never know. I'd better find out." She hurried toward the door, then turned around. "Wait. I'd better bring some food. Never know how long he'll be sick."

Jim heard a soft knocking but was too tired to get up from bed and instead called, "Who's there?"

"Jim, it's me. May I come in?"

Surprised and pleased she had called him Jim, he answered, "Is, of course."

Isabella opened the door, stopped and stared at him under the bedcovers.

Jim shivered slightly before saying, "Excuse me for not giving you the proper greeting. I'm feeling a bit under the weather."

She put her hands on her hips. "You look terrible."

"Thanks, I needed to hear that."

Isabella closed the door and stomped over to the bed. She felt his forehead with the back of her hand. "You've got a fever."

"Tell me something I don't know." He coughed into

his hand. "I developed a cold while hunting."

Isabella frowned. "A cold? It seems a lot more than that."

"It went into my chest. They're worse there because of my old arrow wound."

"You never told me about an arrow wound to your chest."

He sneezed and blew his nose into a handkerchief. "It was during my scouting days. Some Indian caught me by surprise. I can tell you about it later; right now I need to rest."

"Yes, yes, of course. What can I do to help?"

"Just you coming to visit helps, and I mean it." He looked up at her and tried to smile but started coughing again.

"I came as soon as I heard from Mr. Althoff that you were sick."

"Oh, that's why you're here. I thought maybe you wanted to see me. Well, I'm glad you came, but you should probably leave now."

Isabella shook her head bewildered. "Why would I do that?"

"I don't want you to get sick from me."

"Nonsense. I brought the fixings to make soup. Would you like some?"

"Is, that would be great, but are you sure you don't mind staying?"

Isabella mockingly sighed, then put her wrist against her forehead as if under extreme duress. "Cooking will be a lot of effort for little reward. Hours and hours toiling over the soup only to have you consume it in a few minutes. But I'll make the sacrifice."

Jim smiled. "Ah, spoken like the Winner of the Best Homemaker contest."

He paused and looked up at her anxiously for several seconds. "So you forgive me?"

Isabella worried her lower lip, all play-acting gone from her countenance. "You mean what you did in the war?"

Jim said quietly, "Yeah."

She briefly looked away, then met his gaze. "Forgive is probably not the best word. I think I'm trying to understand it. It's hard because I have an image of you being kind and sensitive—"

"You do?"

Isabella nodded slowly and sat down on the edge of his bed. "I do. Well, some of the time at least. But what you did was so . . . horrendous." She shook her head.

"It was the drinking. That's the real issue." Jim rubbed his chin a moment. "I've thought about it a lot over the years. Actually tortured myself with it. I'm still working on trying to forgive myself."

Isabella took his hand. "I think that is what I needed to hear from you. I'm not saying I've worked everything out as to how I feel, and we still have our differences, but I *think* I can try to accept what you did in the war as you not being yourself."

Jim looked at her hopefully. "So we're friends at least?"

Isabella nodded. "Yes. But don't ask me for more right now."

"Fair enough. I'll accept that."

She softly smiled. "Now go back to sleep while I cook."

Jim slept while Isabella worked, but awoke to the sounds of her cooking.

Isabella saw him stir and asked, "Are you feeling better?"

"A little. What smells so good?"

"You can't smell anything. Your nose is all stuffed."

Jim coughed and smiled. "I know. I was trying to be polite."

"It's the soup. I tried sips." Isabella's brows raised. "It tastes absolutely splendid. Want some?"

"Sure. What did you put in it?"

"A ton of lard, a bucket of salt, and moldy nuts." She bit back a smile.

Jim chuckled. "Sounds delicious. Can't wait for dessert. Will you stay a while longer?"

"Of course. I don't plan to leave until you can take of yourself."

"I'd have to be a lot worse before I couldn't take care of myself, but if you insist."

Isabella nodded. "I insist." She helped him sit up, fussed with the pillow and covers, then sat on the edge of the bed and served him the soup.

He took a sip. "Is, this tastes great. I'm not used to people showing care for my welfare."

"You have plenty of friends here."

Jim looked down and sighed. "I try to show generosity and kindness to my neighbors, but it's not always returned."

Isabella nodded sagely. "You're so noble." She shook her head wryly. "It's just that most of your neighbors are gone for the winter now, and you know it."

Jim glanced up at her and smiled. "I was trying to get more sympathy."

Isabella straightened his pillow some more. "Tell me about the arrow wound."

"It was stupidity, plain and simple. It happened my first year as a scout. Nothing we need to talk about now. Let's talk about you."

Isabella smiled at him askance. "What happened?"

Jim shrugged. "I was careless one day when I was out ahead of the troop." He took another sip of the soup. "Mmm, this really is very good."

"I know it's great. Now let me guess. You were out ahead of the troop and . . . saw a bird that caught your attention."

"No."

"You were out ahead of the troop and . . . you decided to recite some bad poetry."

Jim chuckled and coughed again. "No. Oh, very well. I was scouting in advance trying to find this tribe."

"I see. So one of the Indians you were looking for hit you with an arrow?"

"Yeah, I was riding over this hill when I got distracted. A young brave caught me unawares, struck me with his arrow and fled. Story over."

"What distracted you?"

Jim took another sip. "Delicious soup. Did I tell you that?"

Isabella laughed. "Now I'm intrigued. Finish the tale."

"You should leave a sick man be."

"Tell me."

"Anybody ever tell you you're annoyingly persistent when you want to be? And let's not forget stubborn." Jim smiled. "Oh, all right. I was gagging and trying to spit out this bug that I accidentally let fly in my mouth."

Isabella gaped. "You have a permanent arrow wound from a bug in your mouth?"

"In my defense, it was a huge fly. I'd say bigger than Ring lying over there in the corner."

Isabella nodded. "Sure."

Jim smiled. "Fine. No great act of heroism, just a pesky insect. The wound healed without festering, but I guess it left scar tissue in my chest that acts up when I get a bad cold."

Isabella was quiet a moment before looking at him teasingly. "I've never read a dime novel where the hero had a problem with a bug. Maybe we should sell your story. It could be a big hit."

"Very funny. But . . . wait a minute! Miss Isabella Lucy Bird reads dime novels. Ha!"

Isabella blushed. "Well, maybe one. But just one."

"Are you squirming again?"

"All right, two. No, three, but no more than three. They help pass the time on long journeys."

Jim chuckled. "No doubt."

"Anyway I'm glad there aren't so many bugs in Estes Park. There were flies all over the plains even in the food people served, and the town of Greeley had all these bedbugs." She shuddered.

"Yeah, that's why I moved to Estes Park. No bugs."

Isabella smiled.

"God, I love spending time with you even when I'm sick." He put the soup on the bedside table and took her hand again.

Isabella angled her head but said nothing.

"What are you thinking, Is?"

She hesitated a moment, then said, "Truthfully, I'm thinking about what you said to me the last time I saw you."

"That I love you."

Isabella whispered, "Yes."

Jim gazed at her steadily. "And have you come to any conclusions now about your feelings?"

She shook her head. "No, I still need more time."

"I'll give you more time, I promise. But you know what I think about it?"

"What?"

"You must love me. Why else would you have done the things you have? You're not the type of woman to lead a man on for nothing."

Isabella instantly stood up and frowned. "What does that mean?"

"I *mean* your actions speak louder than words about how you feel."

Isabella's frown deepened. "What are you talking about?"

"Well, what about all the times you came to check if Griff was coming with the mail? Before you left for Pikes Peak, remember that?"

She placed her hands on her hips. "What about it?"

"Come on, Is. You know it didn't matter if you saw Griff coming with the mail. He was either coming or not."

"So you're saying I was coming to see you?"

"Of course."

Isabella flung her head back to look at the ceiling before meeting his eye again. "Well, of all the conceited, arrogant—"

He cut her off. "And what about coming back here to Estes Park after your Pikes Peak trip?"

Isabella walked over and looked out the window. "I needed a place to stay until I get the money Griff owes me."

"You could have stayed with Griff in Denver."

She looked back at him. "Some of my things I left here. I needed to give you back your gun."

"Somebody else could have retrieved them." Jim shook his head. Just how many more excuses was she going to come up with to deny her feelings? She was being absurd. She had to know it.

She put her hands back on her hips. "So you think you have it all figured out. I suppose the only reason I came today was because I love you. Not that it could be one fellow human being trying to help another."

Jim nodded. "Yes, you love me. Either that or you were falsely trying to lead me on."

Her eyes widened. Uh, oh. He shouldn't have said *that* again.

"You've got a lot of nerve."

Jim frowned. "Well, someone has to wake you up to the truth."

"And you're the one to do it."

"Who better?" Jim sneezed.

Isabella handed him a handkerchief. "I can't see how having this discussion now is possibly going to help you feel better. I refuse to discuss it further until you're out of bed and up and about."

"I'd feel better if you'd just admit your true feelings."

Isabella raised her voice, "Well, I'm not going to. I mean—I don't know how I feel. I need more time!"

Jim raised his hand to pacify. "Fine, fine. Just think about what I said."

Isabella took a deep breath. "I will."

He smiled. "Good. That's all I ask."

She looked at him concerned. "You need to get more rest. I should go."

He tried to reach for her hand. "Stay."

She took a step back. "No. You'll rest better with me gone, I can see."

"Not so, but all right. Let's talk when I'm recovered. I've decided I don't want to go off hunting for the next couple weeks. I want to discuss this with you."

Isabella sighed. "If you insist."

Jim nodded and smiled. "I insist."

Chapter Eighteen

Jim felt better the next morning and was up and about within a few days. Isabella didn't return to check on him during that time, but he wasn't surprised. She was probably scared of her feelings for him and worried he would badger her further about them.

But when Jim thought about it more, he decided that what he needed to do was back off a little. He needed to give her the time and space to come to grips with the situation and her feelings. He decided that when he saw her next he would not even bring up the matter, but wait for her to give him a clue as to when they could discuss it next.

Jim found it irksome that she was living with the young men, but they provided him with an excuse to head over to Griff's. After all, he had been a little abrupt with Mr. Althoff when he had met up with him while sick. He could go to Griff's, with the excuse that he wanted to discuss hunting, and wait to see whether Isabella had developed enough grit to deal with her feelings for him.

After Isabella left Jim's, she spent several days fretting about him, going back and forth about what she should do. At times she was furious that he could even think she was trying to lead him on and wanted to be done with him once and for all. But at other times, she thought about checking in on him again, seeing whether he was well. She missed him and wanted to see him.

A few nights of tossing and turning made the decision easier for her. She was exhausted. She couldn't take it anymore. The thought that she might actually be in love with him was just too much to contemplate any further. Because if she admitted she was in love with him, then what would stop them from being together for always? And if she was with him for always, would she have to leave Hennie, her only close family remaining? And more importantly, would he, sometime in the future, return to drinking binges, wild revelry, and temper outbursts? Would her reputation be in shatters that she married a frontier ruffian even if he did have a gentlemanly background? The thoughts swirled round and round in her head. And if all that wasn't enough, she still found herself angry whenever she thought about his accusations concerning her previous behavior toward him. No, the sooner she rid herself of the vexing situation, the better for both of them.

She decided to write Jim a note. Once she got word that Jim was feeling better, she would ask Mr. Althoff to deliver it to him. After all, she didn't want to upset a sick man. She sat down at the table and wrote:

"Dear Sir,

Although I am not to blame, in view of the way you spoke to me and the subsequent discord it produced, I wish to immediately end our friendship.
Yours truly,
I.L.B."

She was just finishing the note when there was a knock on the door and Jim walked in. "Hello, everybody. Glorious day outside." He smiled at Isabella.

Isabella stood up and quickly dropped her pen on the table. "You're looking much better, Mr. Nugent."

"Feeling better, Miss Bird. A little rest and some good soup did the trick." He turned to Mr. Althoff. "I didn't answer your question the last time I saw you. I thought we could talk now if you wished."

Mr. Althoff smiled. "Perfect. I was trying to figure out where to go hunting today."

"What game are you after specifically?"

"I still haven't bagged any bighorn sheep."

Jim scratched his neck. "Now they can be tricky."

"They scamper up the rocks so nimbly I can't get a good shot."

Jim nodded. "Head to the lake a few miles south of here. They gather on the shores there."

Mr. Buchanan spoke up, "Mary and I rode there several times. Mary loves the views, but I don't remember there being any sheep."

Jim smiled. "I'm sure you had other things on your mind."

Mr. Buchanan nodded and grinned back.

Such a sweet courtship between Mr. Buchanan and Griff's niece. Isabella couldn't help but feel a little envious. She sighed.

Jim glanced her way. "Well, that was an easy question to answer. I guess I should be heading home. Always plenty of work to do there." He looked back at her, expectantly.

What did he want? That she should follow him to his cabin? Never again. This was it. Time to do it and get it over with. Isabella held out her hand to shake his. "Good-bye, Mr. Nugent."

Jim looked puzzled at first, then extended his hand. "Good-bye, Miss Bird. Have a pleasant day."

She discreetly passed him the note while shaking his hand. Jim smiled brightly. He clearly had no idea what the note said.

Much to Isabella's disappointment, for the rest of the

day, she didn't stop worrying about Jim and had not only second, but third, fourth, and fifth thoughts about whether she should have given him the note.

Jim decided to wait until he was back at his cabin to read the note Isabella had passed him. He was nearly certain it was a note declaring her love for him. Maybe she still couldn't say it to his face, but at least she could write it. He marveled at the fact that she had developed some guts concerning them after all.

He dismounted, hurried inside his cabin and plopped down on his bed. He opened the note, read it and burst out laughing. That blasted woman sure knew how to write a snippy note. But he didn't believe a word of it, and he wasn't going to let her get away with this being the final word. He knew he needed to talk to her again. He decided he would wait a couple of days before approaching her.

Jim went over to Griff's when he figured the men would most likely be out hunting, and he could talk to Isabella alone. He saw she was sewing at the table when he knocked softly and entered. Isabella looked up, startled.

"I'd like to talk to you if you'll allow it."

Isabella put down her needle. "I didn't expect to see you again. I don't think there's much to discuss, but have a seat." Her eyes widened briefly at the revolver in his breast pocket.

Did she actually think he'd shoot her for writing the note? He sat down across from her, took the gun out of his pocket and placed it on the table between them.

"Is, I know you're upset about the things I've said to you, but you're wrong. I don't blame you. I would have fallen in love with you no matter what you did or said the last few weeks."

She frowned slightly but didn't say anything.

He continued. "I suppose the courage you showed

climbing Longs Peak started my feelings of attachment. But it's your intelligence, your wit, your kindness, and your sense of humor that decided my fate. I love spending time with you. I love thinking about you during the day and dreaming about you at night."

Isabella's eyes softened, and she whispered, "You do?"

Jim glanced down at the garment she was sewing. "Hell, I even love that ridiculous riding outfit of yours that you keep repairing."

Isabella smothered a smile.

"Is, listen, my feelings for you are not going to change and are here to stay. I just want you to give us a chance. Even if you can't say you love me now, maybe you'll be able to later."

Isabella bit her lip as if she was making an important decision. "If I do give us a chance, you would need to stop overdrinking and end any violent temper outbursts."

Jim nodded and smiled slightly. "I know, and I'd try."

"But where would we live? My home and sister are a million miles away."

"You could move here, bring your sister with you."

"Hennie would never agree. She's . . . scholarly."

"She could move to Boston or New York or any large city in the country. You could take a train and visit her."

Isabella rubbed her forehead. "I don't know."

"I could move to Scotland but since we both love it here I don't see a reason to do that."

Isabella nodded.

Jim reached for her hand, and she let him take it. "Look, even if we didn't get married and live together always, we could at least see each other if you agreed to visit here regularly."

"Or maybe you could visit me."

Jim smiled, feeling hopeful. "That's right. There are a number of things we could do."

Isabella hesitated, then shook her head. "I still don't know."

"Well then, think about it some more. But please don't terminate our acquaintance."

Isabella sighed and pulled her hand away. "You're not going to let this drop, are you?"

"I don't want to."

Isabella looked at the ceiling a moment and then back at him. "All right. I'll think about it some more. Our friendship isn't terminated. But clearly I'm not the only one who's stubborn."

Jim smiled. "That's the spirit, Is. Think about my good qualities."

Isabella smiled while shaking her head and threw her riding outfit at him.

Isabella was relieved after her talk with Jim. The pressure to make any major decision concerning the two of them seemed to be removed. He had said he would always love her and could wait for her to decide what she felt about him. They did not have to get married for her to continue to spend time with him. They could take their courtship more slowly. She could wait to see whether he did stop drinking, or at least slow down. She could watch for any violent temper outbursts. And perhaps, just perhaps, if Hennie ever did meet him, she would be as charmed by him as Isabella and understand her sister's attachment to him. Isabella slept great and woke up happy the next few days.

Jim felt better after his talk with Isabella. She was going to give them a chance; she wasn't ending their acquaintance. It was clear that she had at least thought about the two of them spending time together and seemed willing to consider different ways that they could see each other in the future. He could try to be a better person, stop his overdrinking and temper outbursts. He still felt that she loved him already, but maybe someday she would actually be able to say it. He could be patient. She was worth it.

A few days later Jim stopped by to see Isabella. "I'm on my way to check traps, but I wanted to tell you I miss you." Jim smiled.

Isabella smiled back. "Likewise. Can I come along?"

Jim shook his head. "No. You were right not to come when I suggested it the first time. There are some things not even you should experience. I find it gruesome even after all these years." Jim shrugged. "But it's a living so I do it."

"I just felt like getting out and going on a ride with you."

"Well, that's different. How about tomorrow afternoon?"

Isabella's eyes lit up. "Where should we go?"

"Wherever you wish, darlin'."

Isabella smiled softly and then clasped her hands together. "I'd like to see the lake and the sheep."

"That's an easy ride. Do you want to try your hand at hunting?"

"Goodness, no. It'd hardly be a challenge, considering how great I was at target practice on Eagle Cliff Mountain."

"That was beginner's luck."

Isabella raised her chin. "So you say. But I'll pack a picnic now that I'm such a superb cook."

Jim smiled.

The next day, while sitting next to Jim on a group of rocks that overlooked the lake, Isabella blurted out, "Guess what?"

"You decided to try your hand at hunting."

"Much more brilliant than that." Isabella waved her hands excitedly in the air. "Misters Buchanan and Althoff and I decided to celebrate Thanksgiving!"

Jim could feel the stirrings of jealousy again, but answered, "How do you plan to do that?"

While Isabella chattered on excitedly about the different dishes they planned to improvise with their limited supplies, Jim thought about how irksome it was that those two men got to live with her. And now there was a third guy who'd shown up. Jim was the one in love with her; he should be the one living with her. Every time he ran into one of the men on his own, he could barely hide his jealousy and would usually talk to them more sharply than he should. He imagined they probably went back to her and told her about his bad moods.

He realized she was asking a question. He took her hand and kissed the back of it. "I'm sorry. What did you say?"

"I asked did you want to come?"

"Come to what?"

"You really were woolgathering. I want you to come to our Thanksgiving celebration."

Did he want to spend hours watching her and the men gaily carry on with one another? Laughing and chuckling at the special jokes they had developed amongst themselves? Ah, no. Definitely not.

"Who's this new guy staying with you?"

Isabella snorted. "Mr. James Allen."

"Something wrong with him?"

"Actually, what's not wrong with him. For one thing, he's lazy. The three of us always shared the chores rather equally before he arrived. But Mr. Allen says he will do something and then never gets it done whether it's sweeping the floor or milking a cow. And he's eating everything in sight, going through all our stores of food. At least he provides some entertainment value."

"How's that?"

"He claims he's a writer and read us some of his compositions."

"Not any good, huh?"

"To the contrary: exceedingly good, considering he lifted lines and verses from famous American and English writers. He must think we're idiots not to see through his plagiarisms."

"He's pretty young to be making a living as a writer."

"Nineteen years old. But he claims he recently left a seminary where he was training to become a minister. Some preacher he'd make after—" Isabella stopped short and stared at Jim, wide-eyed.

"After what?"

"Nothing. I don't want you to get mad and ruin our day."

Jim sighed and shook his head. "Now you have to spill the beans for sure."

"Oh, all right. I was going to tell you anyway, but just not today. Mr. Allen was bragging yesterday that sometime in the last few days he got into your cabin when you were away and went through your box of personal papers and writings."

Jim stood up. "Son of a bitch!"

Isabella stood also. "He said he didn't take anything, but was apparently proud of the fact that he'd sneaked in on the famous Mountain Jim."

"What the hell is he doing here?"

"Stop swearing. He said he's moving to Estes Park for his health."

Jim picked up a pebble and skipped it across the lake. "He looks vigorous enough to me. And who the hell moves to Estes Park for their health in the wintertime?"

Like a bolt of insight it hit him—somebody sent by the Earl of Damnraven! But for what purpose? What was Jim missing here? He shook his head. He was getting crazy suspicious, and yet he couldn't shake the feeling.

Isabella tried skipping a rock herself. It fell with a *plunk*. "It is odd coming in the winter, isn't it? And will you stop swearing?"

Jim reached down and picked up a pebble. "Here. Try skipping this flatter one."

"So are you going to come?" Isabella took the rock and looked at him expectantly.

"Come to what?"

She rolled her eyes. "Our Thanksgiving celebration. My cooking extravaganza."

Jim tweaked her nose. "I think I'll pass."

Isabella looked crestfallen. "But why? I really want you to come."

He said the first thing that came to mind: "I'm not fit enough for society."

Isabella frowned. "That's silly and you know it."

Maybe it wasn't silly at all. If she thought him good enough, she might be living with him right now instead of them. He puffed out his cheeks and let the air out with a sigh. He decided it was best to drop that line of thinking.

He elaborated, "I don't really celebrate American Thanksgiving. It hasn't ever had much significance to me."

"Well, obviously, it doesn't have much significance to me either, but that's not the point." She threw the pebble. *Plop . . . plunk.* "I'm getting better at this." She turned back to Jim. "Please? It won't be as much fun without you."

Jim threw another pebble. *Plop, plop . . . plop, plunk.* "I think it's probably a fake holiday anyway. Do you really think the Pilgrims got along any better with the Indians than we do right now? They probably mistreated them just as much if not more so."

"Then don't think of it as Thanksgiving. Think of it as a little celebration and feast we want to give."

"I'll think about it, but don't expect me to come." He knew he wouldn't give it another consideration.

On Thanksgiving Day, Isabella hurried over to the window and sighed loudly. She realized the movement she had seen out of the corner of her eye had just been an elk.

Mr. Buchanan asked, "You feeling tired?"

Isabella pretended she wasn't dejected that Jim hadn't come yet. Putting on a smile, she turned to answer, "Oh, no. Not at all. This is fun; I'm enjoying cooking. I just walked over to the window because I thought I saw something interesting. But it was just another elk."

Mr. Buchanan smiled back and continued stirring the mashed potatoes.

Mr. Althoff did a little jig. "Should I start carving the meat? Is everyone almost finished with their dish?"

Isabella chuckled and walked back over to the oven to check on her bread. "How many times have you asked us that in the last hour?"

Mr. Althoff grinned. "Maybe fifty."

Isabella shook her head and smiled. "I'd say at least a hundred."

Mr. Buchanan put down his spoon and declared he was finished at the same time that James Allen stumbled out of the bedroom and yawned loudly. "Did I hear that the meal is ready?"

Mr. Althoff rolled his eyes at Isabella, then turned to young James. "It depends on whether Isabella is done baking."

Isabella tapped her fingers lightly on the top of the bread. She had learned what sound to listen for if the loaf was done. Reluctantly, she said, "I guess I'm ready also. I'll assemble the bread pudding after it cools."

But she didn't feel actually ready at all. She wanted to give a little more time for Jim to show up and join in the fun.

As Isabella helped put the plates on the table, she admitted to herself that although she appreciated the men's jolliness, the day still lacked something for her. She missed Jim's smiles and teasing and . . . simply his presence.

Isabella looked out the window again and stared at the

scenery. Truthfully, he could have shown up and done nothing but sit like a bump on a log and she would have been happy.

She cherished the man, probably loved him and that was all there was to it. There was no denying it to herself now. She just wasn't sure when she would tell Jim, knowing he would take it as a full commitment on her part that they should be together. She had let him know there were more questions and issues to be answered than just whether she loved him. He had promised to give her more time to think, and she was going to take it.

A few days later, Jim was sitting outside his cabin sharpening a knife when a stranger rode up. "Mr. James Nugent, I presume?"

Jim looked up at the dandified gentleman with a distinct English accent. "Who's asking?"

"Theodore Whyte. I'm working on behalf of Lord Dunraven. I believe the two of you have met?"

Jim frowned. "Briefly, a year ago." Jim walked over and shook his hand. The man was wiry thin with a wiry mustache and a wiry smile. His handshake was limp.

Mr. Whyte smiled. "I was hoping we could find some time to talk while I'm here in Estes Park."

"What about?"

"It concerns a matter I think you'll find most attractive."

Jim picked up his knife to start sharpening again. He wasn't going to miss this opportunity to try to find out what Dunraven was after, but he didn't want to appear too interested. "We could possibly meet, but I'm busy right now."

Mr. Whyte glanced around at the hides and furs surrounding the cabin and wrinkled his nose before saying, "Perhaps you would be available tomorrow. In the afternoon, shall we say? At Mr. Evans's place?"

Jim nodded. "Fine. I'll be there around five."

The next day Jim washed up, shaved, combed his hair and put on his new suit and boots. He figured it was best to meet this man on the most equal terms possible, let him know whom he was dealing with.

He rode over to Griff's and noticed Mr. Whyte's brief look of surprise as he knocked and entered. He glanced around but he didn't see Isabella.

Mr. Whyte coughed. "Mr. Nugent. Have a seat. Would you care for a drink?" He held out a bottle of fine Irish whiskey.

"Certainly. I see we're alone."

"Yes, the men are out hunting. I'm not sure about Miss Bird." So he'd met her. It didn't sit well with Jim. She didn't need to spend time with Dunraven's agent.

He took a seat opposite Jim and poured each of them a shot. Jim studied the crystal glass a moment before taking a drink. Whyte must have brought the glasses with him also. Jim took another sip and watched as Whyte started to raise the glass to his lips, then put it down without taking a drink.

"Cigar?"

Jim nodded. As they both began to smoke Jim leaned back in his chair and crossed his legs.

Whyte blew out a puff. "It's beautiful country here where Lord Dunraven has bought." He brought his glass to his lips and set it down again without imbibing.

"Yes, it is." Jim brought his glass to his lips and set it down without drinking. He smiled. Whyte smiled back. Message received. Whyte wasn't going to get Jim drunk while he stayed sober.

Whyte sniffed. "Your property is of interest to him also."

"How so?"

"It holds a strategic position on the way into Estes Park."

"Its value is obvious. I know who's entering and leaving the area."

"Precisely. Lord Dunraven has a couple propositions he'd like you to consider."

Jim took a puff. "Which are?"

"First, he'd like to buy your property."

"I'm not interested in selling."

"The offer is most generous."

"The place is going to be my home forevermore. There's no offer that could interest me."

"Perhaps this would change your mind." Mr. Whyte reached in his pocket and then held out a piece of paper.

Jim leaned forward and took it. He quickly shielded his surprise at the large amount of money offered. He slid the paper back to Whyte. "I'm not interested."

Whyte took out a pencil and wrote another figure. "This is the highest Lord Dunraven will offer. Take it or leave it." He slid the paper back to Jim.

Jim glanced at the thirty percent increase. He imagined Griff had told Dunraven just what trouble Jim could cause him. By the amount being offered he figured Dunraven didn't just want his property: He wanted Jim gone from the area. These men were the type who probably thought money could buy them anything.

Whyte frowned. "You could settle anywhere in the world with that kind of money."

Jim leaned back in his chair. "Still not interested."

Whyte studied Jim a minute and took another puff off his cigar. "Perhaps his second proposition will interest you."

"What's that?"

"If you plan to stay in the area, Lord Dunraven would like to offer you employment."

Jim cocked his head back. "In what capacity?"

Whyte cleared his throat. "There are many ways a man of your obvious intelligence and capabilities could be useful."

Jim frowned. "Be more specific."

"He could use a man to monitor who's coming and going into the area and help keep track of any potential problems."

"Just what problems is he anticipating? What are Lord Dunraven's plans for the area?"

Whyte tapped his finger on the table. "He'd like to obtain more land. He's interested in a private game preserve. Perhaps you could help run it in the future."

Like hell. Jim refrained from telling him so and asked instead, "How does he plan on obtaining more land?"

Whyte smiled. "Oh, there are many creative ways in which that can be done. Perhaps that interests you?"

Jim leaned forward. "Speak clearly, sir."

"He needs men who would be interested in filing homesteaders' claims. Foreigners can't file."

Jim frowned. Whyte didn't mean *men* who would be interested in filing claims. He meant drifters and loafers such as the type who loitered around Larimer Street in Denver. He meant *anybody* who could sign their name or just an "X" to the homestead records.

Jim cleared his throat. "I already have squatter's rights on my land. Besides, the land hasn't even been surveyed by the government yet to file claims."

Mr. Whyte waved his cigar in the air. "Dunraven will get it surveyed shortly. Have no doubt about the earl's ability to get things done."

"So you get it surveyed and can start filing homesteader's claims, then what?"

"You're a bright man who I'm sure knows the ways of the world. Slight name changes wouldn't be noticed if money is put in the right hands."

Jim nodded slowly and took a sip. The slimy son of a bitch.

Mr. Whyte coughed and rubbed his chin. "Perhaps you

could help him find a few men similar to yourself who understand what we're talking about."

Jim leaned back and rested his arm on the back of the chair. "I don't care for speaking around an issue. What would Lord Dunraven do with these multiple land claims that just a few men have managed to obtain?"

"Well, once the men paid the government their due, he'd buy the claims from them, of course."

Jim smiled and crossed his arms. "Of course. And that way he could have his private game preserve in as cheap a way as possible."

"I see you are a man of understanding."

"Well, let me tell you what I understand—"

Jim stopped as the door opened, and Isabella walked in wearing her fancy blue silk dress. She wore it on days she was washing or repairing her everyday wear including that ridiculous riding outfit.

Jim turned to her, smiled and stood. "You're looking particularly lovely today, Miss Bird."

She stared at Jim a moment, then looked briefly at Mr. Whyte who was rising, then turned back to Jim. "Uh, I didn't mean to interrupt."

"Not at all, Miss Bird. We were just finished with our discussion."

Mr. Whyte turned to Jim and briefly smiled his wiry smile. "Think about what we discussed. I'm leaving here tomorrow, but you can reach me with your answer at the Regency in Denver where I'll be staying." Mr. Whyte turned to Isabella. "Miss Bird, if you'll excuse me."

Jim and Isabella watched him walk out the door.

Isabella looked puzzled. "What was that about?"

"Nothing worth discussing."

"Really? It didn't look that way to me. And why are you dressed like that?"

Jim smiled. "I thought you'd approve. I dress like this on laundry day."

Isabella narrowed her eyes. "Something's up, but if you don't care to share it, you can at least keep me company for dinner. I was just about to get it started." Isabella smiled.

Jim formally bowed. "Why, Miss Bird, I'd be delighted."

Jim sat at the table with Isabella and chuckled.

Isabella smiled. "What's so funny?"

Jim smiled back. "You're staring at me again."

Her mouth dropped open. "That's ridiculous. Why would I be staring at you?"

He turned so she saw only the good side of his face. "Probably because I look so handsome in my new suit and boots."

Isabella bit her cheek. "No, I'm staring because I'm dumbfounded that you're so arrogant and conceited."

"Don't you like my new suit and boots?"

Isabella started brushing the skirt of her dress smooth. "Of course I do. You look very . . . distinguished."

"Excellent, then come sit on my lap."

She quickly looked up. "Like one of your common saloon girls? I don't think so."

Jim gasped. "How can you say that? None of my saloon girls are common. They each have their own unique talents."

She briefly arched her brows. "I'm sure they do, and I can't believe you just said that."

Jim smiled. "I can't believe it, also, because actually they aren't my saloon girls anymore."

She placed her hands on her hips. "Somebody steal them from you?"

"No. You've ruined me. Since I met you I'm not interested in saloon girls."

She dropped her hands to her lap and smiled haughtily. "Well, be glad about that since I'm sure they carry the

French—"

"Miss Bird! You forget yourself. Anyways, I could only be happy about that if you'd become my saloon girl instead."

Isabella shook her head. "Oh, no. Not a chance."

"I thought you were an adventurer."

"Just what exactly does such a position entail?"

"Sitting on my lap for starters."

Isabella tapped her chin. "Hmmm. If I sit on your lap, can we then discuss something more decent? More intellectual?"

"Sure."

"Very well." She got up and sat lightly on the edge of his lap.

Jim smiled and shook his head. "You're not doing it right."

"What do you mean?" Her voice wobbled as he jiggled her with his legs.

When she grabbed his neck for balance, he stopped and said, "Now you're getting the hang of it."

Isabella smiled and shook her head. "Oh, lovely. A saloon girl is just what I always aspired to—"

Isabella gasped and stood as the door opened. She blushed a bright shade of pink. "Mr. Buchanan. Mr. Althoff. You're back."

Both waved and smiled. Mr. Buchanan leaned his rifle against the wall while Mr. Althoff said, "Hi, Isabella. You having fun with Jim?"

Jim knew Althoff had meant the question innocently enough by the tone of his voice, but he couldn't help chuckling. Isabella's eyes widened and she now turned a shade of beet red.

Jim cleared his throat. "I was educating Miss Bird in frontier hospitality." He turned to Isabella who remained speechless. "We can continue your lessons later."

Isabella straightened her dress. "We most certainly will

not. Are you hungry?"

"Yes, but I just ate."

"What? Never mind. I was talking to Misters Althoff and Buchanan."

"Oh, of course. How's the hunting going, men?"

An hour later Jim whistled while he rode home slowly. He would deal with Dunraven soon enough. For now he had a woman he wished to court. He was a happy man.

Chapter Nineteen

The next day Isabella decided to spend some time with the Murells, the English couple that lived near Longmont. They had been her saviors as friends she could visit when she had been forced to lodge with that particularly nasty family after she first came to Colorado. She was sure she could find their home on her own now. She had learned a lot about traveling to and from Estes Park since she had been dependent on Misters Downers and Rogers to guide her.

Besides spending time with a very pleasant couple, she knew that there she could think about what she should do about Jim. She might even be able to share some of her concerns and get their opinion. They were sensible people.

She already knew how much she cared for Jim. But after seeing him in his fine suit, she realized Jim could fit in anywhere. They could live in America or Scotland and be accepted as a couple. He not only knew how to dress the part of a gentleman, but he could be intelligent and well-mannered as well. That was if he wasn't in one of his teasing moods.

Even Hennie couldn't have many objections. His unfortunate past was a scar on his personal history as much as the disfigurement on his face, but Isabella believed he was sincerely contrite about the mistakes he had made. What was important was the type of man he was at this time in his life. The scarring told of hard battles fought, but he had won. In so many ways he was now an upright, honorable man.

There were only two things he needed to prove to her for them to be together permanently: He had to show her that he could refrain from excessive drinking, and that he had his notorious temper under control. They were both intertwined, and one led to the other, but they were the final barrier. Isabella knew she didn't need to say anything more to Jim. He knew how she felt about his drinking and temper. The only thing she needed to figure out was how much time she needed to wait until he had proven his abstinence to her. A month? A year? Two years? She wasn't sure. Even then, there were no guarantees that he wouldn't relapse into his old ways, but by then she figured she would be willing to take a chance. What she needed right now was a break from his overwhelming personality to think.

She headed out from Griff's the following day. The morning started bright and clear and not too nippy considering it was early December. But by the time she was partway to Jim's place, the weather turned cloudy and much chillier. Freezing rain quickly followed. Finally a dense fog developed, and Isabella started to become disoriented. She wasn't seeing the familiar landmarks.

She thought she heard barking. If it was Ring she swore she was getting down on her hands and knees. She would kiss that dog on the face. "Ring? Is that you?"

"Is, what the hell do you think you're doing?" Jim materialized from the fog.

"And to think I was actually thinking some nice thoughts about you. In answer to your question, I'm taking a little trip."

"Oh, no. Now where?"

"Just to visit my friends by Longmont for a few days. Then I'll be back."

"Are you crazy? Nobody in their right mind travels in this kind of weather."

"It wasn't so bad when I started out. You know how the weather can change suddenly." She shivered slightly.

"Well, you aren't going anywhere until you warm up and dry out your clothes. You know the routine by now. Follow me."

Jim didn't wait for her reply and started walking toward his cabin. Isabella followed.

Jim handed her a blanket and smiled. "Can I watch you take off your wet clothes this time? You know, part of frontier hospitality."

Isabella put the blanket on the table and crossed her arms. "You may certainly not. Now turn around."

Jim heard Isabella taking off her clothes. He noted she wasn't loudly sighing as she had the first time she had done this. He heard her walk over to the bench in front of the fireplace and hang her clothes over the back. Jim turned his head slightly to catch a peek.

"I saw that!" Isabella grabbed the blanket off the table and quickly wrapped it around her shoulders.

"You can't blame me for trying." Jim smiled.

"Are you taking off your clothes?"

"Mine aren't really wet. I'm not foolish enough to travel in this kind of weather if I don't have to." Jim arched his brow at her. Isabella frowned.

Jim looked thoughtful. "But, you know? I'm feeling a little chilled. I better join you under the bed covers."

Isabella studied the bed a moment, then turned back to Jim. "Oh, all right. But remember, don't get fresh."

Jim clasped his chest as if he was astounded she had just said that. "Never, Miss Bird."

Isabella smiled. "Will you read to me again?"

"I got a new book from Gertie. Want to start that?"

"Sure."

Isabella lifted the covers, got in and moved over to make room for Jim. He grabbed the book off the shelf and settled next to her.

"Is, you know this bed is kind of small. It's more comfortable if you put your head on my shoulder again."

Isabella hesitated, then nodded. "I think you're right."

Jim inwardly smiled and lifted his arm until she placed her head on his shoulder. He nudged and maneuvered until she snuggled closer, turning into him.

She looked up into his face. "Another sailing adventure?"

"No. This one's supposed to be about pirates at someplace called Isle Morad."

Isabella smiled, then briefly buried her face in the side of his chest. "I'd ask you if you're kidding but I know you're not."

"I like reading about diverse topics. You know that."

She started toying with the wooden button on his shirt. "Books are expensive. You own your fair share. That's good you value them."

"They're worth the expense, living alone as I do." She looked up at him and studied his face a moment before looking back down.

A half hour later Isabella stretched, still snuggled next to Jim. "This book isn't making any sense to me. Why would people build homes on Indian Key if they knew the place was surrounded by pirates?"

Jim frowned and shook his head. "Is, you're not paying attention. They don't know about the pirates yet."

She looked around the room a moment. "Oh. I can't concentrate. I keep thinking about something else."

"Your trip?"

She started playing with his button again. "Not really. That'll go fine as soon as this fog clears. Are you going to kiss me again?"

Jim smiled. "I was hoping to."

She looked up and smiled. "All right. Just one. Like before."

He shook his head. "It'll be just one, but not like before. That wasn't hardly a kiss."

She looked astonished. "It was a kiss *to me*."

Jim smirked. "I know. That's why we need to give you saloon girl lesson number two."

Isabella took a deep breath. "All right, but we're not moving on to saloon girl lesson number three just yet."

Jim smiled. "Why not? I have a feeling you're a quick learner."

"Not that quick."

"Anything to make you happy, Miss Bird."

Isabella smiled. "I appreciate that, Mr. Nugent."

It was technically just one kiss, but it was a very long and involved kiss, more than Jim had dared hope for. She not only was a quick learner but a soft and responsive partner. When they slowly pulled their mouths apart and she looked into his face, she smiled sweetly. Jim couldn't remember ever feeling so content and satisfied. If he could have held on to that moment forever, he would have.

Ring yawned loudly from the corner in the cabin where he had been sleeping. Isabella rose up on her elbow to look at him and then glanced out the window. "Look, the weather has cleared again."

Jim frowned. "You know how the weather can be around here. Today's unsettled. I wouldn't go if I were you. I'm serious, Is."

Isabella shook her head dismissively. "I'll be fine. Now scoot out so I can get going."

Before Isabella mounted her horse, Jim gave her a quick kiss on the lips. "Is, I've survived Indian and grizzly attacks, but I swear you're going to kill me with worry."

Isabella breezily said, "I'll be fine. See you in a few days."

But the skies became cloudy and rainy again. Before long a wind blew with such ferocity that grainy sleet and hail caused cuts in her face. Eventually the trail became obscured by several inches of slippery snow over ice. Isabella relied on her horse to find the way, a bad move, as she started hearing a cracking noise. Her eyes widened.

Oh, no! She looked around quickly and realized she must be on a pond unseen because of the snow covering it. Her horse took another step and the ground cracked louder. Isabella swallowed and took a couple deep breaths, trying to soothe her nerves. Stay calm. She must stay calm.

She reined her horse to turn back and they took another step. *CRACK!* They plunged into icy water.

She gasped. It was sooo cold! Her horse frantically tried to climb out, splashing more frigid water onto her. She couldn't breathe, *she couldn't breathe*, she felt so panicky. She was going to sink down and die, never to be heard from again!

She waved her arms frenziedly, trying to stay afloat, but her clothes were too heavy. Helplessly, she slowly sank. And . . . and . . . touched bottom! Isabella closed her eyes and sighed in relief. It was shallow, thank heavens.

She grabbed her horse's reins and with strength she didn't know she possessed, she mounted. They forced their way to the shore a hundred yards away, the wind blowing and freezing her hair and clothes into icy hardness. At the edge of the pond Isabella started shivering uncontrollably. She rubbed her arms in a futile attempt to get warm. She urged her horse to walk faster; she didn't dare gallop over the icy terrain, but her horse slid repeatedly. Isabella's eyes began tearing in the howling wind. Her lids started freezing shut, and Isabella was forced to take off one of her mittens in order to pick pieces of ice off her lashes so she could at least keep one eye open. Her fingers were stiff from the cold, making the maneuver nearly impossible. She couldn't even feel her feet anymore in her boots. Just when she was sure she would perish, she saw the faint light from the hotel in Longmont off in the distance.

Relief such as she had never known before assailed her. With a final burst of energy, she made it to the inn she had stayed at before, startling the owner who had never expected guests to arrive in such frightful weather.

That night, after a hot meal, in clothes borrowed from the innkeeper's wife, and with multiple blankets piled on top of her, Isabella shook her head while lying in bed. She might have survived, but Hennie and Jim were going to kill her when they heard about this adventure.

The next day a very pregnant Constance Murell greeted her with surprised enthusiasm.

"Isabella, sit next to the stove or you'll freeze like the rest of the house." Constance held up a pail of frozen milk. "The only way I can cook is if I melt everything first on the stove."

Isabella frowned. "Clearly, the West is lucky any women at all have settled here. But it hasn't been this cold in Estes Park."

"Will you spend the winter there?"

Isabella thought of Jim and blushed slightly. "I'm figuring out my plans as we speak."

The door to the kitchen opened. "What plans?"

Ernest Murell stomped his feet and clapped his mittened hands before placing them in his armpits to warm.

Constance dropped her frozen pail on the stove. "Close the door! You're letting in a draft! Oh, sorry. I didn't see you behind Ernest, Mr. Haigh."

Isabella looked over at Mr. Haigh who quickly shut the door. Another surprise visitor to the Murells, Mr. Haigh had arrived just hours before Isabella. She may have been a fool to travel in such weather, but at least she knew how to dress properly for it with her bulky warm coat, felt scarf, and thick wool stockings. This fellow Englishman was dressed as if he were going on a foxhunt. A thin, stylish coat over riding boots just wasn't going to make it in this weather. Even Lord Dundreary, whom she had met on her Pikes Peak trip, had known to dress appropriately, according to local standards. This guy was trying too hard to look prosperous. She figured he probably was new to wealth. Old wealth didn't try so hard to show off their money. They had it and they knew it.

She watched the laughable Mr. Haigh blow on his hands to warm them. She suddenly missed Jim with an aching intensity. No other man would do. They just didn't compare. She had to figure out a way for Jim and her to have a future together and for her to have no remaining reservations.

Think. Think. What was the best way to proceed? With abrupt clarity, she knew what she would do. It would require some time apart from Jim, but it would be worth it in the end if everything turned out as she hoped. But would Jim agree with her decision? She wasn't sure. The thought of asking him made her nervous. So much depended on his answer.

She looked over at Constance still trying to melt the milk. She didn't need her advice in the matter after all. She would spend a couple days here and then be on her way back to Estes Park. "Constance, I can imagine your discomfort at not one, but two visitors, in this weather."

"Ridiculous. We love having guests from the home country. I just wish we had more beds."

Mr. Haigh sat down across from Isabella. "Naturally, you may take the extra bed, Miss Bird. I'll sleep on the floor. Won't be any problem at all."

Isabella eyed him speculatively. "You probably haven't slept on a floor before. It can be cold and drafty. Perhaps we could alternate nights on the extra bed."

"I can sleep anywhere. Just watch me. It'll be fun."

Isabella smiled the next morning when Mr. Haigh appeared at the breakfast table with wrinkled clothes and dark circles under his eyes. He sipped his coffee sullenly and stared into space.

Ernest placed his mug on the table. "Isabella, you never told me your plans yesterday."

"I'll be heading back to Estes Park tomorrow."

Mr. Haigh muttered under his breath, "Thank God."

Isabella smiled over at Constance and raised her eyebrows. Constance grinned back. If one poor night's sleep on the floor caused this kind of reaction, she'd hate to see this man when he was really irritated. She was glad she had only one more day in his company.

The next morning was frigidly cold but the sky was clear, and Isabella decided to head back. By the time she made it to Jim's cabin, her hands and feet were numb and she was shivering.

Jim opened the door and leaned against the frame with a coffee mug in his hand. "I've been keeping a watch out for you. Welcome back or should I say, thank God you're back."

Isabella remained on her horse. "Oh, go ahead."

"Go ahead what?"

"I know you want to say it."

Jim smiled and shook his head. "I don't have the faintest notion what you're talking about."

"Good. I was afraid you were going to say, 'I told you so.'"

"That's too obvious a remark. Now, why don't you get off your horse so we can try to warm you up?"

"I can't."

Jim frowned. "Why not?"

"I'm too stiff to move; I'm an ice statue. You're going to need to crack my arms and legs to get them budging. I think even my eyelids are frozen in place again."

"But aren't we lucky? Not your mouth."

"That's next. Are you going to help me or not?"

An hour later she sat at Jim's table with her coffee and watched him stir some stew. She hadn't been able to bring herself to talk to him about her decision. It was too worrisome what his response would be. For now she just wanted to enjoy his company. When she couldn't put it off any longer, she would speak to him.

Jim glanced over and smiled warmly. Isabella softly smiled back and then sighed.

"Deep in thought?"

Isabella nodded. "Yeah."

"Wanna share?"

She shook her head. "Not right now. Maybe later."

But events happened quicker than she anticipated. Mr. Rudolph and Griff returned three days later, and Griff brought with him the cash that he owed her. She now had enough traveling money to begin her journey back home to Scotland. If she and Jim were going to spend some necessary time apart, she had to leave now while the weather was still permissible.

Jim put down his ax on top of a pile of chopped wood and watched as Isabella dismounted and strode toward him.

"Is, I was just thinking about you. I thought you might like to go riding today."

"Oh, I came over to talk to you about a ride also." She burst into tears.

Stunned, Jim pulled her toward him in a hug and kissed the top of her head. "What's wrong? I hate to see you crying."

She looked up at him. "I need to discuss something with you."

Jim had a feeling he knew what she was going to say.

She was ending any future between them. She hadn't been the same since returning from Longmont. He felt devastated but knew he wanted to get the conversation over with. "Then we'll go inside and talk."

They entered his cabin, and he poured them each a cup of coffee. They sat across from each other at the table. He reached for her hand and said, "All right, tell me. What do you have to say?"

Isabella looked down and sighed. "I've reached a decision about the two of us."

Jim frowned. "I figured. What is it?"

She looked up at him. "First, let me tell you that I know I care for you as much as you care for me."

Jim smiled but shook his head, puzzled. "Then why are you so sad?"

"Because I think I should leave, at least for a while."

Jim closed his eye and rubbed his forehead before looking back at her. "Why? That's nonsense."

"Just listen to me. I've thought about this at length, and I know it's the right decision."

"Go on."

"Before I make the ultimate commitment to you, I want to know that what's between us is strong and lasting enough for a lifetime. If it's real and true love, then it won't be just because we're together in Estes Park. It will endure and not fade on us while I'm back in Scotland."

Jim started to interrupt: "But—"

She held up her hand. "That's not all. Let me finish. Furthermore, if you love me as much as you say, you'll stop the drinking and temper outbursts that I find so unacceptable. If I'm worth it to you, then you'll stop."

"I already told you I would."

"I know, but for how long?"

Jim leaned forward. "Forever."

"I need to know that. I need more time to feel comfortable that you're a changed man."

Jim shook his head and looked down a moment before returning her gaze. "Is, you know for some things it's too late."

She frowned. "What do you mean?"

"I'll always have a reputation as a ruffian, and I'll always have the memories of what I've done. That I can't erase."

She leaned toward him. "I realize that. But it doesn't need to cloud how you proceed with your life from this day forward."

Jim nodded. "True. So what are you proposing?"

She sat back and blew out a heavy breath of air. "Let's give it a year. Let's see how we feel and where things stand in a year. If our affections are real, they'll last. If you love me enough, you'll maintain an honorable way of living."

"A whole year? How about a few months?"

Isabella shook her head. "No. I think a year is about right. Besides, if I do return here, I'll need time to tie up loose ends in Scotland. I don't know what Hennie will do. I'll need to talk to her and give her time to make a decision."

Jim rubbed his mouth, looking at her. "All right."

"All right?" Isabella started to smile.

Jim smiled back. "All right. You're worth the wait."

Isabella jumped up and awkwardly propped herself over the table to grab Jim in a tight hug around his neck. "Oh, thank you. I was afraid you wouldn't agree."

Jim stroked her back up and down. "Uh, darlin', you just spilled coffee all over."

"Oh, hang the coffee. I don't care."

"Miss Bird, your language again. I guess I need a year to verify that you can straighten out your foul mouth. Well, come around the table and sit on my lap. We'll need to figure out how you're getting back to Scotland."

It was a bittersweet few days Jim and Isabella spent in

Estes Park before Isabella left. Both tried to act normally, but their impending separation weighed heavily at the back of both their minds. But finally, Isabella was packed and ready. The plan was for Jim to escort her to the stagecoach station where they would say their good-byes, and she would take the coach to the train station. The train would carry her to the East Coast, and from there, within a few weeks, she would be back in Scotland.

On the morning of her departure Griff decided to accompany Isabella to just where Jim's cabin came into view. He shook her hand. "Isabella, I'll leave you here. You're welcome back with my family anytime you wish. We'll all miss you."

"Griff, I can't thank you enough for all you've done for me."

"My pleasure. I'd take you to the stagecoach station myself, but I know you're in good hands with Jim. He'll guard you well despite his other faults."

"Yes, he will."

After Jim finished packing and saddling his horse, they left his cabin. Jim was quiet, and Isabella couldn't stop tearing up every time she looked over at him.

Finally, when her sniffling became louder, Jim said, "Is, this is your idea. Just stay here. You don't have to go home now. Stay for the winter. You can leave in the spring if you want."

She wiped at her tears. "No, it won't be any easier then. I know I should go."

"Well, do you want to take a break? We could stop for a while."

"No. What I want is just one more day alone with you. Just one more."

"You want me to take the stagecoach with you?"

"No. But isn't there anyplace we could go and spend some time alone for a while?"

Jim looked at her intently. What was she suggesting?

Couldn't be . . . No, he inwardly shook his head. He knew her. She wasn't ready for the level of intimacy that he desired. Maybe when she returned in a year, but he just knew, not now. He tried to joke. "We could camp out tonight."

"You mean like we did at Longs Peak?" She added quickly, "All right."

Jim smiled. "I was half-kidding. Are you serious—you want to do that?"

Isabella nodded. "It would be a cherished final memory."

Jim shrugged. "Well, I was planning on camping out myself on the way back to Estes Park. I guess we could make do with what I brought along if you want to share the food and blankets. Keep in mind, it'll be cold."

She smiled a half smile and shook her head. "I think I know what's involved by now."

Jim smiled. "Yeah, I guess you do. Camping it is, then."

It was a clear, frigid night. Both put on additional clothes, and Jim held her close under the blankets next to the fire with his arm under her neck. The stars were bright, and both pointed out the constellations they knew. They continued to stare at the night sky.

Isabella sighed. "What if something happens? What if we never see each other again?"

"Nothing will happen. We'll see each other again."

"But would you come to me if I couldn't come to you?"

"Absolutely. You know I would, Is."

"Promise?"

"I promise. Even if I'm dead, I'll come visit you from the heavens."

Isabella chuckled. "All right. And I'll do the same."

"You see? No matter what, we'll see each other again."

Another minute later, Isabella said, "Jim, I never told

you something."

"What?"

"My family used to tease me that I've got fairy blood in me. *Please* don't do anything dangerous, but if, God forbid, something did happen, maybe you *would* visit me from the heavens."

Jim chuckled. "If *I* do something dangerous? Look who's talking. Well, anyways, I guess it's better being called a fairy than a witch."

Isabella poked him with her elbow. "You wouldn't be laughing if I told you any of the strange things that have happened to me."

"Like what?"

"Predictions I've made. Things such as that. Have you ever had anything strange happen to you?"

Jim didn't answer right away, then said, "Well, once I saw something that I'm still not sure what it was."

"You mean like a ghost?"

"No. I wouldn't say I believe in ghosts exactly."

"Tell me. What happened?"

"Before I owned Ring I had this other dog named Shanee who I also adored. Shanee started acting ill, and one morning I woke up and didn't think she was going to make it through the day. So I stuck around the cabin to stay with her until she passed away. But you know, after a while I got the impression that she was just hanging on because of me, because I was still there. She wasn't going to let go until I left the cabin. Do you know what I mean?"

Isabella looked over at him. "Yes."

"So I petted her and hugged her and went out for a walk. I never showed you, but by my cabin are three mounds of dirt covered with rocks, probably grave sites. When I was about fifty yards away from them, I looked up and these grayish forms moved over them and then disappeared."

"What were they?"

"I still don't know. They were too big for wolves, didn't look like humans, didn't look like bears. I just don't know what they were."

"Did you run away?"

"No. They weren't scary or threatening, but I headed back to the cabin anyways. When I got there I found out Shanee had died while I was on the walk."

"Oh, that's sad. Maybe those forms were ghosts. That's kind of spooky."

"I know."

She snuggled closer to him. "Tell me another story."

"About what?"

"Anything. I'm never going to be able to fall asleep tonight."

"Let's see. You want to hear about how I got my mare?"

"All right."

Jim hesitated a moment. "But, Is, first give me another kiss."

Isabella whispered, "All right."

Jim lifted his arm out from underneath the blankets and turned toward her. She reached up and touched his cheek before saying, "I'm going to miss you so much."

He leaned over her, looking into her eyes, then lowered his head. He softly kissed her forehead before lightly touching each eyelid with his lips. Then he slowly brushed down her cheek, finally settling on her mouth, putting all the love he felt for this precious woman in that one kiss. Pulling his lips gradually back from her mouth, he raised his head and softly smiled. She gazed back at him as if putting every feature of his face to memory and softly sighed. He laid on his back again, and she adjusted her head on his shoulder. They didn't speak any further as they drifted off to sleep.

They arrived at the stagecoach inn the next afternoon. It

was not the setting they would have wished in which to say their final farewells.

There was a dance planned that evening in the main room. But before that the owners and townspeople quickly found out that the famous Rocky Mountain Jim was among them. They stared and fawned over him the rest of the day. By evening Isabella and Jim decided not to join in the dancing, but stayed by themselves at the kitchen table, holding hands, reading to each other. When the music died down, they went to their separate sleeping quarters for the night.

The next morning the stage arrived early. Jim pulled Isabella to the side of the building out of view of the others.

He took her face in his hands, kissed her softly, then said, "Is, I love you. Have a safe journey."

"I will. I don't know how I'm going to stand not seeing you every day." Her eyes shimmered with unshed tears until she blinked, and they spilled over onto her cheeks.

He wiped the wetness away with his thumbs. "It's not too late to stay. Come back with me."

"No. I need to do this."

"You'll write when you arrive safely?"

"Yes. I promise." She looked at him anxiously. "Will you write back?"

"Of course. But I vow, I'm going to see you in a year."

Isabella nodded, then broke away from him and stood in line before the open coach door, wiping away more tears. Jim walked toward her.

"Miss Bird, I thought that was you."

Jim frowned at the well-dressed stranger interrupting their good-bye.

Isabella closed her eyes and rubbed her forehead once before turning to Jim. "Mr. Nugent, I'd like you to meet an acquaintance of mine, Mr. Haigh. We met at my English friends' house outside of Longmont."

Jim shook his hand before Haigh turned back to

Isabella. "Are you traveling on this stage with me, Miss Bird?"

"Yes. I'll join you in a moment."

Mr. Haigh stepped into the coach, and Isabella turned back to Jim and swallowed. "I don't know what to say."

"Say good-bye, Isabella, and that you'll be back soon."

"A year is so long."

Jim briefly looked away before returning her gaze. "An eternity, but we'll make it."

Isabella nodded silently.

Jim extended his hand. "Well, this is it."

They stared at each other a few more moments, then she took his hand between both of hers. "Good-bye, Mr. Nugent."

Jim gave her a tremulous smile. "Good-bye, Miss Bird."

And that was it. He helped her into the coach, and within five minutes she was down the road, out of sight.

Chapter Twenty

Jim thought about Isabella often. He yearned for her company. He was anxious to receive a letter from her saying she had made it safely back home. But he didn't agonize over her the way he had when she had left for Pikes Peak. He was calmer and more confident in his feelings for her and hers for him. He told himself he just needed to be patient, that all would be well in a year.

In February, a couple months later, the weather turned milder than normal, and Jim decided to make a trip to Denver. The first thing he did was pick up his mail. He sorted through it quickly and found a letter from Isabella. He tore it open without waiting to get back to his hotel room. He read the letter and smiled. It was a formal note as he expected. She wrote that she had arrived safely and said she missed Estes Park and all the wonderful people who lived there. She made no declarations of love or of missing him specifically. But she did add at the end that she hoped to return to Estes Park again in the future. That was all he needed to read; that line had a world of meaning to him.

He went to the hide store and was pleased to receive more money from the owner for the furs and hides he had left on his last trip to Denver.

He thought about next tracking down Dunraven's man, Mr. Whyte, and warning him against trying any land schemes, but decided he was in too good a mood. Besides, he figured nothing would happen until the spring, and he could deal with them then if and when they actually tried something underhanded.

He headed toward the general store to resupply his cabin, but on the way he heard a soft whimpering as he passed an alleyway. He peered into the shadows and saw a slight movement on the ground. He approached cautiously, but when he got closer he saw a tail wag. He reached down and picked up a wiggling puppy with an injured paw. The pooch tried licking his face while Jim examined her paw.

"Well, aren't you a sweet thing."

Jim didn't need another dog, but there was no way he was going to leave this puppy in the alley. He figured he could feed her and try to clean her paw, then find her a home. But a few hours later Jim had already become too attached and knew he would be taking her home with him.

That evening in his hotel room, Jim wrote Isabella a return letter. He guessed she would want him to keep it formal. She was just the type of person who would worry about letters getting into the wrong hands by accident. Well, what the hell? She could always burn the letter if she was so worried about what he composed. He wrote:

"Is, the love of my life,

I received your letter and am pleased you made it home safely. Now get back here. I miss you.

   Yours truly,
   Mr. James Nugent

P.S. I found a puppy today. I thought about naming her Isabella but presumed you wouldn't approve. I therefore am resorting to my one previous love's name and calling her Sally, a nickname for Salme, in case you haven't figured it out. I hope you are jealous."

Jim sealed the letter and gave it to the hotel clerk to mail.

He would write a longer letter to her later.

It was amazing to Jim how much the puppy cheered him up and made the days go by more quickly. Ring snarled at Sally the first few days after Jim brought her home, but the two eventually became inseparable companions. Initially Sally was too young and inexperienced to accompany Jim and Ring when Jim left to hunt or trap. On those days he would leave her in his cabin and for miles hear her wailing to come along. Eventually he conceded defeat and allowed Sally to come with them.

March brought more diversions. Griff brought his family, including his niece Mary, back to Estes Park. For a few weeks Jim stopped by regularly, chatted with the guests, played with Charlie and William, and flirted with Caroline. Mr. Buchanan and Mary resumed their courtship, and Jim thought how lucky these two uncomplicated people were to have each other.

But things started to turn sour in April. Mr. Haigh, whom Jim had met when bidding Isabella farewell, arrived one day in Estes Park. He claimed he was there for his health. Jim was sure he was Dunraven's agent sent to help manage the Earl's affairs in Estes Park. Jim decided to stop by Griff's even more frequently to keep a closer eye on the situation.

The first change Jim noticed after Haigh's arrival was that Griff, who was no lightweight drinker to begin with, started imbibing more heavily than usual in the evenings. Jim figured that was understandable, considering what Griff had done to himself selling to Dunraven.

The next change Jim noticed was that Buchanan started acting more moody and irritable. It took Jim a little longer to figure out why, but he finally noticed that Haigh was paying particular attention to Mary. Acting a bit too trifling towards her affections as far as Jim was concerned.

Jim decided to get into the mix just to irritate Haigh. So instead of innocently flirting with just Caroline, he started teasing Mary also. It had the desired effect. Haigh began engaging Jim in confrontational conversation over nonsense. That left Mary free for Buchanan again.

But the night of Mary's birthday a week later, Jim felt truly inspired. He stood up. "I would like to propose a toast to Mary, one of the fair maidens of Estes Park. May you always find the happiness you desire, and the man of your dreams."

Griff held up his glass and slurred slightly, "Hear, hear."

Jim raised his hand. "One more thing. In honor of your birthday, I hereby declare the lake where you and young Buchanan have spent many happy hours to be called from this day forward Mary's Lake."

Everyone cheered and clapped except Haigh who rubbed his chin and glared at Jim.

But it was the third change Jim noticed after Haigh's arrival that had more serious implications. Men started arriving stating they had staked a homesteading claim in the acres surrounding Griff's—now Dunraven's—spread.

Jim spent several days thinking about what he should do about the beginning of the land swindle. But that was just the problem; it was only the beginning. He had no proof that anything underhanded was going on. He didn't yet know whether the men planned to sell their acres cheaply to Dunraven. And it would take time for him to know whether the men were going to add necessary improvements to the land.

Jim decided to warn people about his concerns and headed to Denver. On the way, he told everyone he knew about what he suspected was happening in Estes Park. Most were receptive to his way of thinking. That was a start, at least.

However, the first thing he did when he actually arrived in Denver was forget about Dunraven and head to the post office. There on the top of his mail pile was a letter from Isabella. He opened it immediately and read:

"Dear Sir,
    I dearly wish to return to Estes Park as it is clear you are in dire need of assistance in naming your future pets.
            Truly yours,
            I.L.B.
P.S. Please refrain from feeding your puppy's delicate stomach any of your bread, but you may consider it appropriate to give a portion of your bear."

Jim smiled all the way to his hotel and then upon checking in was even happier when he realized that at the bottom of the mail pile she had done as he had and written a longer letter a week later. She was planning a trip to Europe over the summer and wanted to see more mountains and go hiking. Her sister had already started editing some of Isabella's letters to prepare them for future publication. Jim wondered how much Isabella had written about her experiences, and how much was being left out. But on the whole, he gathered that Isabella was content and doing well.

    He spent a good part of the evening with his friends but did not celebrate with his usual vigor. A few commented on his mellower demeanor. He told them he was a happy man and was looking forward to the future, but did not elaborate further.

    The following morning Jim was back to dealing with his Dunraven problem. He was unsuccessful in finding out anything concerning Dunraven at the land office. He decided to track down the newspaper people he knew next. They were always interested in a story but agreed that he needed proof. Perhaps he could write another opinion article, the editor suggested, not including any specifics that could get the newspaper in trouble. Jim agreed and decided to write an article about proper land development when he returned to Estes Park.

The next day Jim went to the general store, picked up supplies and headed back to Estes Park. After wrenching Ring and Sally away from "Grandma," who teasingly wanted to keep them, he arrived late and went to bed as soon as he was finished unpacking. It was not until the following morning that he realized someone had been in his cabin while he was gone. Nothing was missing, and his valuables that he kept locked had not been tampered with, but he knew things had been moved around. He had left Gertie's latest book on the edge of the table closest to his bed, and now it was on the other side. And his rifles in the corner were leaning over more than usual.

It wasn't the first time something like this had happened. Griff occasionally had prying guests—take young James Allen, for instance. It was always annoying when this intrusion into his privacy occurred, but this time it was more bothersome, considering who was probably responsible.

A few days later Jim spotted some men herding cattle over toward Griff's place. The animals were unlikely to be Griff's since as far as Jim knew he had gotten rid of most of his livestock when he had sold his homestead. These cattle were probably meant for Dunraven. He watched as the cattle skirted the edges and then came onto part of his property, trampling and chewing some of the new grassy growth where deer and elk and his own small herd regularly grazed. He wondered how long it would be before the cattle were taking advantage of the other settlers' properties. Dunraven probably wanted a huge herd. He doubted the Earl would concern himself with how far and wide these cattle grazed, his property or not. Jim rubbed his forehead. There was no end to Dunraven's invasion it seemed.

A few days later Jim ran into Griff riding by himself, once again appearing tipsy. Jim reined in next to him. "I could just shoot you for what you've done and are allowing to happen to this area." He looked Griff over before adding, "But then again, I bet you could just shoot yourself and save me the trouble. Let me just warn you. I'm onto the bunch of you, and I'm keeping watch."

Griff scowled back. "Shut up, Jim. You don't know what you're talking about. I can't govern what that lord wants or does." Griff looked away. "Besides, I've got nothing to hide."

"Maybe you don't yet, but I'm sure Dunraven does."

Griff turned back. "I told you I don't control the man."

"That's right. You don't. He controls you or thinks he does. But it's not too late to come clean about what he's doing or planning to do."

"It's fine for you to be on your high horse. You don't have a family to consider."

"Don't give me that excuse again. You have a good family; they'd want you to do what's right, no matter the cost."

Griff shook his head. "I've told you it's none of your business. Stay out of it."

Raising his volume, Jim said, "I'm not staying out of it. I know what's going on. They tried to buy me off too."

Griff stared at Jim a moment, then said quietly, "Jim, you don't really know the type of men you're dealing with and what they're capable of."

With a determined sneer, Jim said, "Well, maybe they don't understand what I'm capable of either."

Jim wrote articles to several local newspapers, explaining what was possible when unscrupulous men became involved in land development. But mainly he continued to talk to everyone he knew about what was happening. Most seemed to favor Jim's position on the matter. He was beginning to think public opinion could have an effect, but he wanted to take more direct action and developed a plan.

First, he needed to get done a month's worth of hunting and trapping in a couple weeks' time. He headed out with his dogs and worked grueling hours. Everything that he could possibly do, he did; and everywhere he could possibly go, he went. At night he was exhausted but slept little. Finally, he returned to his cabin, hauling on his mule the rewards of his hard labor. What all this arduous work meant was that he could stay at his cabin for the next couple of weeks and implement the second part of his plan.

The opportunity to do just that came the following day when Jim was working outside his cabin.

Jim heard Ring and Sally barking and looked up. Haigh was approaching his cabin from the path below. Jim walked over, picked up his shotgun and aimed it at the man. "What the hell do you think you're doing?"

"Heading to Estes Park, Nugent; what do you think?"

"I think you're trespassing on my land; that's what I think."

Haigh frowned. "This has always been a public passageway into the park."

"That's because I've allowed it. I'm not allowing it anymore. Correction: I'm not allowing it to certain persons anymore."

"What do you expect me to do?"

"Find another way in."

"How do you suppose I do that?"

"Go back the way you came and divert around my property."

Clearly put out, Haigh said, "That could take hours."

"Do it or I'll shoot you for trespassing the next time I catch you on my property."

Haigh smirked. "That's if I don't shoot you first. You really must think you're the high-and-mighty one." Haigh chuckled and continued. "I heard about you and Miss Bird cavorting with each other. Take it from me: You never had a chance with her." He reached into his pocket and tossed some coins at Jim's feet. "Next time you buy yourself one of your caliber of women, get one for me."

Jim saw red. "You son of a bitch!" He reacted without thinking, butting Haigh off his horse with the end of his gun, then pointing it at a sprawling Haigh on the ground. "Get off my land and don't come back."

Haigh slowly got up, dusted off his clothes and mounted back up. He left without another word. The man probably figured he could just come through when Jim wasn't around, but little did he know that Jim planned on sticking around his cabin for a while.

Jim had several more encounters with strangers trying to cross his property. It was usually easy to tell who was associated with Dunraven. One day, however, Griff's daughter Caroline cautiously rode up to his cabin.

She hailed him from afar to let him know it was just her.

When she came close enough, Jim asked, "Caroline, what brings you here?"

"I thought you'd want your mail. We got some while you were away hunting. I know you and Papa are fighting, and you probably won't be by anytime soon to pick it up."

"Caroline, you are a true friend. I thank you. No matter what your father and I fight about, I hope you know that doesn't change my good feelings for the rest of your family."

"What are you fighting about? Papa won't tell us kids."

"It's best you talk to your father. But what's new with your life, Caroline? Any new swains courting you?"

Caroline smiled. "You're my only suitor, remember?"

Jim smiled back. "If only life were that simple."

"We have some new guests. Lord Dunraven returned.

He even brought his own personal doctor Mr. Kingsley with him this time. I think the Earl must be very rich."

So Dunraven was back. Caroline was clearly unaware that she had just given Jim a jolt.

"Caroline, as much as I enjoy seeing you, I don't think your father would appreciate you spending any time alone with me. You probably should be on your way."

"It's not the same without you stopping by. Can't you come for a visit?"

"Honey, we'll see what happens. Don't worry about your father and me. We've known each other a long time. We'll figure out a way to work it out." But Jim was skeptical that would happen.

Later that evening Jim savored reading another letter from Isabella. She seemed a million miles away from his troubles at home. He missed her terribly and could tell by the words and phrases she wrote that she felt the same about him. He hoped this Dunraven business would be at an end before he saw her again.

For several days no Dunraven men attempted to trespass, but finally one day Griff hailed Jim from afar.

"Come on in, Griff."

Griff dismounted and walked up to where Jim was working on his furs. "Jim, I was hoping we could talk a few minutes."

"What about?"

"You and I have been neighbors for years. I was hoping we could come to some agreement and not let this Dunraven business divide us."

Jim paused in his work. "What are you after?"

"Let my family and me use this pass, and you can use the trails by my old spread."

Jim hesitated only a moment. "Fine. You change your mind about working for Dunraven?"

"No, but you know I never wanted to sell to him in the first place."

"But you did, and look where we're at now."

"Yes, but let's not make things any harder on the two of us. There's no reason for us to take roundabout trails."

"Agreed."

Griff lingered as if he wanted to say something more. Jim waited, but Griff just hung his head and shook it before mounting back up and leaving.

Jim started riding by Griff's more regularly again, but never stopped in to visit. He knew his feelings were too raw to control in front of others. It irked him that he never could catch Dunraven alone. He longed to confront the man personally.

Jim had trouble sleeping evenings. One night, after tossing and turning and barely resting, he got up and felt around in the pitch-dark for the bottle of whiskey he had bought months ago. He opened it and raised it to his lips, then stopped. Would Isabella understand? He needed it to help him fall asleep. Jim frowned, then took a swallow. He lay back down, but after a half hour of staring at nothing, he grabbed the bottle again and took another long swig and then one more.

An hour later he rubbed his forehead and felt guilty, but tried to reason away with his soused mind his behavior that night. The drink calmed his nerves. It didn't mean he was a terrible person, and he didn't care about Isabella's feelings; it just meant he was, uh . . . human. Surely, she wouldn't fault him for just one night of transgression.

By morning he had nearly finished the bottle and was drunk. He unsteadily saddled and mounted his horse. By the time he reached Griff's, after stopping several times along the way to try to get his bearings, he was still inebriated, just less so.

Jim rode up to the main house, reared his horse to look

in the window and shouted, "Dunraven, if you're in there, come out and talk."

He heard the bolt drop into place on the closed front door.

Ellie looked out the window. "He's not here, Jim. Come back another time."

In full roar, Jim yelled, "Like hell he's not."

Mrs. Rudolph appeared at the window. "Ellie's telling the truth, Jim. Go home and sober up."

"Taking his money is no better than you two becoming whores!"

Mrs. Rudolph shook her head. "Go home, Jim. You're not making any sense."

Sober the next morning, Jim realized how foolishly he had behaved. All he needed was Mrs. Rudolph to write a letter to Isabella about his conduct. He poured out his remaining liquor, vowing not to touch the stuff again.

When Griff returned from hunting, he heard about Jim's conduct. It was a sad state of affairs between them. He was filled with regrets over what he had started in motion and what he was a participant in now. For days Griff drank excessively. It didn't help that every time he turned around, Haigh seemed to be handing him another shot. Haigh was brimming with hatred for Jim. Griff knew that, and when he was sober, he could filter out the unreasonable suggestions Haigh was making. But drunk, Griff found himself becoming as vengeful and irrationally fearful as Haigh.

A man interested in hunting hired Jim as a guide. Jim was pleased to be getting back to anything that didn't revolve around Dunraven. It was June, and he wanted to enjoy the warm weather they were having. For two days the two men hunted together and camped out at night. Mr. Karl was quiet, and Jim didn't develop any special rapport with him, but that was just fine with Jim since he had a lot on his mind.

On the third day of hunting, Mr. Karl and Jim were heading back to his cabin when they stopped by a stream near Griff's place in order to allow their horses some water. Jim saw Haigh sitting on the porch of Isabella's former cabin, leaning back on a chair. Haigh suddenly noticed Jim gazing at him, got up and shouted something through the door back into the cabin.

Dunraven briefly appeared in the doorway, but was shoved aside by Griff—holding a shotgun. Griff swayed in the entryway, appearing drunk, then staggered toward Jim before taking aim.

Jim froze, disbelieving Griff would actually harm him.

Haigh shouted, "Shoot him. Shoot Jim. Protect me before Jim shoots me!"

A feeling of terror sliced through Jim. *He wouldn't, would he?*

The first blast ricocheted off a nearby wagon and hit Jim only lightly, but knocked down his horse. *How could he have?*

Jim turned, reaching for his own gun to defend himself.

Haigh yelled, "Give him another. He's not dead yet."

The second blast struck Jim directly. He collapsed on the ground.

Chapter Twenty-One

A few weeks later, in Fort Collins, Jim was still alive; the wounds to his right arm, shoulders, cheeks and upper nose were all healing—painful, but healing. The doctor who tended to him said that Jim had a head wound to the back of his skull where a blue whistler buckshot must have entered his brain. But a lot of people scoffed at the idea. After all, Jim was talking and writing and even sitting on the front porch of the inn where he was staying. In fact, local settlers heard from rumor and newspaper accounts that right after he had been shot he stayed calm and was as plucky as ever. He had refused to let them carry him into Griff's cabin, but had allowed Kingsley, Dunraven's doctor, to care for him.

Shortly after the shooting Griff had gone to the authorities, confessed that he had shot Jim and pleaded guilty to assault and battery with intent to kill. But there was a strange turn of events after that. Within a few days Griff's story to the justice of the peace seemed to change or was expanded; he claimed he had shot Jim in self-defense. The magistrate had then decided Jim should be moved to Fort Collins under the custody of the sheriff for supervision and care.

The authorities wanted to talk to the witness to the crime, the man whom Jim had been guiding on the hunting trip. But Mr. Karl disappeared and could not be found. Many suspected he must have been paid off—or worse. Abner Sprague, a resident of Estes Park, said the witness had stopped by his cabin after the crime and told him what had happened, that Jim was innocent of any wrongdoing, but that was different from hearing it from the man himself.

Meanwhile word spread about Jim. In Grand Lake, Henrietta Schodde, who had cared for Jim after the grizzly bear attack, heard about Jim and informed her husband that she was heading to Fort Collins to take care of him again, whether her husband took her or not. She could stay with her sister Clarisa who lived in Fort Collins. Her husband knew better than to debate the issue.

But after seeing Jim's condition, Charles informed Henrietta that there were other competent doctors caring for Jim in Fort Collins, and although he needed to get back to his work in Grand Lake, Henrietta could remain several more weeks helping to care for Jim while she visited Clarisa before he would return to pick her up again.

Stories swirled about the crime: Griff had acted cowardly. Dunraven or Dunraven's men were behind it. Jim's life was in danger because of English greed. Griff's daughter Caroline and Jim had had a secret affair. Or was it actually Griff's niece Mary and Jim? Haigh's jealousy over Mary was the real reason for the crime. Or was Haigh mad because Jim had taken his money and never gotten him a woman? Jim was still alive, so he couldn't have a brain wound, but why was it taking him so long to get better? Maybe Dunraven was paying the doctors to keep Jim sick. Maybe the doctors were being paid to kill Jim. Kingsley said Jim was called Mountain Jim because of the mountain of lies he told; but who would believe a word out of Dunraven's personal doctor? Griff started sheepishly claiming Jim had insulted his daughter. That's why he had shot him. Few believed that version, but the rumors went on and on.

Mrs. Rudolph made sure she wrote every interesting tidbit down when she sent a note to Dorothy to inform her of the news. Dorothy's husband Charles told her that he just couldn't believe it was in either Jim's or Griff's character to be involved in any attempted murder. Dorothy agreed; other forces or influences were the only way to explain it.

Nevertheless, Dorothy knew she needed to send word to Isabella informing her of the tragic events. She left out all the gossipy information and tried to prepare Isabella in the beginning of the letter for what she had to write, but no words could spare Isabella the devastating news.

Chapter Twenty-Two
Scotland

Hennie found Isabella collapsed on the sitting room floor, sobbing with a letter in her hands.

She crouched beside Isabella. "Tell me what's wrong, pet."

Isabella looked up at Hennie. "He's been shot. I need to go to him."

"Who's been shot?"

Isabella rubbed her eyes. "Jim."

"Jim who?"

"Jim Nugent. Griff shot him. I have to go to him."

"Rocky Mountain Jim? You said he was just a friend. Or maybe a special friend. But why go to him? People there will take care of him."

"I need to talk to him. I never told him."

"Told him what? You're not thinking clearly."

Isabella got up quickly. "Hennie, I have no time to argue. I'm leaving. He needs me and I want to speak with him."

Hennie grabbed Isabella's arm. "Listen to me, pet. You'll never make it in time if the shot proves fatal."

She shook Hennie's arm free. "I have to try!"

Hennie's eyes widened. "Oh, my Lord. You fell in love with him! That's what this is about."

Isabella glanced away. "I told you he's my special friend."

Hennie shook her head. "How could you so foolishly let yourself fall in love with him? How could you two possibly have any future together?"

Isabella started walking towards the front door. "I'm wasting time talking about this with you. I want to see what arrangements I can make to travel back. *He needs me.*"

"No!"

Isabella slowly turned back around, shocked by the vehemence in Hennie's voice.

Her sister stood rigid with her hands clenched. "No. Not this time. No more. I let you convince me a year ago, but not again. You're not travelling because you're feeling ill; we both know that. And you're certainly not running back there as if you were some pathetic lovesick woman. I'll not have you *ruining* our family's reputation."

"I'd be caring for someone who requires help!"

Hennie enunciated each word, "You'd be caring for an individual who has a reputation as a *desperado*. You wrote me that in the very first letter you sent me from there."

"No, Hennie. He's more than that. Much more than that."

"It doesn't matter. He's still *a man*. A man who is unmarried as are you. Can't you see how it would appear? It'd be nothing short of scandalous!"

Isabella opened her mouth to argue, but then hesitated, closed her eyes and sighed loudly.

In a softened tone, Hennie said, "You know I'm speaking the truth."

"I need to sit down." Isabella walked over to the settee, sank down and leaned forward, holding her waist.

Hennie sat on the settee next to her and put her arm around her shoulders. "Pet, I realize this must be hard. But it's the right thing to do. Besides, your running back to Colorado will make no difference at this point. He's either going to make it or not whether or not you're there."

"I just want to be with him and talk to him once more."

Hennie sighed and shook her head. "Of all the impossible situations you could have put yourself in, this has to be one of the most complicated. Well, I suppose we can't control our feelings as much as we would wish. Listen, at least wait a few weeks and see what happens. Take some time to consider your actions. Don't go running off impetuously now."

Hennie paused, then added, "I suppose if he does mean so much to you . . . that is, if he does survive . . . perhaps, you can see him when he's feeling better."

Isabella looked over beseechingly. "I don't know how I'll stand the wait."

Hennie patted her back. "You planned on traveling this summer, didn't you? That'll help keep your mind off the situation."

Isabella shook her head, "I *doubt* it."

"Well, you need to try. Father and Mother never would have approved of you running off now. You know that's for sure."

Isabella took a deep breath and straightened slowly. "You're right. Of course, you're right." Then burst into tears.

Hennie stroked her back. "You just need to stay strong, and you'll make it through this."

Isabella merely nodded.

After several hours of debating the issue off and on with Hennie the previous night and a fitful sleep afterward, Isabella awoke the next morning knowing she would not be traveling to Colorado at this point to see Jim. She dashed off notes to Ellie and Griff, Mr. Althoff and Mr. Buchanan, anyone she could think of to try to get more information about Jim. She received letters with different versions about what actually occurred, but not where he was staying.

Surely, he wasn't at his cabin with a gunshot wound taking care of himself. She dearly wanted to write to him, but didn't know where to send the letter or whose hands it might fall into. Hennie was right; she couldn't appear as a lovesick woman, it would ruin her reputation. Yet, she couldn't endure the thought of not at least trying to communicate with him. She finally wrote:

"Dear Mr. Nugent,
I have been informed of the tragic events that recently occurred. I wish you a rapid recovery and a cessation of conflict between you and your neighbors. My thoughts are with you and unchanged.
Sincerely,
I.L.B."

She addressed the letter to him in Estes Park, then scratched that out and decided to send the note in care of the postmaster in Denver. She fervently hoped her message would somehow make it to him.

She finally left for her planned trip to Europe, but only after Hennie promised to contact her with any news. She would write Jim again from Europe if she learned of a specific address where she could send the letter just to him.

Chapter Twenty-Three
Fort Collins

On a clear day in August, Jim sat on the porch at the Fort Collins Hotel where he was recovering, wishing the dull, throbbing ache in the back of his head would go away. Henrietta had just left after serving him some stew in his hotel room that she had made at her sister's house here in Fort Collins. She planned on returning later in the afternoon to check in on him. But before she had left his hotel room, she had insisted that if Jim went out on the porch that he dress warmly for the chills he was occasionally having, despite the August heat.

Henrietta didn't know that besides bringing a wool sweater, Jim also had brought a loaded rifle onto the porch with him. It sat across his lap right now and gave Jim a modest feeling of security. After being gunned down so viciously while just stopping to let his horse drink water, he didn't know what to expect next.

Jim looked to his right at the mountains thirty miles away and yearned to be home again at his cabin in Estes Park. But until he healed more and some of his legal difficulties were resolved, he would be stuck here in Fort Collins.

"Jim, can I talk to you?"

He turned his head sharply left in shock. A haggard-appearing Griff Evans stood at the end of the porch with his foot on the first step.

"Get back down, Griff. We have nothing to talk about."

Griff hung his head. "I'm sorry, Jim. I drank too much whiskey that day and wasn't thinking clearly."

He raised his head with imploring eyes. "I'm asking you to forgive me. I can't sleep at night I'm so torn with guilt. The kids don't understand it." He shook his head. "Hell, I don't understand it."

Jim glared at Griff. "You don't? I do. You let English greed take over. You played right into their hands, you fool! No, I won't forgive you! Damn you, I'll forgive you with lead when I get well!"

Griff's eyes widened, then he frowned and stared at Jim. He opened his mouth to respond, then shut it, turned and slowly walked down the street.

Jim shook his head in disgust. Did Griff even realize everything he had lost? Besides his health, his horse, and possibly his livelihood, he didn't know how this tragedy would affect his future with Isabella. Did she even know what had happened? He hadn't received any letter from her. If she had heard, what version of the events did she believe? Would she possibly take Griff's and Dunraven's side in the conflict?

He needed to write her a letter explaining just what had happened. Jim started to stand, then sat back down. No, he told himself for probably the thousandth time, until his legal difficulties were resolved in his favor, he would wait to write her. He certainly didn't want to inform her, if she hadn't yet heard about the events, that he currently was accused of attempted murder.

But back in his room later that day, Jim penned a letter to the editor of the local Fort Collins newspaper. He was outraged and wrote:

"Because of English plotting I am being accused of attempted murder. For golden riches, while I innocently passed by one Griffith Evan's cabin with a hunter, who cannot claim himself as witness because this witness has disappeared, I was shot at with a double barrel shotgun, not once, but twice by Evans. From the first shot, my horse lies dead as one Englishman Haigh, who had threatened my life multiple times, shouts "Kill him, he's not dead yet" at which point Evans lets loose another round of buckshot which have injured me and still cause pain.

What does the prosecuting attorney do who is just a mile away? He does not ask me one question but accuses me of plotting to kill Evans while an English Lord sat inside the cabin belonging to him. Haigh and Evans are free as birds to fly away, neither one under any bond obligation, and my property and stock are within reach of men who tried to kill me. Is this how a law-abiding citizen, who has trod the land of Colorado for over twenty years, to be treated by titled Englishmen with wealth in their pockets? James Nugent"

For a while Jim seemed to improve. But by September he was bedridden and delirious, speaking nonsense to Henrietta.

With tear-filled eyes Henrietta stared at Jim, appearing gaunt and weak in the bed next to her chair. Why did he keep saying "is"? He would never finish the thought.

She clasped Jim's hand. "Is what? Tell me Jim, *is what?*"

She watched as Jim opened his eye. He frowned as if he struggled to recognize her. "Isabella?"

"No, it's me, Henrietta."

He weakly squeezed her hand, closed his eye and said so softly Henrietta could barely hear, "I want her."

Henrietta shook her head and waited for Jim to say more, but it never occurred. Henrietta stayed by his bedside throughout the night and into the next morning. By early afternoon Jim's breathing became labored and then erratic. She had taken care of enough sick people to know the end was near.

She got up to briefly look out the window. When she turned back his breathing had slowed measurably. She sat next to him again, took his hand and watched him take his last breath.

She stood, kissed his forehead and covered his face with a blanket. On the seventh day of September, 1874, James Nugent, better known as Rocky Mountain Jim, passed away.

Isabella awoke abruptly from a deep sleep. She turned over in her bed and briefly opened her eyes. She caught a glimpse of a grayish movement in the corner of her hotel room. She blinked her eyes open and then squinted to make out the vague form that seemed as see-through as a light cloud.

The form solidified into a man with trapper clothes. He smiled and bowed. "I have come, as promised."

As if dream walking, she sat up and stood on wobbly legs that suddenly wouldn't move. Helpless, she reached her hand towards the man.

He left like a cloud dispersing.

She lay back down and sighed while falling back to sleep.

Epilogue

Authorities ordered a close examination of Jim's skull. It revealed a putrid pocket surrounding buckshot fragments had eventually developed in the base of Jim's brain, causing his demise. He was buried in Fort Collins, but his grave site was ultimately lost when the cemetery was moved to a different location in the city.

Griff was charged and arrested for his crime, but with a lack of witnesses attesting on Jim's behalf, the case was dismissed. Griff remained in Estes Park and Longmont for several more years. Ellie Evans told people that although she regretted Jim's death, she could not blame her husband; she felt it had been a case of kill or be killed. Not everyone agreed.

Public opinion swayed so heavily against Dunraven that he gave up his plans for a large private game preserve. He maintained land in Estes Park until the early nineteen hundreds when he sold his holdings to businessman B. D. Sanborn, and Freelan O. Stanley of the steamer car fame. His inability to pay his taxes was one of the reasons given for the sale.

Oddly enough, young James Allen was named administrator of Jim's estate. He was suspected by a court secretary of attempting to take some of Jim's possessions for himself. It is not known what became of all of Jim's personal papers and prose, and there is no known photograph in existence of him.

While Sylvester Downer served as a Colorado judge, Platt Rogers was elected the mayor of Denver and later in life wrote how he came to admire Miss Bird despite his initial impression of her looks.

Isabella Bird eventually became a famous author, publishing magazine articles and books about her travels. In 1879, *A Lady's Life in the Rocky Mountains,* a novel about her experiences in Colorado, was published and became particularly popular. It included a reserved version of her adventures with Rocky Mountain Jim that nevertheless contributed to his fame. Later in life Isabella Bird refused to write or discuss anything further about her time in Estes Park despite many requests to do so. She did claim the unusual story, however, that on the day James Nugent died, she briefly saw an image of him in front of her.

Unfortunately, her sister Hennie passed away a few years after Isabella returned from Estes Park. Isabella eventually married the doctor who had taken care of her sister, but as was unremarkable for bereaved women at the time, wore mourning clothes to her wedding. She confided to friends it was her sister who had wanted her to marry him. After several years she lost her husband to illness despite the fact that he was ten years younger than her.

Devoted to helping the needy, in 1876, Isabella established a college in Edinburgh, named after Livingstone the explorer, dedicated to training missionaries to aid the poor in Africa. After extensive travels throughout the world, in 1892, she was elected as the first female member of the Royal Geographic Society.

Griff's homestead was eventually covered by water after the development of a dam and Lake Estes in the 1940's. Jim's cabin no longer stands, however, there is a sign for Muggins Gulch, the valley where Jim lived, on the road leading from Estes Park to Denver.

Due to the continued popularity of Isabella's book about her time spent in Colorado, Jim's memory still survives in the mind of booklovers. But for hikers heading up Longs Peak, there is a sign in Rocky Mountain National Park, near a group of spruce trees that reads simply:

JIM'S GROVE

Dear Readers,

Reaching Rocky Mountain Jim is historical fiction. Any opinions or characterizations expressed in the novel are my own. Names of minor characters were invented or altered slightly. Any resemblance to a living person is purely coincidental. The plot proceeds as closely to known events as possible, but is interpreted with my personal view as to what I think happened.

I was amazed that despite easy access to information these days, I found very little written about James Nugent, just a snippet here and there, forcing me to piece together bits like a puzzle. Even sources claiming to be histories of the area conflicted with one another where Jim was concerned. I was often forced to take a stance, choosing the sequence of events that I thought occurred. I discounted a lot of what was written about him if the source was a known enemy of Jim such as the men associated with Lord Dunraven. I do not believe Jim could be disregarded as just a mountain of lies. It would have helped if his personal papers had not been lost to time.

But it occurred to me early on that if not for individuals such as James Nugent, Rocky Mountain National Park might not exist as it does today. Granted, Dunraven's acquiring, however fraudulently, so much property himself guaranteed the area was not broken into a group of small homesteads, but who would have enjoyed the land? Just Dunraven's friends? Would anyone ever have made the effort to turn the area into a national park? Jim's labors, along with others', helped ensure the area was not just a playground for the wealthy and privileged.

No matter what else is debatable, one fact is indisputable: James Nugent led a remarkable and challenging life. I wish I could have met him.

All the best,
Kari August

Printed in Great Britain
by Amazon